"I'm sorry, Clint. If it counts for anything, I hate the idea of you leaving."

"It does count," he admitted, but the determined set of his jaw told her he wasn't giving up. He gazed into her eyes. "Someone tried to kill me, Jordana. I don't trust anyone but you to find out who's behind this murder plot."

"How do you even know I'm a good investigator? Clint, you don't even know me. I have an investigation on my desk right now that's growing colder by the minute, and I'm no closer than I was when I got the call that two bodies were found walled up in my family's warehouse. Maybe I wouldn't even be that much help."

She wasn't usually insecure about her skills but now wasn't the time for bravado, not with Clint's life on the line.

"You're the one I want. I have a sense about people—I don't know how I know it but I do. From the first moment we met, I had a good feeling about you. You're strong, confident and capable. I want you by my side."

* * *

The Coltons of Kansas: Truth. Justice. And secrets they can't hide.

D0974134

Dear Reader,

When I was asked to contribute to the Colton continuity, I was so proud to be part of such a distinguished lineup of authors, but once I started writing, I fell in love with the characters. There's something so satisfying about watching a story evolve, knowing that it will continue as the torch is passed.

I love big family connections and complicated relationships, which is something the Colton clan has in spades! I hope you enjoy my vision for Jordana and Clint as they push their way toward a much-earned happily-ever-after while struggling to put together the pieces of a deadly puzzle.

As always, I enjoy hearing from readers. Connect with me on Facebook, Twitter or drop me an email at alexandria2772@hotmail.com.

Warmly,

Kimberly Van Meter

COLTON'S AMNESIA TARGET

Kimberly Van Meter

Special thanks and acknowledgment are given to Kimberly Van Meter for her contribution to The Coltons of Kansas miniseries.

HARLEQUIN®
ROMANTIC SUSPENSE™

Recycling programs
for this product may
not exist in your area.

ISBN-13: 978-1-335-62665-3

Colton's Amnesia Target

Harlequin Enterprises ULC
22 Adelaide St. West, 40th Floor
Toronto, Ontario M5H 4E3, Canada
www.Harlequin.com

Printed in U.S.A.

Kimberly Van Meter wrote her first book at sixteen and finally achieved publication in December 2006. She has written for the Harlequin Superromance, Blaze and Romantic Suspense lines. She and her husband of seventeen years have three children, three cats, and always a houseful of friends, family and fun.

Books by Kimberly Van Meter

Harlequin Romantic Suspense

The Coltons of Kansas

Colton's Amnesia Target

Military Precision Heroes

Soldier for Hire
Soldier Protector

The Sniper
The Agent's Surrender
Moving Target
Deep Cover
The Killer You Know

Harlequin Superromance

Family in Paradise

Like One of the Family
Playing the Part
Something to Believe In

The Sinclairs of Alaska

That Reckless Night
A Real Live Hero
A Sinclair Homecoming

Visit the Author Profile page at Harlequin.com for more titles.

Chapter 1

"You're gonna love this," Reese Carpenter promised with a subtle quirk of his lips that pretty much guaranteed his partner, Jordana Colton, would not agree. "John Doe at the hospital, all banged up, unconscious, no ID. And—wait for it—nothing but your name on a piece of paper clutched in his hot little hand."

Jordana, Braxville police detective, looked up from her report and narrowed her gaze. "Come again?"

Reese wagged the phone receiver at her. "Yeah, line four. All yours, practically gift-wrapped."

Jordana rolled her eyes and switched the line. "Detective Colton here."

"Detective, we've got an unconscious male Caucasian with no identification that we might need your help identifying down here at the hospital. Think you can come down and take a peek?"

"Sure thing," Jordana said, perplexed. "I'll be there in a few minutes."

Jordana clicked off and returned to Reese with an annoyed sigh. "Guess I'm heading down to Braxville General to unravel a mystery." Like she had time to spend on a John Doe when there was a case potentially involving her family on the desk. Sidenote: she hated mysteries of any sort.

"Oh, your favorite," he quipped, to which Jordana shot him a look that said, *I'm going to spit in your yogurt if you leave it unattended*, then grabbed her keys to leave. "Hey, call me if you hear back from forensics, yeah?"

"Sure. Let me know if your mystery guy is an old boyfriend looking to rekindle a lost love."

"Screw you. I don't have old boyfriends," Jordana returned, adding with a smart-ass grin, "None here, anyway."

Reese chuckled and Jordana exited the building. The sticky heat of Kansas in September clung to her face and body as she climbed into her car, the steering wheel burning hot to the touch. God, she'd be so happy when the weather turned to cooler temps. She'd had enough of this fall heat-wave crap.

Hot weather made people cranky and mean-tempered. Just last week she'd nearly been clocked by a mean drunk standing in his skivvies outside his place, waving a whiskey bottle, ranting at the world, sweat dribbling down his sun-weathered face.

In a small department, even detectives had to do fieldwork and that meant answering disturbance calls if none of the street cops were available.

As luck would have it, Jordana plucked the short straw on that one.

Heat and booze, a combination guaranteed to bring out the worst in people.

Braxville General loomed ahead and she pulled into the emergency loading zone reserved for cops bringing in perps with medical issues.

She waved at Rosie, the front desk volunteer, a living fossil if there ever was one, but hers was a face Jordana would associate with Braxville General until the day she died.

"Hi there, honey," Rosie called out. "Say hello to your mama for me."

Jordana offered a short smile and a thumbs-up, saying, "Copy that, Miss Rosie," before going through the double doors to the emergency room where her John Doe was being held.

Jordana knew this place like the back of her hand. Before she retired from the Navy and became a cop, as a kid she'd been a regular at this place.

In spite of her mother's ardent attempts to change her, Jordana had been a straight-up tomboy, more content to spend time running with the boys than hanging out with the girls.

As a precocious twelve-year-old Jordana had come to the conclusion that girls were boring. As opinions went, nothing had changed much since she was twelve. Shocker: Jordana didn't have many girlfriends. But that suited her just fine. She didn't have anything in common with most of the women in Braxville and small talk was excruciating.

So, *best to avoid it* was her motto.

Dr. Cervantes saw her enter and waved her over to a bay. "Sorry to break up your day like this but all he had was this in his hand." He handed Jordana a slip of paper.

Sure enough, her name and cell were scrawled in masculine handwriting, plain as day.

Jordana took a closer look at the guy who remained knocked out, an IV drip feeding fluids into his body, but otherwise he seemed in relatively stable condition. "Head injury?" she surmised.

"Yes, concussion with some minor brain swelling. He should regain consciousness soon but I thought you might want to come down and take a look. I was hoping you might recognize him."

But Jordana was looking at a stranger.

Older, best guess in his mid-thirties, some salt-and-pepper seasoning in his sideburns but an otherwise strong head of dark hair. It didn't take a rocket scientist to deduce that this man wasn't from Braxville.

Also, she didn't have a clue who the hell he was or why he'd been looking for her.

"Sorry, drawing a blank on this end," Jordana said to Dr. Cervantes, but offered to run his prints. "Something tells me this guy ain't living off the grid. His prints ought to be in the system." Jordana pulled her fingerprinting device from her pocket. One of the fancier gadgets the department had purchased with some help from a Homeland Security grant. It was all digital and it went straight to the database.

Jordana gently pressed his fingers against the pad, recording his prints. No messy ink, no cleanup. Sometimes Jordana loved technology. Other times she missed the days when everyone wasn't so heavily connected.

While the device ran a search, Jordana asked for details about the John Doe. "So, what happened to him?"

"Someone found him out on Range Road, like he'd been dumped. Looks like someone thought they'd done the job with that crack in the head but he's a lucky bastard because it didn't fracture the skull, just knocked him around plenty."

"He ought to run out and buy some scratchers with that kind of luck," Jordana said. "That blow could've killed him."

Dr. Cervantes agreed. "Like I said, lucky. I wish I had that kind of luck. If it weren't for bad luck, I wouldn't have any."

Jordana chuckled at the doc's wry humor even if he was full of bologna. Dr. Cervantes seemed to live a charmed life. His wife, Valeria, was a Peruvian beauty and his kids all looked like they were plucked from a magazine photoshoot. On the surface, he had it all.

Jordana knew better than to trust appearances. Still, she hoped that all was as it seemed when it came to Dr. Cervantes because she genuinely liked him.

"Your wife is too pretty for you," Jordana quipped with a snort. "Take your blessings where you find them."

Dr. Cervantes chuckled with a nod. "Such wisdom from someone so young," he said, a twinkle in his eye.

She barked a laugh. "Young? I feel every second of my thirty-one years. Some days I'm pretty sure I might be sixty."

"Someday someone is going to turn you from a cynic to a romantic," Dr. Cervantes prophesied. Jordana laughed because it was highly unlikely but the doc was certain of it, saying, "If I were a betting man...you're too attractive to spend your life chasing criminals."

Jordana wagged her finger at him. "Ahhh, watch out, Doc, your sexism is showing. I happen to like chasing criminals."

Dr. Cervantes sighed as if he'd never understand but said, "I stand by my words. I'm never wrong about these things."

A soft ding alerted Jordana that the search was finished. "Saved by the bell," she teased, lifting the device to read the results. *Oh, damn.* She, sort of, did know him. Well, not in person but she'd spoken to him on the phone two weeks ago. "His name is Clint Broderick, thirty-six, from Chicago."

Clint Broderick was the last living relative of the dead body fished out of the wall of a warehouse scheduled for demo by Colton Construction. The body was identified as Fenton Crane, a private investigator with a shady past, with only one living relative: Clint.

"So you do know him?"

She couldn't get into specifics, not with the Crane investigation still ongoing. "Yeah, part of a possible murder investigation. Mr. Broderick was supposed to meet with me two weeks ago but then I didn't hear from him."

"Seems he must've tangled with the wrong people," Dr. Cervantes said.

"So it would seem."

Instead of solving the mystery, the mystery had deepened.

If Clint Broderick had been on his way to see Jordana, what happened along the way? The fact that the only living relative of the dead guy walled up in an old warehouse ended up bashed in the head and left for dead didn't seem like a coincidence.

Did someone want to protect a secret? Did Broderick know something someone wanted to keep quiet?

She had questions only Broderick could answer—but the man was still out cold.

To the doc, she said, "Can you move him to a private, secure room?"

"That can be arranged. Should we post security, too?"

"Might be a good idea. At least until he wakes up."

Dr. Cervantes nodded. "Consider it done. We need the emergency room bays, anyway."

Jordana took one last lingering look at Broderick, noting with reluctance that even unconscious the guy had an impressive bulk about him. Those nice rounded shoulders and well-defined, broad chest gave away his dedication to the gym.

The man had discipline.

Everything about him told a story without his mouth saying a word.

The only thing it wasn't saying was how he'd ended up in a Braxville hospital instead of in her office like he was supposed to.

More questions.

Another damn mystery.

Oh, goody.

Clint Broderick awoke to dimly light darkness in a place he didn't recognize, hearing sounds he couldn't place.

Panic threatened to bloom, tightening his chest as he sat up with a jerk, nearly upsetting the IV cart attached to his wrist by the thin tubing.

What the hell?

Then the pain hit. His head felt as if a badger were trying to gnaw its way free from his skull using nothing but blunt chompers and a will to succeed. He cupped his head gingerly and found a large bandage covering a knot that throbbed like an angry protestor at a political rally. His mind swam as he blinked back the vertigo that threatened to make him puke.

He was in a hospital? How'd he get here?

The night nurse came in to check his vitals and realized with a start that he was awake.

"Oh, goodness, you gave me a fright. How are you feeling? You have quite the nasty bump on your noggin."

He didn't know how to answer, admitting gruffly, "Hurts. Can I get some water?"

"Of course." She filled a cup from the pitcher at the end of the bedside table, handing it to him. "Careful now, you've been out for quite a while."

"How long?"

"Almost twenty-four hours. Are you dizzy? Faint?"

"All of the above."

"Understandable. Head injuries hurt like the dickens and they do some kooky things to the brain. Lucky for you, you only had minor swelling but only God knows what kind of damage that can do. Do you know your name?"

"Of course I know my name," he grumbled, but when he tried to produce it from his memory, there was a scary blank spot. "It's…" He struggled to remember. "My name is, um…"

But the nurse seemed to expect his memory gap. "No worries. Short-term amnesia is also common for a head injury like yours. I can help you out. Your name, according to your fingerprints, is Clint Broderick. Does that ring any bells?"

Clint Broderick. Sounded right but he couldn't be sure. Still, he took her word for it. *Fingerprints don't lie.* "Yeah, sounds about right."

"Well, you try to get some rest. The doctor will see you in the morning."

Rest? He'd just been unconscious for nearly a day. Lying in a hospital bed for another couple of hours until the doctor made his rounds wasn't appealing but what else could he do? He didn't even know his damn name; he couldn't exactly check into a hotel room.

"Where am I exactly?" he asked, wincing against the throb in his brain.

"That would be Braxville General, in Braxville, Kansas. Just outside of Wichita and pretty as a picture if I ever saw one. We have a lot of community pride around here."

He couldn't muster a polite smile; instead, he took a swallow of water to wet his dry throat, then said, "I'm guessing I didn't have my wallet or anything when I was found?"

"Nothing but the clothes on your back, sugar. Sorry about that. Someone must've been right mad at you to do you like that."

Yeah, guess so. Too bad he couldn't remember who the hell he was or who might be so pissed at him that they'd knock him into next week and leave him for dead. Talk about waking up in a nightmare.

He nodded to the nurse. "Thanks. Can I get something for this headache?"

"Sure thing, sugar. Doc has cleared you for light pain meds if you should need them. Be right back."

The nurse left him and he eased back on the pillow, staring up at the ceiling. He had no idea who he was or how he'd gotten here.

But someone had tried to kill him. What if they tried to come back and finish the job?

Yeah, sleep? Not gonna happen.

He lifted his arms to stare at his hands. Smooth, strong and capable but not callused. Something told him manual labor wasn't in his wheelhouse. So, a desk guy of some sort? Did he push paper all day? Had he discovered some shady dealings and someone thought to clip loose ends?

The throb in his head intensified when he tried to push too hard on the memory button.

Ah, hell. He wasn't going to find the answers tonight.

Hopefully, tomorrow brought more clarity—or at the very least an end to this vicious stabbing pain in his brain.

One could hope.

Because that was all he had right about now.

Chapter 2

The next morning Jordana received word from Dr. Cervantes that Mr. Broderick was awake and she hustled back to Braxville General. True to his word, the doctor had sequestered her victim in a private section of the hospital with a security guard at the door. She flashed her badge and entered the room.

The man who'd been knocked out cold the last time she saw him glanced up at her entrance and she was hit with a pair of stormy blue eyes that complemented his brown hair and revealed an intensity she could feel with a glance.

That presence she'd sensed about him bloomed when he was fully aware. This man could probably command a boardroom or lead an army without breaking a sweat. Her military training recognized authority when she saw it, even if he couldn't remember who he was yet.

"Mr. Broderick, I'm Detective Jordana Colton." She

extended her hand and he accepted with a perfunctory shake. "How are you feeling?"

"Confused."

Damn. She'd been hoping perhaps his memory had returned by morning, but she kept her disappointment from her voice, explaining, "The doctor says you have some short-term memory loss caused by your head injury. It should pass with a little more rest."

"Yeah, I guess so. Gotta say, not sure how to think about this situation. I may not know my name but I remember that my mother's name was Daisy. How can I remember that?"

"Long-term memory is stored in a different section of the brain," she answered. "You should be able to remember the parts of your life that are stored in long-term memory, such as your childhood, but anything in the short term will be affected."

Her explanation seemed to make sense as he nodded. "Yeah, I remember the house I grew up in, the street even, but not being able to remember my name? It's messing with me."

"I can only imagine," she murmured in support, but got right to the point. "Mr. Broderick, I was able to identify you through your prints, but actually, you and I had a conversation two weeks ago with plans to meet up."

He furrowed his brow, regarding her in question. "I'm sorry…were we…supposed to meet for a date?"

The awkwardness of his question only made Jordana blush. "No, it wasn't a personal call," she assured him. "I'm afraid I was calling with unfortunate news."

"Yeah? Like what?"

It was some kind of karmic kick in the ass that she was having to deliver this crappy news twice to the same person. "A body was found in the walls of a warehouse scheduled for demolition and I'm sad to be the bearer of bad news but the victim turned out to be a man named Fenton Crane, a relative of yours."

He digested that information for a minute, but in the end he shook his head, saying, "Sorry, doesn't ring a bell. Was he a close relative?"

"Well, an estranged uncle but you came up as his only living relative."

"So, was I coming to talk to you about this dead uncle when someone waylaid me?"

"It would seem that way."

"Do you know who might've done this?"

She shook her head. "No. The investigation is still early. We don't have much information to go on. I was hoping that you could give us some additional insight when I contacted you. You were planning to meet up with me but then I never heard back."

"I guess I must've had some kind of information worth sharing if I was willing to drive here." He paused a second to ask, "Wait a minute…where's my car? The nurse said I was found on the road?"

"Yeah, dumped along Range Road. Sorry, no car, though. Do you remember what you were driving?"

He thought for a minute, then shook his head. "No, sorry. Another big blank." Frustration laced his tone. "How long is this amnesia supposed to last?"

"I don't know. I think it varies. You'll have to ask Dr. Cervantes about the specifics." She wished she could be more helpful but they were both hitting cement walls. Finding Fenton Crane's body in the walls of a warehouse her family's company was scheduled to demo had planted a frenzy of suspicion on her family's doorstep and she'd hoped that maybe Clint Broderick could shed some light into why Fenton Crane was in Braxville in the first place.

"It's possible you might regain your memory within a few days," she said, trying to be helpful.

An awkward silence followed. She should leave. There wasn't much more that could be said until he regained his memory but she wanted to hang around.

Her gaze strayed to his ring finger. No wedding band. At least no one was waiting and worrying about him at home. *Some men didn't wear their rings.* She shifted against the inner dialog in her head. "You don't remember anything? Nothing at all?"

"I remember that I hated strawberries as a kid. Does that help?"

"Not really."

"Yeah, then I don't have much more to share. Sorry."

He had arresting blue eyes, like two vibrant blue paint chips with flecks of variegated color blended in a creative swirl. Or a turbulent ocean reacting to a summer storm, churning the seabed with its violent motion.

Someone had to be waiting for him at home. There was no way a man like him was unattached.

Get a grip, unnecessary personal information. Stop wasting energy on something immaterial to your case.

The realization that she was hanging around for a less than professional reason made her stiffen and refocus. "All right, then. Well, I suppose until you regain your memory…there's not much we can do to help each other."

"I wish I was of more use to you."

The genuine timbre of his voice tugged at her in a disconcerting way. He had no one here and he had no one to help him. Where was he supposed to go? Presumably, he'd come to Braxville to help *her* and then someone had tried to kill him.

Not your problem.

But he could be an important key to the puzzle. In

the interest of the case, shouldn't she keep him as close as possible?

Don't say it, just turn around, keep walking. Don't be stupid and reckless.

But the words fell from her mouth, anyway.

"Look, I don't want you to get the wrong idea or anything, but seeing as you don't know anyone here in Braxville and you don't even know who you are, if you need a place to crash, I have a spare bedroom you can use for the time being. Until we figure something else out."

Had she just invited a stranger to come bunk up with her?

Had she lost her mind?

She could practically hear the incredulous protests of her five siblings when they found out. It was brash. Dangerous, even. And yet she didn't regret offering. It was about the case, nothing else. Besides, it was just for a few days and maybe it could provide a break in the case.

This went against protocol, another voice argued— a voice that sounded a lot like her partner's. No one in their right mind would, or should, volunteer to house a stranger, but her gut was pushing her to do exactly that. She'd learned to trust her instincts even when all signs pointed the other direction. *So, here's putting those instincts to the test...*

"Yeah, so...if you're not allergic to cat dander...my door is open."

The cute cop had just offered him room and board.

His first impulse was to answer with an enthusiastic yes but was that wise? He didn't even know who he was or who *she* was for that matter.

What if she was a dirty cop who knew who'd done

this to him? What if she was keeping him close to protect his attacker?

What if she planned to finish the job and cover up his murder with her cop connections?

Likely? Probably not but he'd never been attacked and left for dead before, either.

Or at least he didn't think this had ever happened to him before.

Damn, paranoia was an ugly thing. But given the fact that he'd nearly died and he didn't even remember how it'd happened, a little paranoia seemed understandable.

The long pause caused her to fluster, saying, "Forget it, I was just—"

He quickly jumped in. "No, I appreciate the offer. I was just thinking, I have no idea if I'm allergic to cat dander. I guess there's only one way to find out, right?"

A short smile and a sudden flush in her cheeks only made her more appealing but he didn't need to be thinking like that about Jordana Colton. *Detective* Colton, that is. Gotta keep the facts of the situation front and center. "Oh, right," she acknowledged. "Well, yeah, you'll know right away whether or not you're allergic because either you'll start sneezing like your head is going to pop off or you'll be fine. I also have Benadryl on hand in case things go from bad to worse."

"Yeah, I'd hate to survive a blow to the head only to die choking on cat fuzz."

Her smile widened, almost reluctantly, and he realized he might not know who he was but he did know what he liked—and he liked Jordana Colton.

"So, the doc should spring me today… It's embarrassing to ask but could you pick me up later this afternoon?"

She answered with a professional nod. "Of course."

"Cool. Yeah, that'd be great. I appreciate your offer. Very kind of you."

She nodded, clasping her hands in front of her as if conducting a very proper business transaction with heads of state. "Um, so, of course, there is nothing romantic offered or expected or solicited. Just to keep things as clear as possible to avoid any awkward moments."

"Got it. I don't think you're my type," he said with a slight tease to his voice. When her brow arched ever so slightly, he added, "Or at least I don't think you are."

"Good." She scribbled her name and number on a piece of paper, pausing before handing it to him, a small wry chuckle escaping, murmuring something about the irony, which was not lost on him, then said, "Call me when you're ready to leave."

He nodded. "Thank you for doing this. I appreciate your kindness to a stranger. I promise I don't think I'm a bad guy or anything."

Her quick smile revealed a nice set of white, straight teeth as she quipped, "If you are, I'll just shoot you and that will be the end of that."

A private thrill chased his thoughts as he watched her leave. She had a trim, athletic figure, strong and agile. She could probably disable a bad guy in seconds. That was a little bit hot.

He probably shouldn't have taken her offer.

The smart thing to do would've been to find where he lived and then get his ass home. But the unexpected benefit of not knowing who he was relieved him of the burden of expectation or obligation.

Hell, he could be the president of the United States and it wouldn't matter because the slate was blissfully empty. Kinda like when he was a kid. No one looking to him to keep their bills paid. No one expecting him to solve their problems. No one badgering him for signatures or payroll.

He was just like a kid again, floating through life, looking forward to the next day or adventure. He liked that idea. He liked it a lot.

Also, maybe it wasn't right or appropriate but Jordana Colton…he wanted to know her better.

Hopefully, with any luck, he wasn't allergic to cats.

Chapter 3

"Any luck with your John Doe?" Reese asked when Jordana returned to the station.

"No, his memory is still shot," she answered, going to her desk. "But the doctor thinks it should only be a few days before he recovers fully. Just gotta be patient, I suppose. Head injuries are tricky."

Reese grunted in agreement. "Back in high school, I took a nasty blow to the head during a football game. My brain was fuzzy for weeks, but I never lost my memory. Kinda wished I had. Would've made my dating history a lot easier to stomach."

She smiled, privately happy that Reese was returning to some semblance of himself. Not that he'd ever be that happy-go-lucky guy again after losing his last partner, but maybe he'd find his smile again.

He was a damn good cop, though, and Jordana liked working with him.

"So, what's the guy going to do in the meantime? Stay at the hospital?"

She swiveled in her chair to face Reese, knowing he was going to hate what she was about to say. "Actually, in the interest of the case, I offered up my spare bedroom for a few days until he got his memory back."

Reese's expression turned into a scowl. "You did what?"

"Calm down, it's just for a few days and he seems harmless. Besides, the guy doesn't have anywhere to go and he doesn't even remember his name."

"You know this is stupid," he growled. "This guy could be a murderer for all you know."

"He's not a murderer," she disagreed, but she could see how her decision might seem brash. "Look, I get it. Under normal circumstances, I wouldn't dream of doing something like this but my gut says the guy isn't dangerous and what he knows about Fenton Crane might be the key to cracking how the hell he ended up dead in that warehouse."

"Your connection to this case is blurring your judgment," he said. "I understand that you're willing to do whatever it takes to clear your family but that's exactly why you shouldn't be running this investigation."

She was well aware of the conflict of interest, but the saving grace was that they were in a small department and there weren't many backups. She'd assured the captain that she could handle the investigation without losing her objectivity, but granted, this decision seemed to fly in the face of that assurance.

"Okay, yeah, on the surface it looks stupid but whatever happened to just being nice to a stranger who got the short end of the stick in a situation? I mean, he's here because of me. He was coming to Braxville to talk to me about this case and then something happened to him."

"You're not responsible for his bad luck," Reese argued, still not on board. "I'm not trying to be an ass but I'm not going to see your side on this. It's reckless and foolhardy—two things I never thought I'd have to worry about from you."

Ouch. "I appreciate your concern but I got this. Don't worry. Besides, if he gets out of line or I get a bad vibe, I'll just kick his ass into the ground."

"So there's no way I can talk you out of this?"

"Not really."

He shook his head. "I guess there's nothing more to say, right? You're going to do what you want to do no matter what I say."

"Pretty much."

Reese exhaled a long breath but knew it was pointless to keep arguing. "If you're hell-bent on ignoring any common sense, at least let me look into his background so you're not walking blind into this situation."

"Fine. If that helps you relax, run a detailed background on him and text me anything alarming."

"More alarming than the fact someone tried to kill him and left him for dead for unknown reasons?"

"Yeah, more than that."

Jordana chuckled and returned to the report on her desk. Yeah, she knew it wasn't protocol to let a stranger into her home who may or may not have information related to the dead body.

What they knew about Fenton Crane was frustratingly little. They knew he'd been hired by Rita Harrison to search for her missing daughter, Olivia.

Olivia Harrison turned out to be Body Number Two walled up in the warehouse.

In a town with a relatively low crime rate, finding not one but two dead bodies in an old warehouse was downright jarring.

They were keeping the details, such as they were, as quiet as possible. They didn't need the crackpots to crawl out of the woodwork with their own theories, but then they also needed leads, and sometimes the most unlikely source turned out to be the key that busted a case wide open.

People were easy to rile up and hard to control, something she learned in the Navy, which was why she kept those "in the know" within a very small circle.

"Forensics come back on Oliva Harrison yet?" she asked.

"Yeah, best guess midtwenties, cause of death likely a blow to the head. Skull fracture shows blunt force trauma. Been dead a long time, though."

"Man, that's rough. So, the vic turned out to be the mother of someone here in town, Gwen Harrison, an elementary school teacher?"

She nodded, chewing on her pen. And then her brother Brooks got involved and, in true Colton fashion, couldn't stay in his damn lane. Like the situation wasn't complicated enough with their dad owning the warehouse where the bodies were found, Brooks had to go and get involved with the dead woman's daughter.

What twisted webs we weave, right?

"I can't imagine how horrible it must've been for her family when she went missing without a trace, only to be found by accident twenty years later," she murmured.

"Yeah, horrible tragedy," Reese agreed. "Do you ever think of how many dead bodies might be hidden right beneath people's noses, walled up in the buildings we enter every day?"

She made a face. "That's macabre."

"But true. Hell, we have no idea how many people have met their Maker early thanks to some evil asshole with a twisted childhood. It's a sobering thought. Probably why I'll never have kids. This world is a dumpster fire."

"And you're a bowl of sunshine," Jordana quipped with a wry expression before reaching for the phone. A text message awaited. Well, it looked like her new roomie was ready to be sprung from the hospital. She pocketed her cell and rose. "I gotta go. Broderick is ready to leave."

"Text me when you get home or I'll show up with guns blazing ready to execute justice with extreme prejudice."

She laughed. "You watch too much television. I'll be fine."

Jordana left and headed for the hospital. She didn't like mysteries but there was something about Clint Broderick that made solving his more appealing.

Was that a red flag?

Probably.

Was she going to stop?

Not likely.

Clint gestured ruefully to his thrift store hand-me-downs the volunteers had rustled up for him so he didn't have to walk out with his backside showing, and Jordana laughed. "I don't know for sure but something tells me I have better fashion sense than this because damn, this is embarrassing," he said.

"It lacks a certain…"

"Style?" he finished for her, staring down at the trousers that looked like they'd been plucked from some old guy's 1970s wardrobe after his clothes had been donated to charity following his death. "I'm pretty sure this hasn't been in fashion since disco was cool."

"You might be right. It might've even come from Rosie's husband's closet, but look on the bright side, at least it's better than the Braxville General blue robe special."

"You got me there," he agreed, dusting his trousers with a gingerly motion that smacked of a little awkwardness and Jordana didn't blame him. This was a little strange. "So, you sure you want to do this?"

"Of course," she answered. "My gut tells me it's the right thing to do."

"Well, I'm thankful to your gut. I've never been in a position like this. I mean, not that I can remember. The emergency techs had to cut my clothes free but they gave me a bag filled with the remnants. I think I started off well-dressed."

"If that's the case, that means you're probably not homeless. My partner is running down your identity to see if we can find anyone who can help put together the pieces."

"Probably also to check and make sure I'm not a lunatic," he supposed, and Jordana grinned without apology. He chuckled. "I don't blame you. I'd question how good of a detective you were if you didn't."

"Glad to know I've passed the test."

"Well, that one, anyway," he said with a wink. Was he flirting? Like he was in any position to flirt with the cute detective. That blow to the head had scrambled his neurons. Something told him that he wasn't usually this easygoing but it felt good.

Maybe he was acting out of character. Maybe before he got jumped he was a stiff, rigid asshole with a chip on his shoulder.

God, he hoped not.

"All right, paperwork is finished. You're sprung, Mr. Broderick," Jordana said, gesturing for the open door.

But before they went any further, Clint had to set down some ground rules. "You have to stop calling me Mr. Broderick. Even though I don't know who I am, I know it feels weird to be called something so formal. Please, call me Clint. Let's pretend we're old acquaintances or something. It might make things less weird. How about we try that?"

She graced him with a curious smile, cocking her head as if trying on his idea in her mind for size. "Okay, that might work for now. Unless I find out you're, like, a serial killer or something."

"Such escalation. What if I'm just your garden variety thief? Or a white-collar embezzler? It doesn't always have to be so violent."

Jordana laughed. "Okay, but if I find out you're anything but the unfortunate victim of a crime, I'm putting you in handcuffs before you can even slather cream cheese on a bagel."

"Mmm, bagels. I think I like those."

All jokes aside, it was impossible to forget that someone had tried to kill him, possibly someone in this town, and he had no clue who to watch for. Not to be paranoid but being bashed in the head and wiped of your memories made for some jittery peripheral glances.

Danger could lurk anywhere—with anyone.

All he had was Jordana Colton on his side for the time being, and having a cop watch his back seemed like something he ought to hold on to.

Now, he just had to pass the first test.

Lord in heaven, please don't let me be allergic to cats.

Chapter 4

Jordana unlocked her front door and welcomed Clint inside. "Well, here it is, in all its glory," she said with a self-deprecating shrug. "I'm not much for knickknacks and frou-frou stuff. I like it clean and simple. Less to worry about."

Her sister Bridgette had once described her personal style as utilitarian and, by her tone, it hadn't seemed a compliment, but Jordana didn't care, which was probably why the military had appealed to her. Everything had a place and a purpose. If only life were that way, it would make solving crimes so much easier, but no, humans were messy and often did things for no particular reason aside from emotion, and emotion was impossible to rein in with logic and reason.

She dropped her keys in the small bowl perched on the table in the entryway. "Okay, so the house is small enough so no worries getting lost. Bathroom is over there, adjacent to the spare bedroom, and my bedroom, which is, of course, off-limits, is opposite the spare." She returned to Clint, who was still surveying his new surroundings. "Any questions?"

"Seems pretty straightforward. I've yet to see this potentially allergenic cat you mentioned," he said.

"Ah, that's Penelope—I didn't name her so don't judge—and she's probably hiding. She's not a huge fan of strangers or anyone aside from me. You might not see her at all."

"Penelope…okay, good to know." He gestured to the spare bedroom, asking, "May I?"

"Yes, certainly," she answered with her own gesture, following him as he walked into the tidy spare. To her trained eye, she saw her military training in action. Crisp, tight hospital bed corners, zero clutter in sight, floors clean and countertops dusted. Keeping things in order gave her a level of comfort. "It's not the Ritz but it'll keep you warm and dry until we find out more about you."

"It's great. You didn't have to do this and I'm grateful for the kindness." He glanced around, adding, "I don't know for sure but something about your style feels complementary to my own. I don't understand the appeal of knickknacks, either. Dust collectors, if you ask me."

"Exactly. If only I could convince my mom the same. She's always trying to fob off her collections of nonsense on to me in the guise of 'family heirlooms.'" Jordana made air quotes with a quick shake of her head. "Nope, it's just junk, Mom."

He chuckled. Jordana's breath caught in her chest at the sound. Time to exit gracefully. "Okay, well, I'll let you get settled and get out of your hair. Feel free to help yourself to the kitchen, though I don't really keep a well-stocked pantry because it usually goes bad before I have the chance to eat it." She clarified, "I eat a lot at the station, late nights."

"Anything is better than hospital food," Clint said with a wry grin. "I might not remember much but I definitely remember not appreciating the cuisine at Braxville General. Much to be desired unless you're a big fan of reconstituted split pea soup with the grainy consistency of a puddle after a hard rain."

She laughed. "Can't say that I'm a fan. I'm more of a burgers and fries kind of girl."

"Me, too."

"Burgers and fries girl?" she teased.

"Exactly."

Jordana smiled until she realized with a start this sounded way too much like flirty banter. "Okay, then. You have my cell. Holler if you need anything. I'm going to head back to the station to catch up on some paperwork."

"Yeah, sure, no problem," Clint said, but a frown creased his brow, prompting her to pause. "What I'm about to say sounds like the opposite of manly but it just occurred to me…what if whoever tried to knock out my lights comes back to finish the job? I'd like to think that I'm a badass with ninja skills when I get my memory back but the reality is… I'm probably not? I guess, what I'm trying to say, really badly, I might add, is that maybe I shouldn't be left alone right now."

That had to be really hard to admit, she realized. Clint also had a point and she was embarrassed that she hadn't thought of it first. For crying out loud, who was the detective in the room? Her cheeks flushed but she nodded in agreement. "Valid point. I'll have my partner bring my paperwork here. I can work from home."

"I hate to be a scaredy-cat about it but—" he rubbed

the back of his head ruefully "—seems kind of foolish to tempt fate with unnecessary risk."

"Right. Very true." Okay, now that she was thoroughly embarrassed for seeming like a rookie— "Like I said, kitchen is all yours"—she disappeared behind her bedroom door.

Maybe Reese was right. Was it reckless to bring Clint into her home like this? She didn't know anything about him and she seemed to forget basic common sense when he was around. Losing her good sense could be a liability for them both.

Clint was a handsome guy—and everyone in Braxville knew she was single as a Pringle. Tongues would wag, which meant if Clint's attacker was still in town, it wouldn't be difficult to narrow down his location.

She'd have to stay extravigilant for many reasons. Some of which had nothing to do with the case and more do with the fact that her heart rate seemed suspiciously rapid when he smiled.

A handsome man with a healthy sense of humor— that's how panties ended up on the floor.

She rubbed her forehead. It'd been a while since she actively dated (translation: had sex) and apparently Clint flipped whatever switch she had inside her brain that regulated that area. No wonder Reese had side-eyed her when she told him her plan. Good grief, she sounded reckless *and* thirsty.

Hot, single guy with no memory? Suuurre, I can take him in—into my bed!

That last part was delivered in her head with a smarmy leer. Great, now she was bullying herself in preparation for the jokes that would invariably happen somewhere down the road.

The best offense is a good defense.

She'd go the extra mile to make sure no one had reason to question her integrity or her motivation. It was all about the case. Not his broad shoulders, muscular build and charming smile.

Definitely not that.

But the fact that he checked *all* her internal boxes? Well, that made for a perfect foundation for potentially awkward feelings to brew.

And that was just Jordana being honest with herself.

Clint closed the door and took a better look around his new digs. Clean, orderly and functional. What's not to love? *Better than a hotel room, right?* And considering that he didn't have access to his money (hopefully, he had some), Jordana's offer came free of charge.

He sat on the bed, testing the springs. Firm yet supportive. Definitely better than a hospital bed. In addition to the knot on his skull, his spine felt permanently kinked from being folded into a bed too small to accommodate his frame.

Speaking of skull, he gingerly touched the angry bulge still deforming his head and grimaced. Definitely not a great look but he was alive so that kept his vanity in check.

So, his name was Clint Broderick. Seemed like a decent, strong name. He opened the hospital bag with the remnants of his clothes. The linen felt fine, maybe high-end. Definitely not a thrift store find like the rags he was wearing right now. First order of business, find something else to wear. He couldn't continue to sport this 1970s ensemble for much longer or else people were going to start asking if he was planning his Halloween outfit early.

But seeing as he had no cash, it made purchasing difficult.

~~He didn't want to borrow money from the only person~~ he knew in this tiny town but he didn't see a more viable option.

Clint groaned. Was the universe going out of its way to emasculate him? The only thing that would further demolish his sense of masculinity was if Jordana discovered he'd been brained in the head by someone's pint-size, rolling-pin-wielding grannie.

He much preferred the theory that he'd been attacked by a hardened criminal or an international assassin.

All kidding aside (sort of), he was trying not to dwell too hard on the fact that someone had tried to kill him. Who had he pissed off so bad that they wanted to snip his thread?

Was he an asshole? Did he do dastardly things to innocent victims? What kind of person was he? The kind of person who used the word *dastardly*? He didn't have any answers. A sense of panic hovered at the edges of his thoughts. Hell, he didn't have a clue as to who he was or what kind of person he was.

For all he knew, he could be a real jerk who never donated to good causes, or sneered at the misfortune of others.

God, he hoped not.

What if he was the kind of guy Jordana would never actually invite into her home if she knew his true character?

Talk about a spiral into serious mental health danger.

Good or bad, a person's identity was everything.

Breathe. Chill out. You're not Hitler.

He'd know if he were a bad person, even if his memories were gone. If he were a terrible human being, he'd be drawn to do more terrible things, right? That's logical. *Right.* Clint paused a moment, waiting to see if terrible desires jumped into his head. When nothing unseemly took center stage in his mental theater, he nodded with satisfaction at his own deduction.

Conclusion: normal guy with memory loss. No hidden Hannibal Lecter lurking in his psyche.

Okay, so time to make a plan. He couldn't sit in Jordana's house like a caged canary, waiting for the next shoe to drop. Jordana's partner was running a background check on him. Details would reveal themselves and he'd hopefully find someone who actually knew him and could help put the pieces together.

And, much like a normal guy, he had eyeballs in his head. Eyeballs that really enjoyed the view of his new roommate.

But that was a hot stove best left alone. He didn't need his memories to figure out that messing around with the cute detective was a bad idea.

She didn't seem attached to anyone, but then, maybe she preferred to keep her house separate. He knew nothing about her aside from the fact that she appeared dedicated to her job, focused on keeping boundaries between them, and that she had the most beguiling smile when she chose to share it.

For all he knew, she could be a crooked cop keeping him close to protect those who had bashed his head in. Sure, it was a theory but he really couldn't give it much weight. Jordana had a straight and narrow sensibility about her. She probably never lied on her taxes or took an extra dinner mint at a restaurant.

She'd also probably never mess around with someone under her care—and he was relieved. Mostly because his conviction toward her wasn't quite as strong. He was way too intrigued by the intensity of her stare and the subtle curve of her lips to say that he wouldn't ever cross that line.

With Jordana keeping the lines tightly drawn, he didn't have to worry about anything unprofessional happening. All he had to worry about was finding who tried to kill him before they tried to come back and finish the job.

Chapter 5

"I got intel on your houseguest," Reese announced, sliding over in his office chair to Jordana's desk, dropping a folder with a grin. "Background check came in this morning. Seems your guy—"

"Not my guy," she corrected him with a warning scowl. "But go on…what about Clint?"

"Seems Clint Broderick is some big fish from Chicago. The guy is loaded. Owns a big tech company. I'm talking easily worth millions."

"That explains the fine threads," she murmured, digesting the information. She returned to Reese, dreading the answer to her next question. "So, is Mr. Moneybucks married or something? Someone waiting and worrying back in Chicago?"

"Nope. Only family was the dead guy walled up in the warehouse. Tough break, that. It's the old trope—the lonely rich boy with only dollar bills to keep him warm at night."

Jordana tossed a balled-up paper at Reese's grinning face. "You're finding way too much enjoyment in this."

"A sense of humor is important to keeping one's sanity," he drawled with a subtle smile. "So where is your rich houseguest? I thought you said he didn't want to be left alone?"

She chuckled at how her answer would be received. "Actually, I lent him some money so he could buy some clothes. He couldn't keep wearing what the hospital discharged him in."

"At least you know he's good for it," Reese quipped, to which Jordana agreed. "It could be worse—he could've been a con artist and just bilked you out of a couple bucks."

"My gut told me he was an acceptable risk and, as it turned out, I was right," Jordana said with a pointed look toward Reese because she wasn't above rubbing in her victory. "What else did you find out?"

"Well, he might not have any family but he does have a business partner, Alex Locke. Contact information is in the file."

Business partner. Immediate suspicion fell to those closest to the victim; that was just standard operating procedure. "Anything come up on Locke?"

"I didn't go deep but from the surface he looks pretty boring. The business seems to be doing well enough. There isn't a giant red flag waving around that points to motive, but like I said, that's just surface values. I can keep looking."

"Yeah, go ahead and poke around a bit. Make sure Locke is clean. I don't want to send Clint from the frying pan to the fire."

"Any particular reason you're so hot to protect this guy?" Reese asked.

"I'm doing my job," she answered, shifting against the implication that she was doing anything above and beyond what she'd do for anyone. But even as the words dropped from her mouth she knew it was a hard pill to swallow. "Okay, fine, I feel bad for the guy," she admitted. "He came here to help my investigation into a homicide that turned out to be his only family and then he gets whacked in the head and loses his memory."

"It's not your fault," Reese reminded her. "You can't carry that burden on your shoulders forever. What are you going to do, marry the guy to prove how sorry you are that he got jumped while trying to aid an investigation?"

She glowered. "Don't be stupid. Of course not."

"I'm just saying, it's a little much what you're doing for this guy. Feels more than professional. There, I said it and you can be pissed but I'm not sorry for being honest."

Maybe she was being a little more accommodating for Clint but she also knew she wasn't going to kick him out or do anything that might jeopardize his safety. "Well, we all have our opinions," she said, scooping up the file folder. "Thanks for the legwork. I have to go."

"Let me guess, Clint needs a ride after his little shopping trip? Maybe share a sandwich for two over at Harvey's?"

Her cheeks heated. She was meeting Clint for lunch but she hated the way Reese made it sound. But whatever, Reese could suck an egg. Jordana lifted the folder, saying over her shoulder, "Thanks for the support, buddy. You're a peach," as she marched out of the station.

Harvey's deli, located within the newly built Ruby Row shopping center, was a convenient place to meet after Clint did his shopping but it bothered Jordana that Reese had framed this meeting like a date of some sort, which it absolutely was not.

If anything, this was a working lunch and there was nothing social about it. She grabbed a table to wait for Clint, her knee bouncing with nervous energy. Maybe she should've suggested that Clint meet her at the station instead of a restaurant. She could've scarfed down a microwave burrito like she's done countless times in the past and Reese wouldn't have had cause to give her the side-eye.

But what did it matter? Clint was already living in her house for the time being; it wasn't as if meeting for lunch was going to soften the reality of her new living arrangement.

A deep throb had begun to pulsate behind her left eye. If everyone would just lay off her decision, that would be great. And by everyone, she meant Reese.

She looked up to see Clint enter the restaurant. Immediately, her breath caught. He made jeans and a T-shirt look like high fashion. She blinked against the very real warm sensation sending tendrils of awareness through her body. *Oh, good grief, so he can rock a casual look, big deal. Nothing has changed.* She schooled her expression before he slid into the seat opposite her with an unsure grin. "Did I do okay?" He surprised her with the question.

She affirmed with an efficient nod. "Jeans and a T-shirt are appropriate for the early fall in Kansas, yes."

"Good, good," he murmured. "Honestly, I don't know if I'm a jeans and a T-shirt kind of guy because I was drawn to the slacks and polos but, you know, when in Rome, right? I think I'll stick out less if I dress like the natives."

"Braxville is not the untamed wilderness," she grumbled, taking mild offense. "If you wanted to wear slacks and a polo, you would've been just fine. No one would've given you a weird look."

"Good to know," he said, seeming to sense that he'd offended her. "I'm sorry if I implied anything—"

"No, you're fine," she said, wanting to move on. She was being prickly and picking a fight for the wrong reasons. *Get back on target.* Jordana produced the file folder. "I have some good news. My partner, Reese, was able to dig up some information that might help jog your memory."

Clint perked up. "Yeah? What'd he find?"

"Well, it seems you're…let's just say you're not worried about how you're going to pay the light bill." She waited for Clint to open the file before adding, "You're pretty much loaded. You own a tech company in Chicago with a business partner, Alex Locke. Ring a bell?"

A part of her hoped she'd see the light of recognition dawn in his eyes but the other part, the inexplicable part, hoped he remained blank.

Girl, you are walking a dangerous path. Get off while you still can.

Excellent counsel. Except she knew she wasn't going to.

And that was worse.

Clint waited for that spark of memory to burn away the fog of his amnesia, but as he stared at the facts on the printed page, he felt nothing. Frustrated, he pushed the folder away with a heavy sigh. "Sorry, I don't remember any of this. Damn it. When is this going to end?"

"Dr. Cervantes said it could happen anytime. It isn't likely going to be permanent," she assured him. "I would wait on contacting your business partner until my partner can do a little background check."

His face screwed into a confused frown. "Why?"

"Because those closest to the victim are usually the first to fall under suspicion," she said.

"That's messed up. Seems like a penalty for being close to the victim."

"Sometimes but it's really just a way to clear away the obvious. Detective work is often a process of elimination until you get down to the most plausible suspects. As much as I hate to remind you, someone wanted you dead. Your business partner needs to be cleared before we can successfully check him off the list of possible suspects."

That made a certain amount of sense, but he didn't like the idea of someone whom he shared a business to fall under suspicion because it called into question his judgment. "Doesn't feel very good knowing someone tried to kill me," he said, settling back with a sigh. "I was kind of leaning on the theory that it was a robbery gone wrong. I mean, they did take my wallet."

"But no charges have been made on your credit cards, which tells me they likely just dumped your wallet."

"Guess that doesn't jive with a thief's mentality to steal something only to throw it away before using it."

She nodded. "Yeah, pretty much, but hey, think of the bright side—you don't have to fill out a bunch of bank paperwork to prove fraudulent charges. You just need to cancel your cards as lost and order new ones."

"Yeah, that's the bright side," he replied, his good mood squashed. He thumbed through the paperwork. "Is there any way you can clear my partner quickly? I need to get access to my funds and I don't even know where I bank. I'm guessing my business partner would know that information."

"I understand that it's hard to accept help, but if you're just patient, we can get this figured out. In the meantime,

I'll keep track of expenses if it helps ease your discomfort and you can pay me back."

"With interest," he added, needing something to lessen the uncomfortable feeling that he was freeloading, even though he knew he wasn't. He might not remember jack about his life but he recognized the prick of pride.

"Interest isn't necessary," Jordana said, ready to move on, but Clint wasn't.

"No, I need to do something a little extra to feel better about landing in your lap. I know this can't be a cakewalk for you. I've completely disrupted your life and I need to do something to make up for it." He held Jordana's stare, feeling her push back, but he wasn't going to budge. He tried a different angle, saying with persuasion, "Look, you said yourself, I can afford to be generous. Let me throw a little extra your way. It's the least I can do for everything you've done for me thus far."

"I'm just doing my job," she protested. "It wouldn't be right to accept money from you above what you owe."

"C'mon, be honest, you've been a little extra accommodating," he said, gesturing to his new clothes. "And I sincerely appreciate the effort even if it's not something you do for everyone."

"I don't like the way that sounds," Jordana said with a subtle frown. "I don't need anyone saying that I'm giving you special treatment. It's hard enough to prove that I'm walking a professional line without you throwing money in my purse. It doesn't look right."

"Not to point out the obvious but you already said I'm liquid and I think there might be a huge disparity between my income and yours. I don't feel right putting the burden of my room and board on your shoulders without properly compensating you."

"Why are we arguing about this? Fine, if it puts an

end to this conversation, I can donate whatever you give me to charity." She relented with an exasperated exhale. "Can we move on?"

Clint could tell Jordana was at her tipping point. If he pushed any harder, she'd shut down and he didn't want that. Besides, he'd earned the victory, no sense in belaboring the point.

"Yes." He nodded, satisfied and ready to eat. "I'm starved. What's good here?"

Chapter 6

Jordana wasn't accustomed to having another human being rattling around in her house. She struggled with the need to play the hostess at all times—something her mother had never failed to point out was not her strength—but Clint was surprisingly chill about their unorthodox situation.

She'd brought home case files, but as she sank into the sofa, her head still throbbing from the stress of the day, she couldn't bring herself to look at the files just yet.

Clint was in the kitchen making an awful racket. *What is he doing? Remodeling?* She rose to investigate and found Clint wearing a cooking apron her sister Bridgette had bought her as a gag gift (because Jordana hated to cook) and making a huge mess in her usually orderly kitchen.

"What's happening?" she asked, trying to hide her dismay. "Looks like the apocalypse blew through here."

"Yeah, turns out I'm a bit of a messy chef," he agreed with good humor. "But I think I'm doing an okay job on the actual cooking front. I think I know what I'm doing. I mean, I'm kind of going off instinct but it smells pretty good, wouldn't you say?"

It did. "I don't feel the need to vomit if that's what you're asking," she said, sliding into the barstool at the island. "So what are you whipping up, Gordon Ramsay?"

"Pasta carbonara with bacon and peas tossed with garlic and olive oil." He paused to ask with alarm, "Are you a vegetarian?"

"Nope. All meat for this girl," she answered, countering with, "How do you know *you're* not vegetarian?"

"Well, the bacon smells pretty damn good so I'd say if I were vegetarian I'd be repulsed, right?"

"Sounds plausible. What if you're not eating meat for ethical reasons and not for reasons of taste and texture?"

"I'll just have to take the risk," he said. "If it turns out that I am a vegetarian, I'll find a way to repent, but until then, I'm going to eat my weight in this pasta because it smells like carb heaven."

She laughed. "Judging by your physique, I don't think you carb-load very often."

He grinned in acknowledgment. "Then today is my cheat day, I guess, but you know the best part about losing your memory?" He paused for dramatic effect before answering. "You don't remember anything to feel guilty about."

That was an interesting way to look at his situation, she mused. Rising, she pulled a bottle of red wine and uncorked it to pour a glass. She gestured and he nodded. "Guess we'll find out if you like wine, too," she said, raising her glass in toast before taking a much-needed sip. *Ahhh, good stuff.* She watched as he took an exploratory drink. When he nodded in agreement, she smiled.

Was she really sitting in her kitchen drinking wine with Clint Broderick while he made dinner? This smacked of inappropriate. Nothing about this situation was protocol. She didn't know the rules. Everything felt suspect and out of joint. She ought to excuse herself and get back to work but she didn't get the chance.

"I hope you're hungry," Clint said as he dished up her plate and slid it over to her. He took a minute to dish his and then took a seat at the island with her. Clint rose his glass for a toast. "Here's to discovering who the hell I am and why someone wanted to kill me."

She clinked her glass with his, murmuring, "Here, here," and took another fortifying sip. Jordana knew she ought to thank him for dinner and then excuse herself to her bedroom for the night but she didn't want to.

For one, she liked spending time with Clint. For two, it seemed rude to grab her plate and scurry off like a raccoon stealing someone's dinner.

People had to eat. Simple biology. She stabbed the pasta with her fork with a little too much force, startling Clint.

"Whoa there, careful. There's enough for seconds if you're that hungry," he teased.

She blushed, mortified. "Sorry. It's not… Forget it. Smells delicious. Thank you." When in doubt, fall back on good manners. At least her mother would be proud. "Oh, that's really good," she admitted, surprised. "I was a little worried it might be inedible."

Clint chuckled. "Thankfully, it seems I do know my way around a kitchen, which is a relief. I'd hate to think I was completely useless in a real-life sort of way."

"What do you mean useless?" she asked, confused.

"Just the stereotype of a bachelor being all thumbs in the kitchen. Especially a bachelor with means. I like knowing that I can navigate a hot stove without panicking and calling for takeout. Feels good. I don't know, maybe it's stupid but losing my memory has made me insecure about a lot of things. This—" he pointed at his plate "—makes me feel a little less so."

She smiled. "You have nothing to feel insecure about— you are a very good cook." To prove her point, she took another bite and moaned with genuine appreciation. "Don't tell my mom but this right here might have replaced her mashed potatoes and meat loaf as my new favorite dish."

"I've replaced a mother's meat loaf? That feels like high praise. I'll take it. Sorry, Mama Colton."

Jordana broke into a giggle midbite. "Lord help me, but my mom would probably love you."

"What's not to love?" he said with a grin. "I seem pretty damn awesome to me."

Jordana rolled her eyes at his cheesy confidence but the guy had a point. A beat of silence followed as Jordana pushed around her pasta, thinking. Was this his actual personality or was this a consequence of his memory loss? She looked up to find Clint watching her.

"Where'd you go?" he asked as if he could see right through to her personal thoughts.

"How do you know I went anywhere?" she tried teasing. "Maybe your amazing pasta has rendered me speechless."

He shook his head. "You're a terrible liar. Do you know that everything you think and feel flows right across your face? I don't advise you take up poker. You'll lose your shirt."

"And are you a good liar?" she countered.

Clint shrugged. "I haven't a clue. Maybe. Maybe not. I guess I won't know until I regain my memory. Is that what you were wondering?"

"No," she admitted. "I wondered if this is who you really are or if this is just a consequence of the memory loss. People who sustain head injuries…personality changes aren't uncommon."

"I've heard that, as well." He took a moment before adding, "But I can't imagine that I'm so different than I am now. I think some things are just part of who you are."

"Yeah, but you don't even know what that means for you."

"It's hard to describe but I can tell when something feels off. It's like trying to put on a shoe that doesn't quite fit—everything feels wrong."

"But how could you possibly know?" she insisted. "You literally have no clue who you are or who you *were*. You don't know why you were coming to see me or what information had been so important that you'd make the trip."

"All I can do is give you an example," he said, moving to face her. "When you first offered up your place, my first instinct was to say no. Even though I had no idea where I was going to stay or how I was going to manage, I didn't want to put you in a bad position. That's an inherent value that I think is part of your long-term imprinting, which wasn't affected by the head injury."

Jordana was surprised by how relieved that logic made her feel. "I suppose that makes sense," she said, breaking into another smile. "I'm sorry you haven't regained your memory yet. I know it must be aggravating."

"It's no picnic but…having you around makes it easier to bear."

His admission created havoc in her belly that had nothing to do with the fact that she was mildly sensitive to gluten.

On that note, Jordana knew she ought to gracefully excuse herself but she remained rooted to her stool, loath to leave, wanting to stay.

Yeah, this was definitely a problem, but at the moment…she didn't really care.

Clint knew he shouldn't have dropped that truth bomb but there was something about Jordana that made him want to be honest and raw with her. He found her blunt pragmatism invigorating, and her badass sensibilities turned him on.

Yeah, as in completely aroused when she was around, but he was trying to keep himself in check. She'd been pretty clear: nothing romantic was offered or appreciated.

He wasn't going to ruin her trust in him but that didn't mean he wasn't fantasizing about her lips on his behind closed doors.

Keep things on solid ground.

"So, tell me what you can about the Crane case—that's the one you were investigating, right? The one with my relative?"

She seemed relieved to switch gears. Detective Colton was back in the room. "Well, it's an active investigation so I can't share too many details. I can tell you what I initially told you when we spoke on the phone."

"It's all new to me so go for it," he said, winking. "Every time is like the first time right now."

Jordana chuckled but quickly sobered, saying, "It feels disrespectful to joke about the circumstances. I mean, Fenton Crane was your relative."

"Yeah, but even if I did remember him, from what you told me, we weren't very close. I mean, it sounds like I never really knew the guy. Don't get me wrong, it's terrible that he ended up in a wall—that sounds like a bad way to die for anyone—but I don't feel any grief or loss."

Jordana accepted his explanation. "Yes, it seems Mr. Crane was an uncle but that in itself is really sad." She leaned against her elbow to regard him with curiosity. "What's it like to be such a lone wolf? I can't imagine not having brothers and sisters or extended family all around me. Actually, it might be nice at first but after a while… I would imagine that it would get lonely."

His childhood had been lonely. His parents, decent folk, if not a little absent, had figured out early on that having a clutch of kids wasn't in their wheelhouse. It was probably a blessing that he'd grown up an only child. He didn't like playing the lonely kid card, though. "It was fine. Being an only child gave me certain advantages. I never had to share my toys," he said with a playful smile.

"How many siblings do you have?"

"Ready yourself."

His brow arched. "Go on."

"I am one of six Colton kids," she admitted. "And there's a set of triplets in that number."

"Triplets? Holy crap. What a handful for your parents that must've been."

"Yeah, I think it made my mom neurotic. My dad was a workaholic so he wasn't around much for the child-rearing part. I can't remember my dad ever changing a diaper. Not his generation, I guess. My mom shouldered the load. It made me want to never have kids, that's for sure."

"Seriously?"

"Yeah, maybe. Well, maybe that's too harsh. I'm just not cut out for that life. I prefer chasing criminals to toddlers."

He laughed. "Is it sexist that I assumed all women at some point want to get married and have kids?"

"It is and you know it," she said, calling him out. "I can tell by the way that dimple pops out on your right cheek that you're full of shit and you know that, too."

He laughed. "Okay, guilty. I guess sometimes I'm a sexist asshole," he confessed, shrugging his shoulders with mock apology.

"Well, you had to have some kind of flaw," she said, rising as she gathered their plates. "Because a man who can cook like this and looks like you…is some woman's dream."

Some woman? But not yours? Ah, Jordana, you kill me. But he liked it.

Chapter 7

Jordana returned to the house at lunch with good news. She found Clint reading the local newspaper with an expression of amusement. "There's a section in the local paper called 'Cop's Corner' that lists select calls to Dispatch. Listen to this one—'11:25 p.m. Report of petty theft on Georgia Lane. Reporting party saw neighbor take lawn ornament.' This is hilarious! Is this for real? Or is this someone's column full of made-up stuff?"

She sighed. "It's real. Some people are very invested in what goes around. A lot of nosy neighbors calling in their grievances, honestly."

"Oh! Here's another one—'2:30 p.m. Report of suspicious circumstances on Mockingbird Lane. Reporting party wants to report an unknown person parking in front of his house. Wants officer to tow unknown vehicle.'" Clint looked to Jordana with eyes brimming with laughter. "This is what constitutes crime around here?"

"Aside from the two bodies that were found walled up in an old building owned by my family? Yeah, it's pretty quiet around here."

Clint sobered. "Ah, right. Something tells me that discovery wasn't printed in Cop's Corner."

"No, we asked the editor if she would respectfully keep that entry in the dispatch log, out of the media."

"Only in a small town would that work," he said. "If you tried that in Chicago, you'd get laughed out of town."

"Privileges and perks," Jordana said, adding, "And I know exactly what that Mockingbird Lane call was about. You'll find this funny. So there's this old man who thinks he owns the street in front of his house. He calls every time someone parks there. We've tried explaining that the street is owned by the city and anyone can park there but he's stubbornly refused to listen. So we get a call each time. It's a pain in the ass. He needs a friggin' hobby. We actually draw straws to determine whose turn it is to talk to old man Bryce."

"That's his name? Bryce?"

"Yep. Bryce Riggens. You don't need a neighborhood watch with old man Bryce peeking through his blinds at all times." She chuckled. "Not sure how many people will show up to his funeral when he finally goes. He's pissed off quite a few people."

"Sounds like an unhappy man," Clint said. "Ah, well, too late to change that leopard's spots. So, what was your good news?"

Jordana smiled, happy to share something positive. "Seems you did have someone waiting and worrying at home—your assistant. Reese tracked down some names and numbers and came across your personal secretary, Jeana—does that ring a bell? Jeana Erickson?"

His brow furrowed as he searched his memory. "It

sounds vaguely familiar, but when I push harder for details, the information slips away," he said, his tone laced with frustration. "So, did she realize I was missing? Why didn't she file a missing-persons report?"

"She wanted to but, according to her, she was afraid you might not approve, especially if it turned out to be nothing. Apparently, you don't like untoward attention."

Clint digested that information before saying, "Well, that makes sense. I own a big company. I probably have investors, and investors need to feel safe and secure in order to keep the flow of money going. I think she did the right thing not filing. Besides, I'm clearly not missing, just my memory is."

"That's circular logic but okay," she said derisively. "Anyway, I have her contact information for you." Jordana handed Clint the paper in her hand. "Feel free to contact her. You can share what happened to you, but if you could keep details to a minimum, that would be helpful."

"Right," he agreed, staring at the name and number on the sheet. "It's weird to stare at something you should know but have no recollection of its importance. I feel bad for my assistant."

"A suggestion if you wouldn't mind," she said, waiting for his nod to continue. "I wouldn't mention the amnesia. I don't know anything about your business but knowing the boss has lost his memory might affect your company. I'd just keep that intel on a need-to-know basis until you recover."

"Solid advice," he said. "Makes sense. Thanks."

Jordana nodded and headed for the kitchen to find a deli sandwich on sourdough waiting for her. "What is this?" she asked.

"Unless that's a trick question, it's clearly a sandwich,"

he answered, joining her. "I've got nothing but time on my hands when you're at the station and I like to tinker in the kitchen. It's the only thing that makes me feel a little normal."

"But you shouldn't feel you have to make me dinner or lunch every time I turn around," she said, biting her lip. "Although that looks pretty good and I'm starved. I was going to pop a burrito in the microwave but now that doesn't seem very appealing."

"Please, eat." He gestured to the barstool. "It's the least I can do to help out, okay?"

She understood the need to feel useful but she was wary of the tickle in her stomach when he did things like this. It was hard to keep lines drawn when they kept inching closer and closer past the point of no return.

And what exactly did that look like?

Well, if it looked like the dream she had last night, then it looked like two naked people twisted around each other like there was no tomorrow.

Her breath hitched in her throat at the memory. *That does it, no more chocolate before bed.* She slid onto the barstool and pulled the cellophane free. "How do you manage to make a roast beef sandwich look like art? Are you sure you're a tech guy?"

He chuckled. "Well, maybe I made my money in tech but secretly yearned to be the next culinary sensation."

Jordana smiled with amusement before taking a bite. She nodded with appreciation, "Okay, yeah, this is pretty good, damn it," she said around her bite. "If you keep this up, I might not want you to ever get your memory back."

Clint laughed at her joke but a part of her—the part she kept under lock and key—realized she was a little serious.

She liked having Clint around.

More than she wanted to admit.

* * *

He liked feeding Jordana. There was something primal and caveman-ish about his enjoyment of "providing sustenance" to the woman he found attractive, but he kept his feelings in check with a simple reminder: she'd stated her boundaries and they excluded anything romantic.

So, he'd have to satisfy his growing feelings by stuffing her face as often as possible.

And he wasn't lying when he said it made him feel useful. He might not remember his life but he knew that he didn't like being idle.

"Any movement on the case?" he asked, biting into his own sandwich.

"No, not really. It's a challenge when the victim doesn't remember anything," she answered with a teasing smile that tested his ability to keep his lips to himself. "We've got some feelers out, to see if anyone saw anything on Range Road where you were found, but these things take time. People have a tendency to keep to themselves, especially when dealing with something like this."

"What happened to the small-town stereotype of neighbors helping neighbors?" he asked.

"If you were local, that stereotype would apply, but there's nothing more cliquish than a small town," she said.

"That's discouraging," he admitted. "What are the odds you'll be able to catch who did this?"

She winced a little. "Not very good."

He accepted her answer, appreciating her honesty. Now it was his turn to be forthright. "Can I be frank with you?" At her nod, he continued. "I'm not really expecting anyone to come forward with information, which means at some point I'm going to have to admit that my case might go unsolved and I have to get back to my life in Chicago."

"That's a healthy expectation but I'm not ready to give up just yet. Someone might still come forward."

He wanted her to want him to stay for reasons that had nothing to do with the case. *Ugh. Pathetic, much?* Was he a stage-four clinger in his normal life? Was that why he didn't have a wife or a girlfriend? The paranoia was hard to shut down when you knew next to nothing about yourself.

"I appreciate the effort," he said, switching focus. "Maybe if you told me more about Fenton Crane, it might help jog my memory."

"What we do know about Fenton isn't all that flattering. Are you sure you want to know that kind of detail about your family member?"

He assured her with a smile he could take it. "I didn't know the guy, remember? Just because we shared DNA didn't mean he was coming over for Thanksgiving dinner. Go ahead, hit me."

"Okay, from what we know, Fenton was a bit of a sleaze. Definitely no moral boundaries. He was motivated entirely by money. He'd take any job for the right amount of cash."

"Just playing devil's advocate here, aren't we all motivated by money?"

"Fenton was a private investigator who set the bar pretty low if the money was good enough," Jordana said.

"Yeah, but the PI business…not exactly a cash cow. Sometimes you gotta do what you gotta do to survive."

She cast a wary look his way. "You sound pretty defensive for a guy who claims he didn't know the victim."

He held his hands up, laughing. "I swear, I didn't know

him. I'm just saying, passing judgment on the poor guy for trying to make a living seems a little harsh."

"Some of us have higher moral and ethical standards, I guess," she said a bit stiffly.

Was this their first disagreement? Was he weird for enjoying that flash of spirit in her eyes? The thing about Jordana that he was starting to realize was that she kept a lot under lock and key. He sensed a passionate woman hiding behind that buckled-down exterior.

It wasn't his place to try and jimmy that lock but couldn't fault a man for trying, right?

"Sorry, sorry, didn't mean to offend you," he promised. "Just trying to offer perspective."

Jordana's expression lost some of the tension but he could tell the energy between them had changed. "I appreciate your help," she said, rising to clear her spot. "And lunch was great but I have to get back to the station."

He didn't want to leave things ruffled between them. Clint reached out to gently grasp her hand. "I shouldn't have stepped on your toes. It's your investigation and I don't know what I'm doing so take my opinion with a grain of salt."

Her smile seemed strained around the edges as she slowly eased her hand free. "It's fine. You did nothing wrong. Maybe talking to your assistant will jog some memory loose. I'll see you tonight."

And then she was out the door.

Maybe he shouldn't have pressed those buttons. He didn't want to ruin the trust they were building but something inside him urged him to push a little.

Was he a jerk in his pre-memory-loss life? According to Jordana, he'd built a large, successful company. Success came at a cost. Sometimes you had to be aggressive.

Maybe that's why someone had tried to kill him. Maybe he'd pushed the wrong person too far.

Not a far-fetched theory. People have turned violent for lesser reasons. But he was grabbing blindly at anything in the dark and it didn't feel good.

He grabbed the paper. Time to see if a voice from his past triggered some recovery.

Chapter 8

Jordana liked to think of herself as calm and rational, definitely not prone to theatrics or melodrama. As the second oldest in a family of six, there simply wasn't room for a personality that sucked all the oxygen out of the room.

But there was something about Clint that made her feel irrational. It definitely made her want to act in a way that was out of character.

When he grasped her hand, she nearly froze. Her heartbeat practically shattered her rib cage. His hand, smooth and warm yet big and commanding, felt perfect against her skin. It was all she could do to calmly and reasonably withdraw without looking like a crazy person.

Her knee-jerk reaction was to yank her hand free as if scalded. But not because his touch repulsed her. No, quite the opposite.

You need to encourage him to return to Chicago, her inside voice reasoned.

That was the last thing she wanted. She liked having him around.

Aside from his awesome kitchen skills, she liked coming home knowing he was there. The smile that found her lips the minute she pulled into the driveway was hard to smother.

You're losing objectivity, that damned voice chided her, *time for him to go.*

All good advice, and yet, she kept finding new justifications to keep him there.

But not every justification was personal, she wanted to protest. She currently had two unsolved crimes on her desk: the warehouse murders and Clint's attack. What if they were related? It was foolhardy to send him packing because she was harboring some misplaced attraction that would surely fade with a little distance.

All she needed to do was to stay the course, keep her head on straight, avoid doing anything that would blur the lines and everything would work out.

She didn't dare confess her concerns to Reese. He'd tell her to pull the plug, *pronto*, on their living situation because he hadn't been a fan from the start.

Jordana hated being wrong and Reese loved being right.

That's what we call an impasse.

She'd have to buckle down and figure things out on her own.

When in doubt, focus on work.

Jordana strode into the station, heading for her desk, when the brand-new captain pulled her into his office. After her previous boss left the position, longtime lawman Michael Placer was put in charge.

Captain Placer, a man with a stern Wilford Brimley look about him, left his officers to their jobs and rarely micromanaged, but she could tell by his expression he'd heard that Clint was living in her spare bedroom.

Damn that small-town gossip.

"What can I do for you, Captain?" she asked, standing at attention, her naval training demanding nothing less when speaking to a commander.

"At ease, Detective," he said, going straight to the point. "Is that amnesia guy, Clint Broderick, living in your house?"

No sense in lying. "Yes, sir. I thought it prudent to keep him close given the circumstances of his assault."

"Your house is not a certified safe house," Placer reminded her. "If you've located his people, turn him loose. The department can't afford the liability of you harboring him under your roof."

"The department didn't assume any liability. I took him in under my own recognizance."

"Did you run that by me?" he returned pointedly.

"No, sir."

"Right, because you knew the answer would be no."

"He didn't know anyone or have access to any resources. It seemed…cruel to toss him onto the street."

Placer waved away her explanation. "Be that as it may, it wasn't your job to house him. You don't know anything about the man. It was foolish and reckless on your part, and frankly, I find that surprising coming from you. You're not usually this foolhardy. Do I need to worry about you, Detective?"

"Of course not," she answered with a clip to her tone. "As it turns out, Broderick is a respected businessman in Chicago. We only just discovered his contact information, which I gave to him today. I respectfully ask for a little leniency in this regard. It should only take a few more days before he can safely return to Chicago."

That seemed to soften the captain's hard line. "A few days?" he repeated.

"Yes, sir," she answered, assuring him, "I understand your concerns. I promise he's been a perfect gentleman and a polite houseguest."

"That's not the issue. I'm concerned that you made the offer in the first place."

"Sometimes you have to listen to your gut," she said, refusing to allow herself to be second-guessed. "Besides, his case is still unsolved. Someone tried to kill him. I'm still the detective on his case. I thought it best to keep Broderick close for his own safety."

"We're not the FBI, Colton. We're a small-town police force with enough resources to keep the peace, but we're not equipped to take on cases that require that level of protection for the witnesses. Look, I admire your heart. It's one of your best qualities, but I can't have you set a precedent of bringing home victims to lodge at Chez Colton. It's just not sustainable or smart. Understand?"

"Of course," she answered, but she felt the captain was making a bigger deal out of her decision than it warranted. It wasn't as if she were opening her doors to every person in Braxville with a sad story.

"So we're clear? Broderick goes home ASAP?"

"Unless I have a break in the case, yes," she replied.

"Detective," Placer warned, irritated by her stubbornness. "I'm not playing around here."

"Understood."

He sighed as if knowing she was going to do what she felt best, no matter what he said. "I can tell by that look in your eye that you're gonna do what you damn well please. Look, the only reason I'm not putting Broderick on a plane right now is that your gut is usually right, but I don't like this, not one bit."

"I feel a certain level of responsibility for what happened to Broderick. He came to Braxville to tell me something about the Crane case. He got whacked and left for dead because of me. Letting him crash in my spare bedroom, for the time being, was the least I could do. As it turned out, it was an acceptable risk."

"Lucky for you he didn't turn out to be a serial killer."

"That would've worked out badly for him if he were."

Placer's gruff expression broke around a grudging smile. "Can't argue with you there." He leaned back in his chair, his girth causing the chair to groan. "Okay, you've got your few days to put the pieces together, but after that, I'm pulling rank and putting Broderick on a plane back to his people."

"That's fair," she conceded. "Was there anything else?"

"No, one shitshow a day is my limit. Keep me in the loop if anything pops up on either case. I've got too many eyes on our department and it's giving me indigestion."

She smiled. "Or it could be the pastrami on rye that your wife has told me you shouldn't be eating."

"And I'll tell you what I tell her, 'Don't waste your breath. Some things ain't worth living without.'" With that, he shooed Jordana out of his office.

When she sat down at her desk, she narrowed her gaze at Reese and mouthed the words, *Big mouth*.

Reese just grinned without so much as a mouthed *Sorry* back because she knew he wasn't, and he wasn't going to pretend otherwise. Okay, she kinda liked that about Reese but not when it backfired on her.

She only had a few days to produce some kind of results.

Nothing like an impossible goal to galvanize one's motivation, right?

* * *

Clint stared at the paper with the phone number. He'd spent the last fifteen minutes vacillating on whether or not to place the call.

Sure, it seemed an easy decision—make the call, possibly trigger a memory, maybe even go home.

But what was waiting for him back in Chicago? Who was he? Did people like him? Was he a jerk boss who everyone secretly hated and talked about behind his back? The loss of his memory wasn't a cakewalk but it certainly freed him up to be whomever he chose without the burden of the past.

He was being a baby and delaying the inevitable. He couldn't play house with Jordana forever. At some point he had to face the music back in Chicago.

No matter the tune playing. With a heavy sigh, he picked up the phone and dialed. Within the first ring, a female voice answered.

"This is Jeana Erickson, may I ask who's calling?"

Well, that was the name Jordana had given him. He supposed he was on the right track. He cleared his throat and threw his cards out there. "Hi, Jeana, this is…uh, Clint Broderick. I heard you might be looking for me."

The sharp intake of breath on the other end wasn't surprising. "Mr. Broderick! Where have you been? When you didn't answer your phone for several days I became worried. Are you okay?"

He waited a beat for recognition to hit him like a thunderbolt, and while there was something about the timbre of her voice that sounded familiar, he couldn't picture her face or recall any memories.

Clint smothered his disappointment by assuring the woman he was fine. "I'm sorry, Jeana, I didn't mean to worry you. I had some business here in Kansas and then lost my wallet and cell. I've had a bear of a time trying to sort the details in this town but I can't leave just yet. I still have some unfinished business to take care of."

"Oh, heavens! Do you need me to call and cancel your bank cards?"

"Yes, that would be great. Thank you. Also, I can't get access to my accounts right now. Can you wire me some cash?"

"Right away. Just tell me where to send it."

Clint gave Jeana the information for the Western Union in town with the amount. When she didn't seem to blink an eye, it seemed to support Jordana's intel that he wasn't hurting.

"Is there anything else you need?" Jeana asked. "How long will you be staying in Braxville? Should I cancel your upcoming meetings?"

He must've told his assistant where he was going, but had he told her why? "Yeah, go ahead and cancel. I'm going to be here for a few more days."

"Yes, sir. Oh, Mr. Locke has been asking for you. Should I let him know that you're still in Braxville?"

His business partner. Jordana hadn't cleared Locke of being a suspect. He hated to be so paranoid but losing his memory had made him second-guess everything. "No, I'll give him a call later, tell him myself," he told her. "Hey, quick question, what did I tell you about why I was going to Braxville?"

The confusion at his question was evident in her voice as she answered, "I don't recall you saying why. What I remember you saying was that you had private business to deal with and that you'd be gone a day or so. Did I miss something?"

Clint let the poor woman off the hook. She sounded

like she ate antacids for breakfast. "No, no, you're fine. I was just wondering. You're good."

Her relief was evident. "Thank you, sir. I'll get that wire transfer to you immediately and take care of your bank cards. Is this a good number for further contact?"

"No, I'll get in touch after I buy a new replacement phone."

"All right," Jeana said. "I'm so happy you're safe. Everyone will be so relieved."

"Thank you, Jeana. You're a big help."

"Oh! Gosh, yes, of course, I'm on top of things on this end." Then the flustered woman clicked off. Clint replaced the phone on the receiver, silently amused that Jordana still had a landline and wondered if Jeana's reaction was proof that he was seen as a real jerk back at the office.

She'd been practically tripping on herself to please him. If that were the case, maybe the list of people who wanted him dead was deeper than he thought.

And that wasn't a nice feeling at all.

Did he have more in common with his dead relative, Fenton Crane, than he cared to admit?

He had to find out.

Chapter 9

Jordana planned to spend her day off working on background files for both cases but Clint had other plans.

"We need to get out of this town for the day," he announced, causing her to look up from her notes with a quizzical expression. "Now that I've rented a car for the time being and I have some cash in my pocket, I say you let me treat you to a distraction."

"You really shouldn't draw so much attention to yourself," she warned, worried that whoever had been after him still hadn't left town. She had a hard time believing someone local had perpetrated the crime but she remained open to the possibility.

"What? I needed a car to get around."

"Yes, but did you need to rent something so…flashy?"

"A convertible Mustang was the only vehicle they had in an upgraded coupe," he apologized. "I'm not trying to be flashy. It was either the Mustang or some kind of boxcar that looked like it wouldn't withstand a stiff wind. At least the Mustang is made from steel."

She supposed she could understand that explanation. The rental agency in town was notoriously small without much of a selection. "You're lucky you didn't end up with a Buick LeSabre. That's Bonnie's favorite car in her fleet, which no one wants to ever rent but she won't replace it."

"Do they even make LeSabres anymore?"

"I don't think so." She shook her head.

He clapped his hands, rubbing them together, excited to get back on topic. "Back to my original suggestion. Let's distract ourselves from the noise and do something fun."

She frowned. "A distraction is the last thing I need. I need to focus," she said, pointing at the piles of paperwork all around her. "I need to double down if I'm going to find answers."

He immediately countered with, "Actually, you'll be *more* productive if you give your mind a break to recharge. Right now you're spinning in mud and not getting anywhere."

"How would you know this?" she asked dryly. "You can't even remember if you like pineapple on your pizza much less what makes someone more productive."

He paused for a minute to give her statement some thought, then decided definitively, "I do not like pineapple on pizza. Just thinking about it gives me hives. Seems unnatural. And, Miss Negative Nelly, I actually just read about a study conducted by the University of Illinois that concluded taking breaks helps the brain to reboot and aids in the formation in critical problem-solving."

She regarded him with a curious frown. "Are you pulling my leg?"

"Not even a little bit. So, it's science. Time to take a break."

The warning from the captain rang in her head, but

if Clint was right and taking a break actually helped her with the case, it seemed warranted.

A break would be great, though. Her eyesight was swimming from all the paperwork she'd been wading through with little to show for it.

"Let's say I was open to the idea in theory—what did you have in mind?"

"I did a little digging around and there's an indoor climbing place in Wichita that looks right up your alley."

"Like, rock climbing?" she asked.

He nodded with a grin.

"What if I'm afraid of heights?"

"Are you?"

"No, but what if I was?"

"Then I guess I'd say, time to conquer your fears," he answered, his grin widening.

Jordana bit her lip to keep from smiling. She knew all about the place he was suggesting. She actually went there when she could spare the time away. Since the warehouse bodies were found, it'd been a while since she could sneak away.

Was she impressed that Clint had accurately guessed what she'd find relaxing and enjoyable on her day off?

Okay, yes, a wee bit.

Was she going to take him up on his offer?

Not sure.

"I probably shouldn't," she hedged, still mulling the idea in her head. "I'm not sure it's a good idea to be out socially together."

Clint balked. "Am I not good enough for you, Detective?" he asked with mock offense. She couldn't stop the laugh that followed. Jordana shook her head and rolled her eyes. His gaze met hers, a twinkle matching the dimple in his cheek. "Look, it's just an offer to climb a fake rock and sweat our asses off, not a marriage proposal. It'll be good for both of us to blow off some steam. I may not remember much but I do recognize the signs of cabin fever and I definitely have it."

Jordana should say no but she wanted to go. A day away from Braxville at her favorite place to hang out and, as Clint put it, "sweat their asses off" seemed like the perfect plan to her.

"Fine," she relented, but not before reminding Clint of the ground rules. "This isn't a date by any stretch of the imagination. We'll pay our own way. I can pitch in for gas. Understood?"

"Buzzkill," he teased, but nodded. "Understood. Like I want you slobbering all over me, anyway. You probably kiss like a Saint Bernard."

She laughed harder at his obvious overkill in that department. Popping from her seat, Jordana grabbed her purse and jacket, saying, "I guess you'll never know."

Clint smiled. "Guess not," he agreed, but there was something about his tone, or maybe it was his expression, that told a different story.

She suppressed a shiver and forced a bright, completely unaffected smile, saying, "I can't wait to critique your driving skills. Not to make you nervous or anything but I'm a harsh critic. Between military and police training, I'm a stickler for the rules of the road."

But Clint just laughed, taking her challenge with a level of confidence she found alluring. "Bring it. I'm impervious to intimidation."

That shiver she was trying ardently to keep under wraps morphed into a full-body warmth that raced from her toes to the top of her head. She recognized trouble when she felt it but it was like trying to fight a food craving when she was starving. Even though she knew she ought to stop, Jordana couldn't fight the urge to reach for the very thing she knew was bad.

Bad for so many reasons.

The man had amnesia, for crying out loud. He couldn't possibly know what was good for him. It didn't matter that his energy matched hers—he wasn't in a position to act on those feelings.

But even if he wasn't working on two instead of four cylinders, the fact didn't change that she was investigating his case. There simply wasn't any wiggle room for *feelings*.

"Ready?" she asked.

"Woman, I was born ready… I think," Clint answered with a wink.

A change of scenery was just what the doctor ordered—a fact hammered home the minute they got out of Braxville. In spite of her promises to the contrary, Jordana was quiet and seemingly relaxed as a passenger. He liked to think it was because she trusted him but it was likely because he hadn't been the only one needing an escape.

"What's it like to grow up in Braxville?" he asked, making conversation during the drive. "Is it stereotypical to think that small-town life is all bake sales and community picnics?"

She chuckled, admitting, "Sometimes. I did go to my share of community barbecues and picnics. Also participated in quite a few bake sales." Jordana smiled in memory. "I've definitely eaten my weight in chocolate chip oatmeal cookies in my day."

"Are you an oatmeal raisin fan?" he asked.

Jordana made a face. "God, no. Throwing a raisin in a cookie is a quick way to ruin a perfectly good cookie."

He laughed. "Okay, so tell me more about being a Braxville native."

"Well, growing up in a large family in a small town is very insulating. It's like you can't breathe without someone asking you about your business. It's bad enough when you have your siblings poking their nose into everything you do, but it's made ten times worse when the neighbor down the street does, too."

"Sounds like hell."

"For a kid who wanted some space, it was, which was why I left and joined the Navy."

"That must've been a culture shock," he said.

Jordana nodded. "At first, yeah, it was overwhelming, but I liked the idea of a new adventure, seeing places I'd never been and meeting people outside of my bubble."

"So you enjoyed your time serving?"

"Mostly, yeah."

"So why'd you leave?"

"Because at the end of the day, I realized I wasn't cut out for a lifetime in the military. I wouldn't say I have a problem with authority but I definitely don't like someone telling me what I can and can't do every single moment of the day."

"Makes sense. Do you miss anything about the service?"

"The structure," she answered wistfully. "I liked that there was order, which was something I never had growing up. No matter how hard my mom tried, a houseful of six kids is going to be chaos at a certain level. I craved structure when I left home. I definitely got that and more from the Navy."

"Why'd you come back to Braxville?" he asked.

"Turns out I missed home," she replied with a small laugh. "And I wanted to go into law enforcement. When an opportunity to join the Braxville Police Department popped up, I took it."

"Are you happy with that decision?"

"Of course," she answered, but there was the faintest hesitation he sensed. Everyone had regrets, even people who said they were blissfully happy. "Sometimes I wish there was more action, but now I've got two cases without easy answers and I'm wondering if I should be careful what I wish for."

"There's a possibility my case is a simple robbery gone wrong," he reminded her. "If it weren't for the knot on my head and the amnesia, you probably wouldn't be spending so much time on trying to find who did it."

"You were assaulted. In a town as tight-knit as Braxville, an assault doesn't go unnoticed. People feel safe here for a reason. I can't just shrug off your case on the assumption that it was probably a failed robbery."

He admired her dedication. There was a lot to admire when it came to Jordana. Damn, he wished he could remember more about his own life. It felt like half a person with his memory gone. "I thought this amnesia thing was something they made up in the movies. I didn't know it happened to real people," he said. "Being on the receiving end, I can tell you, zero stars. I do not recommend."

She laughed. "I can only imagine. I'm sorry your memory hasn't kicked in yet."

"Yeah, me, too. It's disconcerting not being able to tell if I like raisins or not."

"Take from me, raisins are gross. Shriveled up little husks of former grapes…they're not only gross but macabre, too."

At that, he laughed. "Maybe I'll take your word for it."

They arrived at the place and exited the car. Jordana gave him a quick smile before saying, "You passed your driving test. You might not remember much about your-self but you remember how to drive. I consider that a good sign."

He gestured to the massive building. "I guess we'll see how good I am at climbing. If I fall on my face, prom-ise not to laugh?"

"I promise no such thing."

"Harsh."

She winked as she pulled the door open. "Don't fall."

Excellent advice.

Don't fall. He watched as Jordana walked with easy familiarity to the counter, throwing down some cash to enter. She wore tight leggings and tennis shoes and a formfitting top that showed off her trim figure. He didn't know what he liked as far as women went but he liked what he saw in Jordana. Why was she single? Were all the men in Braxville dumb and blind? A lesser man might be intimidated by Jordana.

He found her breathtaking.

She turned to him, waving him over. "C'mon, pay up! I'm about to show you how it's done."

Clint grinned. "I love a woman with balls bigger than mine," he quipped, throwing down his own cash. "But don't worry, honey, I'll go easy on you."

"Challenge accepted, big man," she taunted with a darling smile that made him want to throw her over his shoulder and claim her as his. Damn, it was a good thing he was about to get his sweat on because he had way too much testosterone pickling his brain.

As he watched her attack the hardest climbing wall in the place, lithe muscles working, determination etched on her expression, that reminder came floating back.

Don't fall for her.

What if it was too late?

Chapter 10

Jordana was covered in sweat, muscles loose and worked out, her hair a damp mess—and she couldn't stop smiling.

For one, she smoked Clint on the climbing wall, and two, a shirtless Clint was an image she'd savor for months to come.

"Not bad," she told him, throwing him a bone as she wiped herself down with a small towel. "I think you can respectfully hold your head up in mixed company."

"You're too kind. You shimmied up that rock wall like you were a monkey in a past life. I was just trying to keep up so I didn't lose my man card."

She laughed, tossing him a clean towel. "Your man card is safe," Jordana assured him, her gaze lingering a little too long on the firm muscle cording his stomach. A whole lot of man was hiding beneath those buttoned-down shirts. Jordana forced herself to look away as he finished. Once he'd thrown the used towel in the bin, they checked out, the mild fall air caressing their faces, practically inviting them to take a picnic at a park.

What would people say if they saw them? That niggling voice of doubt was less strident away from Braxville but it was still there.

"You're an amazing woman, you know that?" Clint said, that grin sending tendrils of need and want curling through her body. He was so damn nice to look at. She couldn't remember the last time she felt drawn to another person like she was drawn toward Clint and she didn't know how to handle herself.

"You're no slouch yourself," she murmured, glancing up at him through her lashes. She never flirted but she was doing it now. *Kiss me, damn it, before I come to my senses and shut you down!* The energy around them crackled with tension. She could almost hear their heartbeats beating as one.

"Am I off base or…" He looked to Jordana, his gaze fastening on hers with the same energy. When Jordana gave him the green light with a small, breathless nod, he looked like he'd won the lottery. He reached, pulling her into the cove of his arms, saying, "Thank God. I've wanted to kiss you for longer than I should admit but, you know, *boundaries*."

"Shut up and kiss me," Jordana said, lifting her mouth to meet his. His lips, soft and firm, brushed across hers, setting her soul on fire. She willfully ignored that anyone could see them, taking the chance that the odds were slim that someone from Braxville might recognize her. His tongue swept her mouth and she rose on her tiptoes to deepen the kiss. The sharp musky smell of man rose beneath the notes of his aftershave, tickling her senses.

He tasted and smelled like a snack she could happily enjoy for the rest of her life.

They broke the kiss but she continued to cling to him, his arms around her feeling like the home she never realized she was missing. "We've really done it now," she warned with a breathless laugh. "I can hear rules breaking all over the place."

"I only care if you do," he said.

She met his gaze and realized with wonder, "I don't really care."

"Good because I know exactly what I want to do with you," he said, slipping her hand in his as they walked briskly to the car. She laughed and eagerly followed where he led.

Climbing into the car, fastening her seat belt, she asked, "And what did you have in mind?"

"The closest hotel."

Her opportunity to cool the heat between them flashed before her eyes but she didn't want to stop. In one breath, she tossed all the good reasons why this was a terrible idea right out the window.

You barely know him.

You're breaking all the rules—yours and the department's.

You shouldn't open a door you can't close.

The gossip hounds will eat you alive!

Oh, yeah, all excellent reasons to pump the brakes but Jordana couldn't imagine a better idea than to end up skin against skin with this man. The heat between them could warm a small country and she couldn't wait to throw more kindling on the fire.

She ignored the shrill little voice at the back of her head and instead played his willing navigator. "There's a small motel off Greenberg Avenue. It's quiet and off the main road. It's also clean and cheap."

"And you know this because…?"

Jordana laughed. "Because a few officers from the department stayed there for an interagency conference. It was easier than driving home each day."

"Works for me," he said, pulling onto the main road, the tension between them humming.

A few minutes later—after a hurried detour to the closest pharmacy for condoms—they were checked into the motel, and before they even reached their door, they were all over each other. Hands, mouths, breath mingling and fingers fumbling for the door. They finally burst through the door. Clint kicked it shut with his foot, tossing the keys to the dresser, and they tumbled to the bed.

Hunger and desire blotted out rational thought as she stripped out of her clothes, watching with rapt anticipation as Clint shed his, as well. She rose on her knees, admiring God's handiwork on the male canvas before her. A light dusting of hair furred his chest, traveling down his belly to pool in a dark but neatly trimmed nest where his erection sprung, hard and ready.

"You might not remember who you are but I like who you are right now," she said, gently cupping the warm, soft flesh of his sac while she nuzzled the spicy length of his manhood. She wanted the taste of him, her mouth hungering for the feel of his length. He groaned as her mouth closed over the soft head, her tongue playing with the slit at the top, tasting the faint saltiness of his excitement. "Mmm, I love the way you taste," she said, thrilling at the feel of his fingers threading through her hair, his breath short.

After a few moments of teasing, taking his length down her throat, he groaned and gently pulled away, his gaze dark and consuming as he stared down at her. "Not so fast, you little devil. Your turn," he said, giving her a gentle push and sending her tumbling backward into a soft cloud of bedding. He opened her legs and stared with hungry appreciation before saying, "Damn, woman, I think I died and went to heaven."

She didn't have time to roll her eyes with a blush because Clint was serious about taking his turn, only he was determined to make her climax. Jordana twisted her hands in the bedding as Clint's tongue worked masterful strokes against her swollen nub, sucking, nipping and pushing her ever closer to that cliff, only to pull back and start over.

Oh, God, had she ever been so thoroughly mastered by a man's mouth? No, never, but Clint was quickly proving he was a man above all others.

Fresh sweat broke out across her skin. A low moan escaped her parted lips. Her hips lifted as he held her against his mouth. She couldn't escape what was building. Her nipples pearled, tight and hard, as she crashed into a climax so hard her toes curled and a cry fell from her mouth as she gasped his name over and over. Everything inside her clenched and released in a rhythmic dance that stole her breath and left her shaking.

Holy hell, what'd just happened? The answer came swift and with stunning clarity as she struggled to catch her breath.

I think I just fell in love.

Hearing Jordana keen her climax was music to his ears. Going on instinct, he followed her cues as he drove her closer to that edge so that when she finally tumbled over, she would lose her ever-loving mind in the fall.

And it was sweet.

She tasted like honey, and he already wanted more. He didn't care about anything but this moment. Clint couldn't say for sure but this felt different than anything he'd ever known. He wanted to consume Jordana, to become one with the delicious woman beneath him until neither knew where one stopped and the other began. It was the craziest feeling but he also knew he could trust it as genuine.

But now, he needed to be inside her. He climbed her body, pausing to slip a tight, budded nipple in his mouth, sucking and teasing as he'd done to her clit, and then continued on to seal his mouth to hers. She groaned against him, her tongue darting to taste herself on his lips.

The heat between them seared the air. After sheathing himself, he positioned himself at her entrance and slowly pushed deep, groaning as she swallowed him whole. *Oh, God, it felt so good.* He wanted to make her climax again but his eyes were crossing from the pleasure. She clenched herself around him, sending stars whizzing across his vision. "If you keep doing that, I won't last long," he bit out a rueful warning, sweat dotting his hairline. "You feel so damn good, woman."

Jordana giggled, low and throaty, pulling him deeper inside her. "You can make it up to me," she said, nibbling at his neck as his muscles strained.

He kissed her long and deep as he slowly thrust against her, building that heat again. Before long, she was clinging to him, whimpering as he kept hitting a good spot.

And damn, was it good for him, too.

Just a few more minutes, he pleaded with himself, clenching his jaw, as the pleasure ramped up, building to that inevitable moment. *Puppies, kittens, basketball, runny oatmeal*—he tried pulling anything and everything into his mental theater to stall his orgasm but it simply felt too good between her thighs; that wet heat was more than he could ignore and he came hard.

"Jordana," he gasped, thrusting against her like a wild man, losing all semblance of control. He finished with a gasp and collapsed against her, his member throbbing inside her with residual waves of pleasure. He groaned and rolled off, his heart beating with the speed of a runaway train. "I think I'm about to have a heart attack," he said with an exhausted grin. "But man, but what a way to go."

She laughed, shaking her head. "You know we've really screwed things up by doing this, right?"

"Don't care."

Jordana rolled to her side, propping herself up on her elbow. "Is that so?"

He wasn't lying. "Nope. It was worth it. You're worth it."

She sobered, her eyes like twin seas after a storm. "You say that now but…"

Clint met her gaze. "And I'll keep saying it. Nothing will change my opinion on that score." He sealed his mouth to hers before she could launch a counterargument. Something about her felt right, more true than anything he'd ever known. Given that his life had been turned upside down and he could trust very little, he was going to be greedy about holding on to what felt real. Breaking the kiss, he murmured, "Any questions?" and Jordana shook her head in answer. "Good."

He knew all the arguments against what they'd done—as well as the ethics—but none of that mattered to him. He may have come to Braxville for different reasons but Jordana was his reason to stay.

At least for now.

It seemed his business partner, Locke, had things well in hand back in Chicago, so who was to say that he couldn't take a minivacation with Jordana? He was the boss. He could do as he pleased. And nothing would please him more than spending days in bed with this incredible woman.

"Do you think we could get a restaurant to deliver here?" he asked in all seriousness. "I'm starved."

"This isn't the Ritz," she reminded him with amusement. "But I think there's a vending machine down the hall. You might be able to find some chips and a soda."

"That's not good enough for the fuel we're going to need," he said, bounding from the bed, aware of how she watched him with unabashed hunger. "We can order a pizza, then."

"And just what exactly do you plan to do that you need to carb-load?" she asked with a provocative slow roll to her belly, glancing at him with playful seduction.

That beautiful, heart-shaped ass with its soft, rounded cheeks begged for his hands, lips and tongue, and he had to swallow first before he could rejoin her with a promise. "Oh, woman, the things I'm going to do to you might be illegal in some states."

He was suddenly thankful he'd grabbed the big pack of condoms because damn if he wasn't ready to go again right now.

"Ah, hell, food can wait."

And suddenly he wasn't thinking about his stomach anymore.

Chapter 11

"You know we can't stay holed up in this motel forever," Jordana said around a hot bite of take-out pizza. "At some point we have to go back to Braxville, or at least I do. My boss might start to question if I've been kidnapped if I don't clock in within a few days."

Clint responded with a regretful sigh. "I know but let's enjoy our illicit moment a little while longer."

Jordana and Clint had spent the night and following day hiding from the world, having sex, showering, ordering takeout and starting all over again, but Jordana knew reality wasn't too far behind.

"I don't want this to end," he said.

"I don't, either, but I can't have people questioning my integrity if they find out we're sleeping together. I just want you to know, I've never done anything like this before," she said, worried Clint might think this was a normal thing for her. "I'm straight as an arrow, most days.

I don't even claim an extra shirt on my uniform allowance like most people."

He chuckled, "Calm down, Dudley Do-Right," he said, putting her at ease "I know you're not that kind of person. We have insane chemistry and that's hard to fight."

"Insane is right," she agreed with a worried frown. "But what does that mean? I mean, what's happening right now?"

"Do we have to define it?"

"Yeah, I think we do." She wasn't the kind of woman who did things spontaneously or rashly, and the fact that she'd fallen into bed with the victim in an assault case she was investigating left her feeling off-center. "I'm not saying I want you to put a ring on my finger but… I don't know, this is outside of my comfort zone."

"I like you," Clint said. "I want to keep seeing you. To me, it's that simple."

"There's nothing simple about that at all," she disagreed. "If my captain finds out about this, I could get kicked off both cases. I shouldn't have done this. I don't know what I was thinking."

"Do you want to keep seeing me?" he asked.

"Of course I do, but—" Clint cut short her tailspin by pulling her to him and kissing her quiet. Jordana stilled, surprised at how easily his touch calmed her overactive brain.

"It's going to be fine," he promised, and when he said it, she believed him. "The thing about not growing up in a small town? You don't worry too much about the opinions of strangers."

Jordana wished she had that freedom. "If only it were that easy." She exhaled a short breath, refocusing. "We have to keep this on the down-low. You might have the freedom of not caring about what people are saying but

I have to care. My reputation is on the line. You understand that, right?"

Clint sobered. "Of course I do. I will keep my hands to myself when we're not in private," he said, but added as he pulled her into his lap, "but when we're not in the public eye, that's a different story."

She melted beneath his touch. "I'm good with that compromise."

"Excellent," he said, brushing his lips against hers, "because I plan to spend as much time as possible in your naked company. Have I mentioned you have the most amazing body?"

She blushed. "You have. Several times."

"Well, it bears repeating. Over and over and over again."

Jordana laughed. "You're too much of a charmer to be completely single. Are you sure you don't have someone waiting for you back in Chicago?"

"Not that I'm aware. I think Jeana would've mentioned something, like, 'Oh, Tina has been calling nonstop,' or 'Do you want me to let Rhonda know you'll call her soon?' but she never said anything similar, which leads me to believe I'm footloose and fancy-free."

Jordana was skeptical. "That's not a convincing argument. She might just be respecting your privacy."

"I could just ask Jeana if I'm seeing anyone. As my assistant, she'd probably know."

"That would be a really weird question to ask, don't you think?"

Clint shrugged. "If it eases your concern, I'll do it."

"No, I'm fine. I don't want you to do anything that will tip off your people that you've lost your memory. Something like that could affect confidence."

He tightened his embrace, pleased. "I love that you care. You're really sweet."

"I'm not actually," Jordana confessed with a chagrined expression. "*Sweet* is definitely not a word used to describe me."

"I disagree," he said, his voice dropping to a husky murmur.

She blushed again, saying, "That's not what I meant."

Clint chuckled, the sound a low rumble against her body. "When you blush, it shows off the tiny smattering of freckles dancing across the bridge of your nose."

Jordana rubbed her nose with a gasp. "I do not have freckles."

"You do and I love them." He grinned. "You also snore a little."

Now she was truly mortified but she didn't have time to dwell on it because Clint was determined to make good on his promise of keeping her occupied when they were alone.

Her head fell back on a groan as he nuzzled her neck and nipped at the tender skin. Goose bumps rioted along her forearms and her nipples stood at attention, ready for his mouth.

To which he obliged.

Oh, good God, did he oblige.

As much as Clint wanted to hole up in that tiny motel room, they had to check out and return to the real world—a world that left him still wondering who had knocked his lights out.

After another round of naked fun, a shower and a quick bite to eat on the road, they headed back to Braxville. Each mile closer to town brought a change in Jordana. Away from the stress and expectation, Jordana was a different person. She laughed more easily and the tension coiling her in knots disappeared.

He hated that he felt half a person with the loss of his memory. Clint liked to pretend that he was taking the situation in stride but, deep down, a niggling sense that he really needed to return to Chicago was becoming more insistent.

The doc had suggested memory exercises, which he wasn't sure was helping. The truth of the matter was, the best way to trigger his memory was to return to the place where he'd made memories. Braxville was an empty slate.

But he didn't want to leave Jordana. She created a light inside him that felt new and intoxicating, brightening all the dark spots that he hadn't known were there.

"I'm going to leave a five-star review on Yelp for our little motel," Clint said, winking at Jordana.

She laughed. "Make sure you use an assumed name. I don't need people connecting the dots."

"You are thorough," he said with an appreciative whistle. "Have you considered a career in the FBI?"

"I did," she replied with a cheeky grin. "I decided to stay local but I like to keep my options open."

"I love a dangerous woman," he quipped.

"That's what they all say until she's better with a gun than he is."

He didn't know about other men but that excited him. "Maybe you've been hanging around the wrong men."

"Maybe so," she agreed.

They got back to Braxville by evening and Jordana was already in work mode, as if feeling guilty for taking a few days off. He sensed he ought to keep his thoughts to himself at the moment because Jordana had a wall up around her in spite of everything they'd shared.

Something about that drive felt familiar to him. Maybe in his previous life he'd been a workaholic, too. While

Jordana buried herself in work files, Clint found a quiet place to call his assistant.

"Hello, Mr. Broderick," came her pert reply even though it was considered after-hours. Maybe he always expected his assistant to work the same hours as he did, no matter how late. That pinched at his conscience a little, but in this instance, he needed to ask a few questions.

"Sorry for the late call," he said.

"No trouble at all," Jeana assured him, which told Clint he probably needed to make some changes in his life for the benefit of his most trusted employee. He'd have to work on that later. For now, he had more pressing issues. "Jeana, I need to trust you with something that no one else knows. Can I trust you?"

He was taking a risk in confiding in Jeana but he had to start trusting someone who knew him from before the assault. If he couldn't trust his assistant, he was in sorry shape.

"Of course, Mr. Broderick," Jeana replied without hesitation. "Is there a problem?"

"Yeah, a pretty big one actually," he admitted, glancing up at the ceiling with a sigh. "Seems I lost my memory."

"Come again?"

"Yeah, you heard me right. I was assaulted when I arrived in Braxville and the damage to my head was enough to knock my memories sideways. Mostly short-term memory. I can remember stuff about my childhood, but I can't remember much about my adult life, especially within the last year."

"Oh, Mr. Broderick," Jeana gasped with genuine horror. "What can I do? Shall I call your doctor? What do you need? How can I help?"

"That's the thing, I don't really know what I need except that I need someone I can trust to help me through this without alarming anyone within the company. The doc here says it's temporary so I just have to find something to jog my memory back into place."

"Perhaps you should come back to Chicago," Jeana suggested, which wasn't far from what his own counsel had advised, but he didn't want to leave.

"I appreciate the advice and you're probably right but I have things I need to do here for the time being. I need to ask, what's my relationship like with my business partner?"

"Mr. Locke? Well, you seem like close friends. He's been your right-hand man since you started the business. Why do you ask?"

"Just trying to get the lay of the land." He didn't want to admit that Jordana had planted a seed of suspicion in his head because he couldn't remember much of his relationship with Locke to defend him. Now, to the next awkward question. "Uh, okay, so I'm just going to come out and ask, am I currently dating anyone?"

God, that was hard to get out of his mouth. *Please say no.* It was going to get real ugly real fast if it turned out he had someone waiting for him when all he wanted to do was be with Jordana.

But Jeana gave him wonderful news. "No, sir. You were dating a woman named Iris Yearly but you broke it off about three months ago. Since then, you've preferred to bury yourself in work rather than date."

Relief coated his voice as he said, "Thank God." He hastened to clarify, adding, "I just mean, I'm glad no one's sitting at home worried about me."

"Of course, sir."

Another question popped in his head. "Are you always this formal with me? All the 'yes, sir, no, sir' makes me feel like I'm from the IRS or something."

Jeana answered carefully. "Well, you do prefer a certain level of decorum between us but I don't mind, sir. I appreciate your professionalism."

"How long have we been working together?" he asked.

"Going on six years."

"Six years and you still call me 'sir'? Good grief, Jeana, was I an asshole?"

He didn't expect her to be truthful but the answer was evident to his eyes even if his memory was faulty. "Look, can I apologize for the person I was before I got knocked in the head? I sound like a real jerk. No wonder someone was trying to kill me."

"Oh, no, sir. You're very kind and a good boss. I can't imagine who would want to hurt you. I enjoy working for you and most of everyone who knows you seem good with your authority."

He ought to drop it but he was bothered. Maybe the person who tried to kill him was a disgruntled employee? What if he'd been ruthless and cold to the wrong person? Had he brought this on himself?

The only way to find out was to return to Chicago. But he wasn't ready. Not yet.

"I'll be in touch," he told Jeana. "Remember, keep this between me and you. Don't tell Locke, even."

"Of course, sir."

And stop calling me sir.

But really, that was the least of his problems. Going forward, he needed to figure out who he wanted to be and if that was the same person he'd been when someone tried to put out his lights. Hell, who was he kidding? Right now, all he wanted to do was fall asleep with Jordana in his arms and think about all this crap tomorrow.

Good plan.

Chapter 12

Jordana walked into her parents' house and found her mother, Lilly, in the kitchen, scrubbing a pot with an agitation she recognized from her childhood.

Lilly Colton had always exorcised her stress through the power of elbow grease—a coping mechanism Jordana had inherited, as well—but seeing as their home had always been spotless in spite of six kids, that said a lot about the level of stress her mother had endured.

And now she was back to scrubbing.

"What's wrong?" Jordana asked, going straight to the point.

Lilly looked up with a warm but strained smile. "Nothing, darling, so good to see you," she answered, presenting her cheek for a kiss, which Jordana dutifully provided. "I just needed to get these pots cleaned before starting dinner. You know I can't cook in a dirty kitchen," she reminded Jordana.

"Mom, by no stretch of the imagination would anyone dare to call your kitchen dirty. I'm pretty sure your kitchen is cleaner than most hospitals."

"Hospitals are dirty places," Lilly said with a scowl. "That's hardly a welcome compliment."

"Sorry." Jordana shook her head, knowing she wasn't going to win. "So, what's new? Aside from Bridgette being here again. Are you two getting under each other's skin yet?"

"I love having Bridgette home," Lilly insisted. "It's been so long since we've had any decent visit with that job of hers."

"Well, being a public health official has its demands on her time," Jordana said, defending her sister, but added, "Don't you think it's interesting that a cancer cluster popped up in Braxville?"

"Oh, whatever." Lilly waved away Jordana's comment. "Can't hardly blow your nose somewhere without someone saying something is going to give you cancer. Can't drink the water, can't eat the vegetables, can't breathe the air…it's exhausting if you think about it. For my own mental health, I've resolved to *stop* thinking about it. If the good Lord sees fit to send me home, that's what happens."

"Mom, I hardly think people getting cancer is God's will. That's pretty macabre, don't you think?"

"Jordana, let's not argue," Lilly said, resuming her scrubbing. "Did you come over to snipe at me or did you come to actually visit?"

A wave of guilt made Jordana soften her tone. She reached for a freshly baked cookie from the display plate. "Of course not, Mom. I wanted to pop in and say hi, see how you're doing. By the looks of the force you're putting on that poor pot, I'd say something is bothering you."

"Nothing is bothering me," Lilly insisted with a slight clip. "Just trying to get this house in order in time for your uncle Shep, is all."

She paused with the cookie midway to her mouth. "Uncle Shep? What do you mean? He's coming home?" Jordana's uncle Shep was an infrequent visitor to the Colton homestead because he was too busy with his naval career, a path she'd followed, in part because of her admiration for her uncle. "Why didn't you tell me he was coming?" she asked, excited.

"I wasn't sure until yesterday. Your father offered the carriage house, though I don't know why Shep can't find his own place. He has plenty of money seeing as he had no children of his own."

True, Uncle Shep had never married but Jordana had understood because Uncle Shep had been married to the military—happily, one might argue—given he'd risen through the ranks with a stellar reputation.

And Jordana idolized her uncle Shep. "I can't wait to see him," she said with a bright smile. "So I'm guessing he finally retired, then?"

"Yes," Lilly answered, wiping away a small bead of sweat with the back of her hand. Her restless gaze swept the kitchen as if searching for something else to direct her attention but everything gleamed as if on display, a fact which dismayed Lilly. "Yes, retired. And he'll probably be underfoot the whole time, pestering me."

"Pestering you? Mom, Uncle Shep is hilarious and sweet. I doubt he'll pester you for anything," Jordana disputed, shaking her head at her mother. "Did you and Uncle Shep get into it or something?"

At Lilly's sudden sharp look and subtle flushing as she murmured, "No, don't be silly," Jordana recalled a hazy memory that popped in her head for no reason she could figure.

It was the summer her dad was working long days and nights—barely home at all—and Uncle Shep was helping out around the house, filling in the gaps for Fitz. She remembered her mom laughing a lot with Shep, something she rarely did with Dad. Dad was a hard man to please and that critical eye fell on his wife often, particularly after the triplets arrived.

To be fair, triplets would've put a strain on any family. And then her baby sister, Yvette, came along—it was a lot of kids.

But there was love, too. There had to be for Lilly to stick around; that was always the argument Jordana made when people whispered under their breath about Fitz Colton being a raging maniac.

Fitz was as different as one could be from his half brother, Shep. Maybe that's why Jordana had gravitated toward her uncle. Uncle Shep had been encouraging and entertaining whereas her dad…well, he was so focused on work that he'd had little time for the six kids all clamoring for a bit of his attention.

Again, six kids was a lot.

She didn't fault her dad for being overwhelmed.

"You don't want Shep moving into the carriage house?" Jordana surmised, curious as to her mom's reaction.

"I'm too old for a roommate, Jordana," Lilly said stiffly.

"Mom, the carriage house isn't even attached to the main house. You're hardly roommates. You and Dad had talked about renting out the carriage house for extra cash."

"Yes, and ultimately we decided against it," reminded

Lilly, straightening the dish towel for the third time. "Honestly, I just don't understand why your dad couldn't have encouraged Shep to find a nice apartment in town."

"Maybe because we're family and there's no reason? The carriage house isn't doing anything but collecting dust. It'll be fine, Mom."

But Lilly looked more agitated than ever. "Yes, of course. You're right. I'm just feeling out of sorts today." And then she did what she always did, pasted a blinding smile on her lips as if nothing had happened because Lilly Colton had the steel spine of a soldier who made living through chaos look like a walk in the park.

While Jordana was out, Clint made use of the empty house to study his own business, Broadlocke Enterprises. He figured it was time to make that call to his partner, Alex, but he wanted to have some kind of idea what they might have to talk about.

Dialing the number Jeana gave him for Alex, he made the call.

Alex picked up on the fourth ring, as if he were on the other end trying to figure out who was calling.

"Alex Locke," he answered.

"Hey, Alex, it's me, Clint. Thought I'd reach out to you and see how things are going without me barking orders all the time."

The surprise in Locke's voice was evident as he answered, "Clint, where the hell have you been? No one's seen or heard from you in days. I was starting to get worried. Not even Jeana knew where you were."

"Needed a few days off to decompress," he lied. "The stress was getting to me. It was either take a few days or start drinking my breakfast. I figured I've earned a few days of R and R but I'm sorry for worrying everyone."

"You take a few personal days? Who is this pod person? Clint Broderick doesn't take vacation days unless ordered to because he's banked up too many," Locke refuted with a chuckle. "Seriously, are you okay?"

"I'm fine. Went rock climbing two days ago," he said, amending, "Well, indoor rock climbing but it counts. It was hard as hell and my fingers are still jacked up. Not sure I'll take it up as a hobby."

"Rock climbing? Little early for a midlife crisis, don't you think?" Locke teased. "You should stick to golf, even though a five-year-old could beat your swing."

So he golfed? Golf sounded boring. Hit a ball and chase it. Over and over. It was aggravated walking. But he played it up to Locke. "Yeah, maybe you're right. So, everything good while I've been gone?"

"See, there's the guy I know and love—can't keep business off the brain," Locke said. "Yeah, of course. I've always told you that the world wouldn't stop spinning just because you weren't there to micromanage it."

Micromanage? "I'm a changed man," he told Locke. "I've had…an *epiphany*."

"Yeah?"

"Yeah. I know I was a workaholic and a bit of a control freak," he said, taking an educated guess at his own habits, "but you know, life is short and you can't take it with you. I'm going to start spending more time making memories that matter."

"Are you joining a cult? Oh, God, you joined a cult, didn't you? Please tell me you didn't pledge your assets—*our* assets—in your initiation?"

"What the hell is wrong with you? I said I wanted to create memories and you think I've joined a cult?"

"Hey, if you were on this end, listening to Clint Broderick wax philosophically about stuff he generally didn't care about until now, you'd start to freak out, too."

Clint was beginning to realize maybe it wasn't far-fetched to theorize that whoever had tried to kill him probably worked for him.

Jesus, talk about a rude awakening.

"So, when are you wrapping up your little impromptu 'Finding Clint' tour and returning to Chicago?"

"Not sure. I still have some things to do here in Braxville."

"I don't understand how you managed to find your zen in a small nothing town in Kansas. As far as anyone is concerned, the only thing you can find in Braxville is tumbleweeds."

He chuckled. Locke had a good sense of humor. "Actually, Braxville is kinda nice. The small-town atmosphere is a nice change from Chicago."

"I'll bet you can't get a decent deep-dish there," challenged Locke, and to that Clint couldn't argue.

"The pizza situation here is marginal at best but I did have an incredible burger the other night and that made my taste buds happy."

"You, the foodie? I don't believe it. You're impossibly picky. You made the chef at Harold's want to quit."

Clint didn't remember the chef or Harold's but he played it off. "Well, if you're going to call yourself a chef, you better be prepared to accept criticism."

"The man fed heads of state but apparently your palate was more sophisticated," Locke returned dryly. "Anyway, kudos to the burger man for managing to please Clint Broderick."

Ouch, there it was again, proof that maybe he'd been an insufferable ass before getting the stuffing knocked out of him.

He shifted, discomfited. Maybe getting assaulted would turn out to be a blessing in disguise?

Never in a million years would he ever have imagined thinking or saying anything like that statement.

But here we are.

"Okay, I gotta run. This is my new number. Lost my old phone. Call me if there are any issues you can't handle."

"Enjoy your tumbleweeds and five-star burgers."

"Will do."

And Clint clicked off. So, Locke sounded like a decent guy—the opposite of himself apparently. Maybe that was their dynamic. Locke was the good cop, Clint was the bad.

Their dynamic must've been successful. If he wasn't that same guy anymore, would their dynamic still work?

He supposed he'd just have to play it by ear.

Chapter 13

Jordana was at her desk while Clint did some business around town when Reese popped in, dropping a blue file on top of the papers she was reading. "What's this?" she asked, opening the folder.

"Information on Broadlocke Enterprises." He gestured for her to start reading. "The business owned by your roomie and his partner, Alex Locke."

"Yeah? Is there something amiss?"

"Well, just that someone has been siphoning cash off the top for years."

"Who?"

"That is a bit trickier. I don't know. Whoever is doing it is pretty sneaky about it. Almost didn't catch it. I happened to call in a favor with a forensic accountant who works for a law firm in Wichita and they pointed out the discrepancy in the books."

"So whoever attacked Clint could've been the one cooking the books."

"Or Clint could be the one and someone found out."

She frowned. "That makes zero sense. Why would someone try to kill Clint if he was the one stealing from his own company?"

"Maybe it was his business partner who tried to off him, pissed off because he was stealing."

"Stop saying that Clint had something to do with the books," she said, irritated.

"What if he did? We don't know this guy from Adam. Need I remind you, he's a stranger with one helluva weird situation. Who gets amnesia? Is it even real? I heard somewhere that true amnesia is so rare it's practically almost fiction."

She dead-stared Reese. He was getting on her nerves. "You're acting like a jealous boyfriend. Dr. Cervantes diagnosed him with amnesia because he treated his head injury. I didn't make up his diagnosis and Clint certainly didn't. Is that what this is about? What is your deal?"

Reese immediately went on the defensive. "I'm just saying, you're putting a lot of faith in a guy you don't know. Seems unprofessional at best and dangerous at worst. I'm trying to look out for you."

She couldn't exactly admit that her feelings were personal. Sleeping with Clint may have been a bad idea, especially now with this new information. But her instincts said Clint wasn't the one behind the embezzling and Reese was grasping at straws trying to find a way to paint Clint in a bad light. "Look, it makes more sense that someone connected to the business is behind the embezzling. A disgruntled employee? Maybe even his partner. What do you know about Locke?"

"Common garden variety upwardly mobile white male," Reese answered with a shrug. "On paper, pretty boring. Competent but nothing particularly extraordinary jumps out at me."

"And you think he doesn't have motive?" Jordana asked, exasperated. "You and I both know that anyone closest to the victim falls under suspicion first."

"Yeah, well, I can't exactly check his alibi when you've told me to keep the details of Broderick's attack under wraps." He affected a mock questioning tone, saying, "Sir, can you tell me where you were the night your business partner may or may not have been attacked on Range Road in Braxville, Kansas? Why do I ask? No reason."

She knew the right thing to do would be to question Locke but Clint didn't want his partner to know the details of his injury. Ordinarily, business concerns would take a back seat to her investigation but she justified honoring his request by saying that they were waiting to see if Clint's memory returned before questioning Locke.

It was flimsy at best and she was embarrassed.

Worse still, Reese knew she was handling Clint's case with kid gloves. "All right, let's question Locke," she said with a sigh. "We need to get some movement on this case."

"Finally!" Reese dropped into his seat, ready to rock and roll. "Now we're cooking with gas."

But she stopped Reese just as he scooped up the phone. "Can you wait until tomorrow? I want to give Clint a heads-up that it's going to happen."

Reese frowned. "Why?"

"As a courtesy."

"He could be a suspect," he returned, exasperated. "C'mon now. Get real."

"No, in the embezzling," Reese answered, equally irritated.

"Yeah, well, we're not investigating that part. We're investigating his assault. Stay on task, okay?"

"Stay on task?" he repeated, incredulous. "I'm not the one stalling and making all kinds of excuses not to follow the usual protocol."

"I'm asking for one day," Jordana said, gritting her teeth. "Not a month."

"If I didn't know better, I'd say you were letting your personal feelings get in the way of your judgment," he muttered, clearly not on board with her suggestion. "I don't understand why you're going soft on this Clint guy. You let him move into your place and now you're giving him undue courtesy. Is he blackmailing you or something?"

"Do you really think I'd let someone blackmail me?" she asked. "No. I just feel bad for the guy. He's a victim, try to remember that. Think of it this way—what if he'd been a woman assaulted on Range Road and I offered her the same deal while she recovered? Would you be all up in my business, accusing me?"

"A woman is different," Reese answered with a shrug, not caring that he sounded sexist as hell.

"So because it's a man, I can't control myself?" she asked, getting hot under the collar. "Seriously, you can shove your sexist BS up your ass, and while you're at it, stop worrying about my personal life and what I choose to do with it."

"If the situation were reversed and I was the one offering up my place to a female victim, would you be good with it?" he countered.

Jordana hated that he made a fair point and she didn't have an equally strong counterpoint. She grabbed her stuff. "I'm taking a half day," she muttered, needing some fresh air and to get away from Reese.

Jordana exited the building, still fuming. Reese had never been such a jerk before. She gave him some latitude because he'd lost a partner and that made him a little overprotective but she was fully capable of taking care of herself. She didn't appreciate being coddled or managed and Reese had put it upon himself to do both.

Everything about this case had flipped her on her head and she was done feeling out of control.

She saw Clint coming toward her, two shopping bags in hand, ready to meet her at the car parked alongside the main road.

In slow motion, she noticed Miss Ruthie Garrett—a little old lady that should've had her license revoked years ago—career toward Jordana's car in her beat-up Buick like a drunken sailor on leave, neatly clipping the driver's side door before tootling off as if nothing had happened.

Jordana opened her mouth to shout at Ruthie but seconds later a loud explosion threw her to the ground as her car burst into flames.

Clint's ears were ringing. It took a moment to realize he was lying on the ground, smoke all around, shouts and sirens finally piercing the fog in his brain. *That can't be good*, he thought muzzily as he climbed to his feet. The scene was something of a gangster movie, except this wasn't 1930s Chicago but a small town in the middle of nowhere Kansas.

And Jordana's car had blown up.

Dropping the bags, he half ran, half stumbled to where Jordana was lying on the ground, unconscious from the blast. She'd been closer to the explosion and the blast wave had knocked her back a few feet.

"I need an ambulance," he shouted, gently cradling Jordana's head where a giant gash seeped gobs of blood onto his hands. "Goddamn it, I need a doctor! Somebody call 911!"

Jordana's partner, Reese Carpenter, skidded to a stop and helped Clint carry Jordana to the sidewalk and out of the street. "What happened?" Reese asked, waving over the paramedics. "Did you see anything?"

"No, man, she was walking to the car and then this other car, a freaking boat, came out of nowhere and sideswiped Jordana's car and seconds later it was in flames."

"Goddamn Ruthie Garrett," Reese cursed under his breath. "The woman needs to get off the road but her damn family has a lot of money and somehow she gets to keep her license."

"If this isn't enough proof that she's a menace, I don't know what is. I thought cars only blew up in the movies. Was it the gas line or something?"

"I'm not a mechanic," Reese snapped, moving so the paramedics could load Jordana onto the stretcher just as her eyelids start to flutter open. Reese pushed Clint out of the way, saying, "Jordana, can you hear me? You're going to the hospital. You've got a head injury and they need to check it out."

Clint knew Reese wasn't deliberately trying to be obnoxious, but he felt a little territorial at the most inappropriate moment. He forced himself to take a step back and let Reese handle things.

But then just as the paramedic was about to shut the doors, he popped his head out to ask, "You Clint? She's asking for you. Hop up, you can ride with her."

And he didn't have to be asked twice. He ignored the look of suspicion clearly stamped on Reese's face and climbed aboard, going straight to Jordana. He didn't care what it looked like; he needed to be with her.

The double doors closed and Clint gently grasped her

hand. She squinted against the pain. "Hurts," she admitted as the paramedic prepared an IV line. "What happened?"

"I don't really know. Some old lady in a giant Buick hit the car and then it blew up. You're lucky you weren't closer when it blew, otherwise…" He didn't even want to finish his sentence. Clint looked to the paramedic, needing reassurance. "She going to be okay?"

"Head wounds bleed like the dickens but her vitals are good. She'll need a CT scan to be sure there's no bleeding on the brain."

"I doubt it's that bad," she said, her voice a weak croak. "I don't need—"

"Will you let the doctors do their thing? You were just nearly blown to smithereens and I need someone to tell me you're going to be okay."

Maybe it was the shake in his voice or the fear in his gaze but Jordana quieted and gave a small nod of understanding. "Maybe it's not a terrible idea to get checked."

He knew she was doing it for his benefit but he didn't care. Whatever it took to get her to the doctor and treated was fine by him.

"I'll buy you a new car," he promised, kissing her hand. "One that's supersafe and not prone to blowing up."

Was that even a thing? How would he know?

"State of the art, the safest on the market," he said, kissing her hand again. "I swear to God, the safest I can find, and if I don't find one that is deemed safe enough, I'll hire engineers to build me something."

She had the wherewithal to chuckle because he was being ridiculous but it was good to see her smile through the pain. "It was probably just a fluke. I was planning to buy a new car, anyway."

Logic told him yes, it was likely a fluke but a tiny,

scared voice whispered the possibility that someone had meant that fiery end for him, and Jordana was simply collateral damage.

He wasn't sure he could live with the possibility that something he was tangled up in had endangered Jordana.

First things first: fix his girl.

Then, like it or not, it was time to go home.

He couldn't afford to walk around in the dark anymore.

Chapter 14

"That's one hard head you have there," Dr. Cervantes said with a smile. "But one completely normal brain scan. You conked your noggin and you're bound to have a nasty headache but otherwise you're good to go home."

Jordana smiled with relief. She hated hospitals. Clint exhaled, looking as if he'd been holding his breath the entire time. She was tired and her head was throbbing but she wanted to go home.

She didn't want to think about anything aside from a soft pillow and falling asleep in Clint's arms. Tomorrow would come soon enough and all the trouble that came with it. For one, she had to talk to Reese. She'd jumped on him when he'd called her out for doing things that were out of character. He was a good detective and a great partner. He didn't deserve her guilty conscience.

She'd have to come clean and let the chips fall where they may.

Clint hadn't left her side. Tears crowded her sinuses for no good reason. The head injury was making her loopy. Dr. Cervantes signed her discharge paperwork and she was dressed and ready to leave when Reese appeared.

Clint shared a look with Jordana and she gave him a subtle hint to give them a minute.

Once Clint left the room, Jordana was surprised when Reese folded her into a grateful hug. "Jordana, I thought you were going to die in the street. Puts things in perspective real fast."

She felt awful for Reese. Seeing her like that must've triggered some really bad memories of his last partner. She pulled away to regard him with a solemn apology. "I'm sorry I was so awful to you. You were right. Your instincts were right. I am sleeping with Clint and I've lost some objectivity. I didn't mean for it to happen but it did and I don't regret it. I only regret not being honest with you."

Reese took a minute to absorb what she'd said and then nodded, accepting her apology and her confession. "You're a good detective, too. If you think he's a good guy, I'm sure you're not wrong. I just want you to be safe."

"I know you do. I'm sorry I put you through needless worry. I appreciate that you've got my back. I'm sorry I didn't trust you with the truth from the start."

"It's okay. You're forgiven. So what's your next move?" he asked.

"Honestly, my bed. My head feels like it's about to pop off. Now I know how Clint felt when we pulled him off Range Road. Head injuries are no joke."

Reese affected a mock-serious tone as he asked, "Do you know who I am? Do you know who you are? Do you have amnesia?"

"I remember that you're a smart-ass so I must be okay," she said, smiling, glad that things were good between them again. She needed her partner. Fighting and keeping secrets from him hadn't felt right.

Clint reappeared, peering around the corner to see if the coast was clear. She motioned for him to enter. "It's okay. Reese knows," she told Clint.

"Thank God. I'm not very good at keeping my feelings a secret apparently," Clint admitted, assuring Reese, "I'm not a bad guy, I promise."

"You better not be or I'll take you down without losing a minute of sleep," Reese said with a smile that was both good-natured and a little dangerous. Clint might not know it, but Jordana did—Reese meant every word. He took his partners very seriously. "All right, I'll leave you two kids to it. You don't need a ride?"

"I left and came back with my car. We're good."

Reese gave them a thumbs-up and then left.

"I think he likes you," Jordana said.

"Yeah, well, what's not to like, right? I'm practically a basket of kittens."

She laughed and then winced. "Oh, please, don't make me laugh. My head is killing me."

Clint left and returned with a wheelchair, which he directed her into in spite of her protests. "I can walk perfectly fine. There's nothing wrong with my legs."

"Oh, I know that," he said with an appreciative glance that made her blush. "But you're getting the royal treatment. I mean, check out these wheels. Top of the line chrome and medical-grade leather. This is—" he fiddled with the brakes until they disengaged, pushing her out the door "—the only way to travel."

Jordana waved at Dr. Cervantes as they headed out, trying not to laugh as Clint made a terrible nurse, but even as she climbed into the car and waited for Clint to return after he took the wheelchair back into the hospital, she couldn't shake the sinking feeling that Ruthie Garrett's vehicular mishap hadn't caused the explosion.

Because cars didn't just explode.

Someone had either tried to kill her or Clint.

The question was…who?

Clint tucked Jordana into bed, fussing over her like he would an injured bird until she glared at him with exasperation. "Okay, okay," Clint conceded, and climbed into bed beside her. "I'm so glad you're safe." Wrapping his arms around her, she settled into the cove of his chest. The warmth of her body against his soothed his ragged nerves. The subtle scent of her shampoo tickled his nose. When he thought of how badly things could've ended, fear curdled his guts. "I'm so glad you're okay," he murmured, brushing a kiss across her crown.

"You were knocked out, too," she reminded him. "Maybe you should've had your head rechecked. You're the one with the preexisting head injury."

"I'm fine," he promised her. "My concern is for you."

"You heard Dr. Cervantes. My head is too hard to sustain any damage."

"Yeah, well, that blast was intense."

Jordana fell silent and he tightened his arms around her, her head lying on his chest. In such a short time this woman had become so important to him. How that'd happened, he'd never know, but he couldn't question the way he felt because it was as real to him as the blood flowing through his veins. But with that realization, he also felt the crushing weight of guilt. If he was the cause of Jordana getting hurt, he'd never get over it.

"So, cars don't usually blow up like that, right?" he

asked, half joking even though it wasn't funny in the least. When she affirmed what he already knew with a small shake of her head, he exhaled a long breath and said, "I didn't think so."

"Does that mean you're not buying me a new car?" she teased.

He chuckled. "I probably have a fleet of them somewhere in Chicago. I'll have one shipped to you."

"I'm kidding and don't you dare. I have insurance."

"I've never thought to check—does your insurance policy cover explosions?"

"I guess I'll find out tomorrow," she murmured with a sleepy yawn. "Let's go to sleep. Tomorrow will be here soon enough with all its problems."

That was the truth.

Tomorrow he had to tell Jordana the news that he was going to return to Chicago but he hoped he could persuade her to come with him. It was crazy—they hadn't known each other very long—but the idea of leaving her behind was unsettling and he knew he couldn't stay.

He needed answers. It was selfish of him to hide out in Braxville knowing that he wouldn't find the answers he needed here. Chicago held the key to regaining his memory and he couldn't afford to ignore that fact any longer.

Life gets real when cars start blowing up. But even more real was the way he felt about Jordana. He knew it was fast but there was something about her that felt right. His gut said, *Hold on to this one*, and he knew he had to do just that. He had no idea how he was going to convince her to leave Braxville, though.

She was stubborn and attached to this place. Her roots went deep. Asking her to uproot herself to follow him to Chicago felt selfish on his part, and yet he couldn't bring himself to leave without her.

Damn, maybe the old Clint was slowly rising to the surface. A certain level of ruthlessness urged him to say or do whatever possible to get her on that plane with him.

He wouldn't manipulate the situation, he told himself. If she didn't want to come on her own, he wouldn't force her hand. Not even if it killed him to leave her behind.

Jordana was fast asleep in his arms, making those soft noises that he found adorable but fairly mortified her when he brought it up.

Good night for now. Tomorrow is a big day.

Clint let his eyes drift shut, joining Jordana within seconds.

Chapter 15

"Go to Chicago with you?" Jordana repeated, staring dumbfounded at Clint from across the island bar in her kitchen as the morning sun cast golden light around her and the coffeepot gurgled to life. She may have bonked her head but surely Clint wasn't asking her to run off with him? What about her job? What about her life here? Stunned, she replied with a shake of her head, "I can't. I have responsibilities and a life. I can't just drop everything to go play house with you in Chicago."

"That's not what I'm asking you to do," Clint said. "I'm asking you to come with me to Chicago to help me sort out who's trying to kill me. I can't find answers until my memory returns and my memories won't return until I leave Braxville. Somewhere, deep down, you know I'm right."

Of course she knew he was right. Didn't mean she liked the idea of him leaving or that she could traipse off into the sunset without a care in the world. Frustration laced her tone as she shut him down. "Clint, as much as I would love to be with you, I have a job here and people who rely on me. I can't leave with you."

Clint bracketed his hips, his lips pursed. He wasn't a man to take no for an answer. He tried a different tactic. "Okay, I get it, your job is important to you—as it should be—but what if your captain signed off on your absence as part of the investigation?"

"He won't."

"But what if he did?"

She sighed with exasperation. "Trust me, he won't. It makes zero sense for me to follow you to Chicago on Braxville's dime. We don't have that kind of budget."

"What if I contributed to the Braxville personnel budget?" he said.

"That's not even funny. It's also illegal. Private citizens aren't allowed to make contributions or donations to city budgets," she said, casting him a short look. "You can't buy me, Clint."

He realized he'd made a misstep and quickly tried to correct. "Of course, you're right. That was crappy of me to even suggest such a thing. Can you tell I'm desperate to have you with me? It's not a good look or feeling but I'm being honest. I don't want to leave without you but I have to leave."

Jordana rose from her seat to wrap her arms around him, truly sad that he was going. "I'm sorry, Clint. If it counts for anything, I hate the idea of you leaving."

"It does count," he admitted, but the determined set of his jaw told her he wasn't giving up. He gazed into her eyes. "Someone tried to kill me, Jordana. I don't trust anyone but you to find out who's behind this murder plot."

"How do you even know I'm a good investigator? Clint, you don't even know me. I have an investigation on my desk right now that's growing colder by the minute and I'm no closer than I was when I got the call that two bodies were found walled up in my family's warehouse. Maybe I wouldn't even be that much help."

She wasn't usually insecure about her skills but now wasn't the time for bravado, not with Clint's life on the line.

"You're the one I want. I have a sense about people—I don't know how I know it but I do. From the first moment we met, I had a good feeling about you. You're strong, confident and capable. I want you by my side."

Jordana felt it was necessary to point out an alternate theory. "Look, I know the circumstances are unusual but there's still a possibility that it was an unfortunate coincidence. My car might've been a ticking time bomb and all it took was one swipe from Ruthie Garrett to set it off. It might have nothing to do with you. If forensics doesn't come back with anything that suggests someone tampered with the vehicle, we have to accept the possibility that coincidence was in play."

He released her with an exhale filled with irritation. "C'mon, Jordana, don't patronize me. You and I both know that someone rigged that car to blow with me and you in it. The only reason I wasn't in that car when it blew up was because I made an impromptu decision to pick up a few things at Ruby Row Center. That car was going to be our funeral."

He was right, she had patronized him when he was strong enough to handle the truth and they were running in circles. Maybe her reluctance to follow him to Chicago had less to do with the reasons she gave and more to do with her reluctance to admit that she had deep feelings for a man she barely knew.

"I need you, Jordana," Clint said, reaching for her hands. "I don't trust anyone else. You're the only person I have in my life that I trust one hundred percent. Given the fact that someone is trying to kill me, that gives you the number one spot in my life."

"What would I do in Chicago?" she asked, wavering. "I don't have any privileges with Chicago PD and they certainly wouldn't appreciate me poking around without clearance."

"I know. What I'm asking is for you to be my second pair of eyes. Tell me what your gut instinct tells you about the people around me. I'm too close to the situation. I'm not asking you to walk away from your career—hell, that's the last thing I would ever ask of you. I'm just asking for a little help and a little time to figure this out together."

He made a damn persuasive argument. She had some personal time banked up seeing as she never used her vacation or sick days. Human resources would be overjoyed to see her use up some of that banked time. But it felt foreign to skip off with a man she'd only met two weeks ago to go undercover without permission or clearance to catch a criminal. If she was considering this wild idea, Clint had to know everything.

"Someone is embezzling from your company," she blurted out.

Clint drew back in surprise. "Come again?"

"I was going to tell you but then the explosion happened. Reese found some banking discrepancies in your books. He had some fancy forensic accountant take a look and they found that someone has been siphoning money off the top for years. It's easy to miss but it's there."

"Why was Reese poking around in my books?" Clint asked, frowning. "Seems a little bit of an invasion of privacy."

"He was looking for motive. An investigator always looks to the financials. Money is a great motivator to kill someone."

Clint regarded her with wary curiosity. "And what do you think about that? Do you think someone within my company tried to kill me over money?"

"I can't deny it's a compelling lead."

Clint accepted her answer with a nod. "About how much money are we talking?"

"Hard to say exactly but a rough estimate is in the millions. I mean, your company has been doing well for years. It's no wonder no one caught the siphon."

But Clint looked ready to punch something. She could only imagine how it must feel to realize someone was dipping into his bank account. It might even bother him more than the murder plot, judging by the storm building behind his eyes. His gaze swung to her, determined more than ever. "I understand if you don't want to come but I could use your help."

Jordana felt herself slipping. Was she going to do this? And if she did go, was she going for the right reasons?

From the moment Clint Broderick had come into her life, nothing had been the same.

Someone was stealing from him. He narrowed his gaze, cursing his inability to remember jack shit about his own life. His memory loss was a coup for whoever was putting their hands on his cash box.

The knowledge that someone was embezzling from him felt like a double insult. The attempt on his life had to be connected to the theft. He was a loose end. Had he discovered who was dipping in the books and everything that'd happened to this point was simply someone trying to cover their tracks?

Hell, he'd become a TV crime drama plot. That didn't sit well with him.

The urgency to return to Chicago was like a dull roar in his brain.

He took some solace in that Jordana had agreed to leave with him. Her agreement left him with no small amount of gratitude. There'd been nothing he'd said that wasn't true. He trusted no one like he trusted her.

He'd sift through the meaning of that understanding later. For now, he was just overjoyed that he wasn't facing what was coming alone. And he was under no misconception that he was walking into a storm with blinders on.

How had he let this happen? What kind of man had he been before his head injury that someone would do this to him? Was Alex a part of this? From what he'd gathered, he and Alex went way back. They'd built the company from scratch. Why would Alex steal from their company? He couldn't imagine how any scenario with Alex at the forefront of a murder plot made sense, but he was holding on to what he knew with a tight grip.

A part of him was starting to understand that he used to be ruthless because for a split second it had been second nature to try and bend Jordana to his will. That wasn't right. If he was that man before coming to Braxville, he sure as hell wasn't leaving as that man.

But with someone gunning for him, he was going to have to bring some of that edge to the fight if he wanted to survive.

Jordana returned from the station with a tension he recognized. He knew he was the cause of that turmoil.

"Everything okay?" he asked.

"No." She didn't sugarcoat it. "I asked for the time off. My captain agreed to it, but in the meantime, Reese is going to take over the Fenton case."

It made sense but he knew that must've stung. He went to her and grasped her hand, making a point to meet her gaze. "I know what you're sacrificing to come with me and I want you to know I appreciate it more than I can put into words. When this is all done, I swear I'll make it up to you."

"I made the choice," she said. "I believe it's the right decision but it still stings, I'm not going to lie."

"I won't say I understand but all I can say is thank you and mean it."

Some of the tension left her shoulders and he pulled her into his arms, holding her tight. "You are an amazing woman, Jordana Colton. I think getting bashed in the head was a blessing in disguise because it brought me to you."

"I wouldn't go that far," she said with a rueful chuckle against his chest. "Let's just get this done so we can move forward. Hopefully, the minute we set down in Chicago, your memory comes back like a ton of bricks so we can make short work of who's behind the attempt on your life. I'm only willing to put *my* life on hold temporarily."

He understood and accepted her terms.

"You and me both," he murmured, hoping for the same shock of memory rushing back. If not, he didn't know how he'd hold on to the life someone was trying to take from him.

Chapter 16

After winning an argument with Dr. Cervantes to clear her for flying, Clint arranged a first-class flight to Chicago, which in itself was a culture shock for a girl who lived a more modest life.

Sure, her parents had money on paper but everything was always tied up in their assets and her father's business. Plus with six kids, there'd been times Lilly had had to get creative to make ends meet. So traveling in the lap of luxury wasn't something Jordana was accustomed to and she wasn't sure if she liked it, either.

Champagne during the flight, soft, comfortable chairs with ample legroom and a little curtain divider to separate the Haves from the Have-Nots…it was all too ritzy for her tastes.

But Clint seemed to settle into the comfort as if he were born to it, which made her a little anxious.

Reese had warned her that she didn't really know

Clint. He owned and ran a multimillion-dollar company; he wasn't a lost stray without a family to care for him.

And even if he seemed lost and alone at first, that'd been temporary.

Now, they were headed back to his world and Jordana hadn't a clue what that world looked like, except she was willing to bet her eye teeth it looked nothing like her own.

They touched down at O'Hare International and immediately a sleek black town car awaited them. Clint's assistant, Jeana, had made all the arrangements and Clint fell right into step with every accommodation as if using muscle memory. Already he seemed different, more confident and assured of himself, but also colder.

His gaze took on a sharp look and that smile she'd come to love was replaced with a tight, contained set of his jaw that spoke of control and authority.

She suppressed a shiver. Seeing him like this was a different kind of sexy but the change made her wary.

Would she like the person he truly was when he regained his memory? What if this entire relationship they'd built in record time was an illusion that wouldn't stand up to the glare of reality? Had she put her life on pause for something that was doomed to fail?

There were too many questions in her head to enjoy the flight. By the time they landed, she was rigid with tension, a fact Clint noticed.

"I'm nervous, too," he admitted, slipping his hand into hers. "We'll face this together."

That helped a little bit. Some of her tension melted away. She risked a short smile as she nodded with a murmured, "Together."

The town car, drenched in understated wealth and privilege, looked like something a movie star would find appropriate. Jordana felt underdressed in her comfortable jeans and sweatshirt but she tried to keep her insecurity at bay. She didn't like the idea of people staring at her, which would no doubt happen as curiosity provoked interest.

Clint might not remember his life here but everybody else in his world did.

Not only had the king returned but he'd brought a plus one.

The town car pulled up to a stately building and a sharply dressed doorman promptly helped them exit the car.

"Pleasure to see you home again, Mr. Broderick," he said.

"Thank you, good to be home," Clint said, handing the man a crisp bill for his troubles. Clint waited for Jordana and then, holding her hand, they walked into the building, which his assistant, with whom he'd shared his secret, provided all the relevant information to gain entrance to his penthouse.

The *freaking* penthouse.

Yes, of course Clint lived at the very top of a very posh building. Where else did she expect him to live? A hovel? A small shack in a depressed neighborhood? Of course not. But again, the shock of reality was a sharp one. Everywhere she looked, she saw evidence of extreme wealth, a world she'd never get used to being around.

"Not bad," Clint joked as he opened his front door to reveal a spacious, tastefully decorated but definitely masculine decor. Tones of gray, black and white with steel accents dominated the space with cold, hard marble countertops that gleamed in the overhead light. "Too bad I don't have any family to impress because this is worth showing off, am I right?"

She forced a smile. "It's pretty top-shelf. Where's the bathroom?"

"I haven't a clue but let's find out together." He gestured and they traveled down a long hallway. Art created by artists she couldn't identify hung on the walls but Clint barely noticed. They found the master bedroom and Jordana sucked in a wild breath at the vision of male dominance and sexual prowess that practically dripped from the room.

"Jesus, Clint, who the hell were you? Christian Grey?" she muttered with a grimace. Definitely not to her tastes. She turned to Clint. "If you have a secret room of pain hiding behind a closet door, I'm catching the first plane out of here."

"It's a little much, isn't it?" Clint agreed, glancing around. "Very 'executive privilege.'"

"Yeah, not to be rude but it's not very homey."

"I agree. I like your place better," he said, shocking her. He smiled for the first time in a way that reminded her of the man she'd fallen head over heels for and reached for her. "I don't know the guy who signed off on this pleasure palace but I do know that you being in it automatically makes it ten times better."

She grinned as he sealed his mouth to hers. His tongue darted to taste her and she opened willingly, needing something to ground her in this new environment. His touch, his scent, the way his mouth fit perfectly against hers, was exactly the touchstone she needed to breathe more easily. "I needed that," Jordana said, smiling. "Thank you."

They ended the kiss, somewhat reluctantly, because both had to use the restroom after the long flight, but after a quick shared rinse in a massive shower that looked bigger than her entire bathroom back at home, Clint was ready to put that sumptuous bed to good use.

"Let's break it in," he said, dropping his towel to reveal his ready erection. The lustful grin curving his lips was predatory and sexy as hell. He gestured to her own towel covering her. "Your turn."

She cast him a sly glance and then, turning, let the towel slide slowly to the floor. "Come and get it," Jordana said with a demure glance over her shoulder.

Clint growled. "Oh, baby, consider yourself *gotten*."

He was on her in seconds.

Damn, the man was fast—and oh so good with his hands and mouth.

Clint stared up at the darkened ceiling of his bedroom, Jordana sleeping softly beside him. Moonlight caressed her half-revealed naked body as she lay twisted up in the silk sheets.

They'd christened this bedroom with extreme prejudice. Bits of memory came to him unbidden at unexpected moments. He'd known about the stash of condoms in his bedside drawer. Remembered putting the fresh box in the drawer. He remembered that the hot water spigot was sensitive and would pour lava if he twisted it too hard.

He remembered the doorman's name—Fred—and that Fred had a wife and two grandchildren. He also remembered that he always gifted Fred a thousand dollars for a Christmas tip.

So, he could be generous when it suited him, it appeared. Or maybe he was generous with those he deemed worth the extra effort.

Tomorrow he was going to the office. Jeana had it arranged so that she could brief him on the business end.

She'd already pushed his business meetings for another two weeks to give his memory time to bounce back with familiar immersion. He made a mental note to compensate Jeana generously for her discretion and her invaluable help.

Clint also had a meeting with Alex at some point but he wanted more time before meeting with his partner. There would be no way he could hide his memory loss from Alex and he wasn't comfortable revealing that handicap just yet.

Maybe it was his ingrained sense of competition or maybe he wasn't sure how secure he felt about Alex's loyalty but he felt it was the right decision to hold back details.

Or maybe he was just being paranoid and Alex would never do a thing to hurt him.

It could go either way. The downside to amnesia was he couldn't tell who was trustworthy and who was likely to stab him in the back when he wasn't paying attention.

The upside to amnesia? Well, it might sound crazy but when he was in Braxville he felt more relaxed than he ever thought a person could with the whole of their life wiped away.

But now that he was back in the Windy City, he understood. He could feel the responsibility settling on his shoulders, the familiar weight of expectation weighing on him. Getting away from all that? Felt pretty good. Even if he had to get bashed in the head to achieve it.

He was Clint Broderick—CEO and cofounder of Broadlocke Enterprises. By all accounts, he was a very wealthy and powerful man with questionable design tastes. He couldn't imagine signing off on this look now. After staying with Jordana in her cozy little house, the penthouse felt cold and detached.

Did he really *live* here? As in, did he come home from a long day at the office and find sanctuary here? Nothing about this place felt relaxing. Sure, it was a great place to host cocktail parties to schmooze with powerful people and it certainly made for a perfect place to hook up with women he didn't plan to keep around but it wasn't a place he'd happily bring someone he wanted to build a life with.

Again, his gaze strayed to Jordana and a warm smile immediately followed. She made love like a voodoo priestess summoning an unearthly force but there was something sweet and tender about her that she tried to hide.

She didn't trust easily or quickly and yet, for some reason, she'd taken a chance on him.

He didn't want to do anything to lose that trust. He'd also do anything in his power to make her stay with him more comfortable. If she wanted, she could rip out everything in his place and start fresh with her own vision of comfort and security.

Hell, he clearly had the money, and what good was money if you couldn't spend it on the things that mattered most?

Jordana mattered to him.

All this—his stare perused his bedroom—meant nothing if Jordana wasn't happy.

Sighing, he pulled her sleeping body against his. She snuggled against him, those lovely, perfect breasts baring to his gaze. Immediately, he hardened but he'd already exhausted his pretty, long-legged detective and she needed some rest.

He chuckled as she moaned softly, the sensual sound sending the blood pounding to his already hardened member, but he deliberately closed his eyes and forced himself to relax.

There'd be plenty of time tomorrow morning to remind her how happy he was to have her here.

And he couldn't imagine a better way to start the day
than inside Jordana.

After that, he could conquer the world—with or without his memory.

Chapter 17

Within minutes of waking, Clint's head was between her thighs, lapping at her sensitive nub and sending sweet pleasure cascading through her body. She moaned, threading her fingers through his hair, barely able to breathe as he pushed her toward that cliff before she'd even had a chance to chase the wispy remnants of her dreams away.

In such a short time, Clint had learned her body's language and he spoke it fluently. He teased, sucked and nipped at her most sensitive spots until she had no choice but to succumb to the thigh-shaking pleasure that only Clint could provide.

She came quickly with a tight gasp, her body spasming with release, a moan rattling in her throat. *Holy Mother of God*...she was nearly delirious.

Clint rose from beneath the bedding, his mouth slick, a grin curving his lips. "Good morning, gorgeous," he said before kissing her fully awake.

He had this way about him that drew her like no other. If she were smart, she'd pack up and leave. She wasn't stupid or naive. These kinds of love affairs burned bright and hot and left scars when it was all said and done.

But she wasn't going anywhere, not yet.

"That's better than pancakes," Jordana said with a satiated grin as she wrapped her arms around his neck. "You're going to spoil me. That's how I want to wake up every morning from now on."

"How can I say no?" he asked.

"You can't."

"Good, because I can't imagine anything better than tasting you for breakfast every day."

She blushed, teasing, "I bet you say that to all the girls."

"I don't think I do," he said with genuine honesty, "but even if I did, I only mean it with you because I don't remember anyone else."

Jordana laughed. "That's terrible."

"But truthful."

He kissed her again and her hand moved to remove his boxers but he stopped her. "That was just for you," he said. "Besides, if we start that engine we'll never get out of here. I have to get in the shower. Care to join me?"

She glanced at the alarm clock and realized she'd better get up and moving, too. "Sure," she said, stretching like a cat. His gaze heated and she caught his full erection barely contained behind his boxers. With a quick movement, she pulled him down until he tumbled to the bed. Jordana rolled on top of him, grinning with a counter: "But you need to get dirty first…"

"Oh, I'm already plenty dirty—" Clint lightly tapped his head "—but I like a woman who goes after what she wants," he said, his hands bracketing her hips as she rubbed against his hard length.

Everything about Clint felt so good, so addictive. She'd never been one to place such a high priority on sex but that might change with him. In a blink, his boxers were off and a condom was on.

"So much for not starting the engine," he said with a groan as she slowly sank down on his length.

"Stop talking," Jordana demanded, her eyes fluttering shut on a moan as she seated herself fully on top. He drove up, his hips flexing as he anchored her with his big hands. "Oh, God, yes, just like that!"

"Bossy woman," he bit out with a sexy grunt. "I like it."

Yes, she realized with a groan, sex like this was addictive.

And like most addicts, she was willing to do things she never thought possible just to be with him. It was heady, dangerous and thrilling.

He rolled her over, skewering her, hitting the best spot deep inside until she panted with desperate need. He made her wild, insatiable. She clutched at his shoulders as he drove into her, his thrusts becoming more and more intense. She tensed as the pleasure built to an indescribable level until she crashed into her climax, shuddering and crying, almost babbling as wave after wave washed over her.

Clint followed seconds later with a growl that she felt deep in his chest before collapsing; the weight of his body while he remained firmly lodged inside her was the best feeling in the world.

"I can't get enough of you," he admitted with a rasp. "My God, woman, what have you done to me?"

Jordana felt the same but she held the words back.

Instead, she smothered the potential of more talk with a searing kiss. He tasted of her, he smelled of sweat and sex. Together, the spicy blend aroused her to new levels.

Was this insanity? Had she tumbled into a crazy new world where chaos replaced order?

Maybe.

It was too late to turn back now.

Slowly recovering, Clint rolled from the bed with a command, "You, me, shower," and he padded naked across the bedroom, giving her a lovely view of his perfect ass as he went. The water started and he hollered, "Are you coming?"

She grinned and bounced from the bed. "Hold your horses, now who's being bossy," she said, pausing to glance at herself in the bedroom mirror.

For a full half second, Jordana didn't recognize herself. She looked the picture of a well-screwed woman. Her hair, tousled and wild, almost to the point of rat's nest territory, fell around her shoulders, and her cheeks were pink and rosy.

Who was this person? She envied her.

The woman in the mirror wasn't afraid to run off and live a life of luxury with the man she adored. The woman in the mirror wasn't plagued with fears and anxiety that her family might somehow be responsible for the death of two people. The woman in the mirror wasn't trying to walk the line between keeping up professional pretenses while secretly screwing the man whose case she was investigating.

The woman in the mirror didn't have any worries or cares.

But she wasn't the woman in the mirror, was she?

She was Jordana Colton—a woman with a complicated family life and a stalled personal life—and at some point, she'd have to leave the woman in the mirror behind.

Clint arrived at his office, Jordana in tow, apprehensive that someone would figure out something wasn't right with him, but as it turned out, everyone was too busy with their own workload to focus much on him.

Jordana murmured as they took in the room, "You definitely had a preferred style."

"It would seem so," he agreed with a slightly pursed frown. He must've used the same decorator for his office as he had for the penthouse because it had a similar executive tone, lots of grays and steel accents. Everything screamed masculine power, in an overt way. Almost as if trying too hard. There was no time to fret about his interior decorating choices but he made a mental note to make some changes when the dust had settled. "Now we'll see where the rubber hits the road," he said, preparing to learn what kind of boss he was.

Maybe they'd been relieved by his absence. He didn't have long to think about that possibility for Jeana appeared, the woman who was his right-hand man, so to speak, and she looked as efficient as she sounded on the phone.

Medium height, brown hair pulled into a no-nonsense bun, glasses perched on her nose, wearing a sensible skirt and light jacket, a scarf tied artfully around her slender neck. Her blue eyes were kind but sharp. "Mr. Broderick, so happy to see you back after your business trip. Shall we discuss your itinerary?"

Of course, that was code for going to his office so that Jeana could debrief him further on his life. He was so glad Jordana was there with him, as well. He'd need the extra set of ears and eyes to keep everything straight. He

felt as if he were cramming for a test on every subject
he'd ever taken in school but he had no idea which subject the questions would be about.

Jeana led them to an expansive executive office with
a glorious view of downtown Chicago, closing the doors
quietly behind them.

More grays, some navy blue and variations of gray
met his eye as he perused his office. It was cold and im-
personal but also imposing, which was probably the tone
he'd wanted to convey in his previous life but now felt
like an ill-fitting suit. *One bump on the head and everything changes*, he mused with sardonic wit.

"You must be Jordana Colton," Jeana said, extending
a hand. "I hear we have you to thank for keeping such
close watch on our intrepid leader."

"Quite by accident, I assure you," Jordana answered,
shaking Jeana's hand. "But I'm happy to help. We're
going to find who made the attempt on Mr. Broderick's
life."

Jordana was playing it cool, keeping the professional
lines drawn, but Clint didn't want to keep his affection
for Jordana secret. To Jeana, he said, "She's my girl.
Anything you can tell me, you can tell her, too. I trust
her implicitly."

Jordana flashed him an aggrieved look but didn't say
anything to the contrary.

Jeana, to her credit, didn't blink an eye. "Very good."
She gestured for Jordana to have a seat while Clint settled
in the high-back leather chair behind the modern executive stainless-steel desk. The desktop gleamed without a
single fingerprint or smudge, the room smelling faintly
of polish. A memory flashed: selecting this desk. He
remembered thinking it looked impressive and intimi-
dating, appropriate for someone of his position. Jeana

handed him a folder. "I compiled some pertinent information you might need. Basic background of the company, current projects, challenges and obstacles, as well as some personal information, as I know it."

Jordana shot Clint a look as if wondering exactly how close he and Jeana had been. He wanted to reassure Jordana that there was nothing between him and his assistant; he wasn't that much of a cliché. He actually knew this to be true. Slivers of interactions with Jeana started coming back as if pushing water through a rusty bucket full of holes.

He snapped his fingers, excited. "I bought you a Hermès scarf last year for your birthday!"

Jeana broke into a pleased smile. "Indeed you did. Such an extravagant gift but much appreciated."

He was nearly giddy. "I'm remembering things. Not all at once but they're starting to fall into place, one by one." Clint jumped from his chair to peruse the library lining the wall. He picked up a leather-bound book, a first edition of *The Adventures of Tom Sawyer*, published in 1876. "I bought this at auction. I narrowly beat out my competition by ten thousand dollars." He grinned at Jordana, adding, "I paid a hundred grand for this book."

Jordana's gaze widened. "Are you kidding me? You paid how much for an old book?"

"What can I say, I'm a huge Mark Twain fan. Reminds me of my childhood. Remember, I was an only child. Kinda lonely. Books made it bearable. This book was the start of my love for reading."

Still, Jordana murmured, "Seems a lot for a book. Just saying."

He chuckled, returning to his chair, feeling much better, more hopeful than before. Clint rubbed his hands together. "All right, let's get started. Jeana, tell me what I need to know."

They spent the next hour going over the tidy file Jeana provided, and by the end, he'd gained more memory just by going over the information. There were still gaps but they were getting smaller by the minute. He'd known familiarity would help jog his memory. All he'd needed was to immerse himself in his previous life and it would all come tumbling back.

"Jeana, I need to take my girl out and celebrate. Would you make us a reservation at Boka? I want to show her a good time."

"Clint—"

But Clint's mood couldn't be dampened. "Wait until you experience the culinary mastery of Chef Pierre, you'll think you died and went to heaven."

Jeana nodded and left them alone. Judging by the frown on Jordana's face, she wasn't on board to be wowed by Chef Pierre.

"Do you really think it's wise to be out and about when your memory is still compromised?"

"That's the thing, it's coming back. I remember things. I remember more and more with each interaction. I think it would be beneficial to go to places I'm used to going, and I remember Boka being one of my favorite restaurants."

It was solid logic, but honestly, his reasons had more to do with treating Jordana than triggering more memories. He wanted to show her a good time. He also didn't want to give her a reason to regret coming with him. He was willing to take out all the stops to impress Jordana. Maybe if he did a good enough job, she might want to relocate to Chicago…permanently.

Chapter 18

Jordana stared at the black floor-length, formfitting dress Clint purchased for her to wear to dinner. Was she going to prom? Who went to dinner dressed so fancy? And it was itchy. She preferred burgers and beers where jeans and a T-shirt were appropriate but she permitted herself a wistful sigh at the sheer beauty of the designer gown. *Okay, twist my arm, it's gorgeous*, but was it her? She wobbled a little in the heels, wincing at the subtle pinch on her toes. Whoever created high heels was a sadist.

She gave a final critical perusal and came to the inevitable conclusion that, even though it wasn't her style or comfort zone, Clint had excellent taste. It was hard not to feel like *Pretty Woman* wrapped in such finery. She didn't want to even know how much this dressed had cost him but she imagined it was worth a small fortune. She could almost hear her frugal-minded mother's voice chiding, "No dress needs to cost that much when there are children going without food in the world."

But when in Rome, right? What was done, was done. Maybe she could donate the dress to charity tomorrow to ease her guilt. Tonight, she was going to wear it with a smile because her date was the hottest man on the planet.

Especially now.

Clint appeared, dressed in a sharp tailored suit, black with a midnight blue tie, dress shoes polished to a shine. He was almost beautiful, too pretty—definitely the most handsome man she'd ever seen—and he took her breath away.

But she wasn't the only one affected.

Clint walked up behind her, his breath on the nape of her neck as he murmured in awe, "You, in that dress, should be a crime. Incredible."

She turned with a shy smile. "It's very pretty, isn't it? You have very good taste."

"To be honest, I think you could wear a potato sack and still turn me on but I'm happy to let the rest of the world be envious of what I have." He offered his arm, "Shall we?"

Jordana drew a deep breath to steady her nerves, and accepted his chivalrous invitation. "You're very charming when you want to be," she told him.

"With you, I always want to be. You make me want to be better."

"What makes you think you're not a good man to begin with?" she asked, faintly amused. "Amnesia doesn't change who you are, just blots out your memory."

"Yes, but memory is an essential part of who we are. We are shaped by our experiences. Without them, how are we supposed to know how to react to a situation?"

Jordana stilled. He made a good point. Clint noticed her sudden disquiet and pressed a lingering kiss on her bare shoulder. "Don't worry, I don't think I was a bad person but I'm beginning to realize I was a workaholic. Now, all I can think about is spending time with you."

She glanced at him, faintly troubled. How did this end happily for either of them? Clint seemed so well-suited to this environment, whereas she felt distinctly out of place. There was no way she could ever picture calling Chicago home, just as asking Clint to adjust to the slower pace of a small town seemed ludicrous.

Clint sensed her disquiet. "Everything okay?" he asked.

Answering to stave off the inevitable, she said, "Just a little nervous about walking in heels." She wasn't going to ruin the night with an argument she knew they couldn't solve. Tonight was about enjoying each other's company. Maybe it was foolish to ignore the elephant in the room but she couldn't help herself.

"If you trip, I'll catch you," Clint promised, and her traitorous heart fluttered a little faster. How could she not fall for a man who knew exactly how to charm the socks from her feet? With Clint, it seemed she was destined to ignore every red flag flashing before her eyes because her usual rules didn't apply.

"You are a ridiculously sweet talker," she teased. "But I'll hold you to it. It would be my luck to be dressed this fancy only to land on my behind."

"And such a fine behind it is." Clint dragged a knuckle lightly down her arm, admitting, "All I know is that you matter to me in a way that shouldn't make sense but feels right." She shivered, angling to receive the most tender brush of his lips against hers. Clint smiled, murmuring, "We should go if we're going to make our reservation."

Right, dinner. She scooped up her clutch, ready to go, but not before reminding him that as fun as it was to get dressed up, it might not be wise. "You look amazing and

I'm proud to be on your arm but I want to go on record to say that I don't know if going to dinner is a good idea. We don't know if it's safe yet."

He chuckled. "Turn off that detective brain of yours and just enjoy a lovely evening with your favorite person," he said, winking.

Turn off her detective brain? Not possible but she'd let that go for now. She dazzled him with a bright smile, determined to enjoy the moment. "Wow me, Mr. Broderick. I'm ready to be amazed."

"That's my girl," he said, causing her to warm all over. They walked arm in arm as if they were a couple used to such outings together, but in the back of her head, Jordana was still struggling with how different his life was compared to hers back in Braxville. How could he ever find Braxville interesting when he was accustomed to this level of opulence?

She supposed the reality was that their time together would end sooner than she would be ready but that was life. Nothing lasted forever.

But as much as Clint wanted her to shut down the investigator in her, that wasn't something she could do. It was just a part of who she was, even when she was wearing an evening gown.

Clint couldn't imagine a more beautiful woman sitting across from him. Jordana had swept her dark hair up into a messy bun with curling tendrils that drifted to frame her face, exposing that long, graceful neck he wanted to spend the evening kissing.

The fact that he had to convince her to leave her gun back at the apartment only made him want her more. She was the perfect contradiction—exquisite lady on his arm, deadly if needed.

The urge to be greedy, to keep her all to himself, was a struggle to keep at bay.

Pride puffed his chest when he caught envious glances as they walked into Boka. *That's right, she's all mine. Keep staring because you can't have her.*

But he immediately tempered that thought process because he knew Jordana wouldn't appreciate being thought of as a possession to be coveted.

She slid into her seat with grace but her gaze remained sharp and on point, as if scanning the crowd, ever watchful for threats.

"No one is going to gun me down before the entree," he assured her with a playful smile. "You can take the night off, sweetheart."

"Force of habit," she murmured with an embarrassed smile. "Of course, you're probably right. This is a very nice place. Do you remember coming here often?"

"I do," he answered, happy to be able to recall that information. "I know it sounds silly but I'm almost giddy that I can remember such a small detail."

Jordana smiled more broadly. "Don't apologize. There's nothing silly about being excited to recover your memory. I think you've handled your situation with more grace than I ever could've. Frankly, the fact that you haven't run screaming into the streets is a miracle."

"Don't let my cool facade fool you. There were some private panic attacks in the bathroom. I just didn't want you to see me break down. I wanted to preserve my manly image."

She rolled her eyes. "That's ridiculous. If your penchant for slippers didn't ruin your man card, nothing will."

He pretended to be affronted. "There's nothing wrong with slippers. Cold toes are irritating. Especially when a certain someone wants to warm said toes against some-one's back when they go to bed," he replied, arching his brow pointedly at her. She giggled, knowing she was guilty. "I know what you're getting for Christmas, Miss Frosty Toes."

"Slippers make your toes sweat. My toes have to be free."

To be honest, he'd endure her cold toes any day but he didn't want to admit too fast that he was crazy about her. Jordana wasn't like any woman he'd ever met. She wasn't impressed with his wealth or stature, which he found refreshing.

Now that his memory was returning, he recalled why his last relationship ended. Iris, a stunning woman with culture and class, had been more in love with his bank account than him as a person. She delighted in extravagant gifts and the glitzy social scene when he'd been more interested in staying home, curled up on the sofa watching a movie or, as in the case with Jordana, spending the day sweating on a climbing wall.

At the end of the day, they'd simply been incompatible.

He privately chuckled at the very idea of Iris breaking a sweat doing anything beyond her yoga class. Her body had been practically perfect—sculpted and pristine without a single blemish—and yet Jordana's body, criss-crossed with nicks and battle scars, strong with hard-earned muscle, made him shake with arousal.

"You have a look on your face that doesn't seem appropriate for a fancy restaurant," Jordana warned, her gaze lighting with conspiratorial understanding. *Oh, yeah, baby, you know what I'm thinking.* But she was right. Damn if his thoughts weren't running like a ticker-tape parade across his forehead. "You're going to set the table on fire if you don't stop."

"Not my fault you look like a smoke show in that dress," he countered, reaching for his wineglass, needing something to put out the fire smoldering between them. "Remind me who's idea it was to leave the apartment when we could've ordered takeout and spent the rest of the time naked?"

She lifted her glass in salute, her expression saying, *That's on you, sucker*, and he wished she were beneath him, naked. It took a minute to calm the hunger clawing his groin but he managed to reach a respectable mindset by the time their food arrived. His taste buds rejoiced as the memory of Chef Pierre's signature culinary style exploded in his brain. Taste, touch, smell, all-powerful catalysts for memory, as Dr. Cervantes had told him.

Jordana groaned as she sampled the couscous. "That might be the best thing I've ever had in my mouth." At Clint's raised brow, she blushed. "You're incorrigible."

"Only with you," he said.

"Oh, my goodness, laying it on a little thick, aren't you, Broderick?" She laughed, her eyes twinkling with wit. "One might think you're trying to butter me up for a little after-dinner action."

"Am I that transparent?" he said, pretending to be shocked until his grin gave him away. "Okay, caught. I want you naked in my bed for all time. There, I said it. And I don't apologize for it, either."

"I hate to be a wet blanket but my captain might have a problem with that," she returned with a wink.

He waved away the unwelcome dose of reality. "No wet blankets allowed." He didn't like to think about Jordana leaving. Maybe he could convince her that Chicago wasn't so bad, after all. But that was a problem for another night.

Clint was riding a high until they went to leave. Climbing into the town car idling at the curb, a plume of exhaust curling into the chilly night air, something caught Jordana's eye, causing her to do a double take.

"What's wrong?" he asked.

"You ever get that feeling that you're being watched? Well, I just got that feeling."

He relaxed. "Of course you're being watched—you're the most beautiful woman within everyone's direct line of sight. Let them stare, you're all mine," he said, kissing her cheek as he helped her into the car.

But Jordana was still troubled. She twisted to peer out the back of the town car window. "My instincts have kept me alive. Something feels off."

"Honey, I love how diligent you are but I think we're okay," he assured her.

Jordana settled in the seat, dragging her gaze away from the rear. "Maybe it was too soon to be out and about," she said, worrying her bottom lip.

Clint chuckled. "My little detective. I told you, tonight we were taking the night off from intrigue and drama. We are celebrating." He pulled her into his lap to kiss her. She gentled in his arms as his tongue swept her mouth. "There's my girl," he murmured with approval. "Do you have any idea how hard it was to keep my hands to myself throughout dinner? I think I deserve a medal."

She laughed, the sound like happiness in his soul. "We didn't even stay for dessert. I had my eye on that tiramisu. I feel cheated."

"I'll have it delivered," he promised, going to nuzzle her neck. "Whatever you want, it's yours."

Jordana dropped her head back with a throaty giggle, giving him better access to the sensitive spot where her neck met her shoulder. She moaned as his lips traveled the soft skin, his nostrils flaring at the intoxicating tease of her unique scent beneath the artfully applied dab of perfume at her pulse points. He groaned, his hand sliding up her thigh, baring the toned skin beneath the thin sheath that whispered across her flesh.

But as his fingers climbed farther beneath her dress, inching their way toward the apex of her thighs, Clint was thrown forward as something impacted them from behind. He held on to Jordana to keep her from falling but she was already twisting free from his grasp to peer behind them.

"Goddamn Chicago drivers!" the driver shouted as he righted the wheel. "I'm sorry, Mr. Broderick. Everyone all right back there?"

"What happened?" he demanded, wiping the sweat from his brow.

"I knew something felt off," Jordana said. "Did you notice if the car was trailing us before it hit?"

"No, ma'am."

"It was probably just a bad driver," Clint said, trying to calm the storm behind Jordana's eyes. "Driving in Chicago is like driving downtown New York—you take your chances."

"You don't think this is connected to the attempt on your life?" Jordana queried, not convinced.

Admittedly, the first thought that jumped to his mind was filled with paranoia, but now that his heart rate was settling down, he didn't think the hit was deliberate. "It was just bad luck that it was our vehicle that was hit. I doubt it was connected."

"I disagree," Jordana said flatly, unwilling to budge. "We need to report it and I need to bring in my brother Ty for additional security."

"Whoa, whoa, let's hold up for a minute. The last thing that will help is overreacting to a situation that's likely unrelated. I don't need your brother showing up trailing my every move."

"Ty owns a security company. This is literally what he does for a living. I'd feel a lot better if he were here watching your back."

Did he really want a shadow? No.

Did he think Jordana was overreacting? A little bit.

Was he willing to do whatever he could to put her mind at ease? Yes.

He sighed, relenting. "Fine. If it'll make you feel better. Get your brother on the line. I just hope it's not a waste of his time."

"Your safety is not a waste of time," Jordana said sharply. "And you're wrong…someone is still trying to kill you. My gut is never wrong."

He wasn't going to argue.

What if she was right?

And just like that, the evening was ruined.

Chapter 19

Money was a great motivator. Jordana asked Ty and his team to come to Chicago to watch over Clint, and after she offered him double his usual rate, he made it happen.

But to be honest, Ty might've come whether she'd offered him money or not because big brothers were like that—even when their little sisters were all grown up.

Or maybe he was just as curious as the rest of the family to find out why Jordana had packed up and split with a guy she barely knew.

Everyone had questions—questions she hadn't answered before leaving town. The thing was, she didn't want to get into a deep conversation about her motivation when she wasn't sure how she'd gotten to this place. Sure, the investigation was an easy excuse, but it didn't take a trained investigator to see that it was flimsy as hell. Jordana didn't relish the idea of admitting to her family that she was crazy about Clint, and yes, it'd happened fast but she couldn't deny how she felt.

Her mom would lecture her about being impulsive, her dad would yell about her lack of professionalism, her sister Bridgette would frown and ask if she'd thought things through, the triplets would grab some popcorn to watch the show, and her baby sister, Yvette? Well, she'd probably watch the ensuing chaos with detached interest without offering much more than a shrug because Yvette was ridiculously contained with her feelings.

So yeah, Jordana hadn't been superexcited about sharing what was happening in her personal life when she didn't know if it was going to last.

Why shake up the fishbowl if this thing with Clint was short-lived?

But now Ty was coming and he'd have questions. If she wanted him to stick around, she'd have to be honest.

She picked up her brother at the airport. His team was taking a later flight. Clint had offered the guest bedroom but Ty preferred a hotel, which suited Jordana fine because it felt awkward to be cuddling with Clint with her brother watching. *Ugh.* Big brothers remained protective no matter how many birthdays she'd had.

"It's been a while since I've been to the Windy City," Ty said, folding Jordana in a hug before they climbed into the town car. She'd missed the big lug. Of her brothers, Ty was her favorite. He had a way about him that was hard to ignore. Between those incredibly dark blue eyes that didn't miss a single detail and that slightly unruly shock of dark hair, it was hard to find anyone who wasn't intrigued or drawn to Ty. His only flaw? The man had a serious streak a mile long that could be a real buzzkill at times. Still, she loved the butthead.

"Thanks for coming," Jordana said, gesturing to the awaiting town car. Clint had insisted they use the car service for traveling around the city, even though Jordana would've preferred to use Uber.

Ty paused at the luxury with a knowing grin. "Moving on up, sissy?"

"Shut up," she growled, climbing into the car.

Today, she was the one cutting short the laughs, which was a change. When he saw she wasn't in the mood for jokes, he sobered quickly. "Okay, what's the situation? You can handle yourself on most days. It must be serious if you're calling me in."

She drew a deep breath, then as quickly as possible, she gave Ty the backstory of their current situation, ending with, "And that's why I think last night's *accident* was no accident—along with everything else that has happened."

Ty took a minute to digest what she'd shared. "I agree," he said to her relief. "I don't think it feels like coincidence, either."

"I'm so glad you agree with me," she said. "Clint refuses to believe that he could be in real danger in spite of everything that's happened. I think he thinks if he doesn't give it the appropriate weight, it'll stop being true."

"Denial is a powerful thing. Maybe he knows you're right but he doesn't want to further alarm you."

"Too late and that tactic does not work on me. If anything, it makes my anxiety worse."

He chuckled. "Well, I guess he doesn't know you well enough yet." Ty paused before saying, "And about that... kinda moving a little fast, don't you think?"

Ah, the big brother talk. She knew it would come sooner or later. It didn't matter that she'd served in the Navy, been on her own for quite some time and worked as a police detective, Ty would always see her as that kid in pigtails. *Boy, that got annoying.* "Yes, it's very fast," she acknowledged, meeting his gaze without flinching. "But I know how I feel and I know myself well enough not to second-guess. The way I feel about Clint is unlike anything I've ever known. I'll do anything to keep him safe. Will you help me?"

It was the simplest way to get Ty to understand that she wasn't messing around nor was she taking her own actions lightly. She knew how it looked from the outside and she knew how she'd react if someone she loved were doing the same. She didn't fault her family for being apprehensive, but in the same breath, she hoped for their understanding.

Ty smiled, reaching for her hand to give it a short squeeze. "I'll do what I can to help your man. I hope he's worthy of your love."

Jordana smiled, so happy Ty was there with her. "Thank you. Your support means everything."

Ty gave a short nod, acknowledging the moment, and then switched to business mode. "Okay, so I'm going to need a list of associates, his itinerary and any pertinent information you picked up during your investigation if we're going to do this right."

"Perfect. I can get that to you tonight after you get settled at the hotel. When is your team coming in?"

He checked his watch. "Flight is scheduled for eight o'clock."

"That gives us some time to squeeze in some visiting. Deep-dish pizza, maybe?"

"Oh, girl, you're speaking my language and I'm starved. I miss the days when flights offered actual food instead of peanuts and a ginger ale."

"Who drinks ginger ale?"

"I do."

She made a face. "Reminds me of Granny when we were sick. Always forcing ginger ale down our throats."

"It's supposed to settle your stomach," he said, chuckling.

"Well, it had the opposite effect for me. Gross stuff."

"You and your picky palate."

It felt good to banter with Ty. They'd always been close even if they had bickered hard enough to bring the roof down. Now, as adults, they were just as close but their lives kept them apart for long periods of time. Ty was always off doing cool stuff with this security business and Jordana was focused on her law enforcement career.

Ty broached a subject Jordana wasn't keen to touch but she supposed it was the hot stove that threatened them all.

"What's the deal with those bodies being found in one of Dad's warehouses?"

"It's been a nightmare, honestly."

"I'm kinda shocked that you're the investigator. Isn't that a conflict of interest?"

"A big one but the department is small and there just isn't anyone else qualified to run the investigation. I have a partner, Reese Carpenter, who's working the case with me. Captain said Reese will keep me honest," she answered with a wry chuckle. "Reese is a good man. He won't let me lose perspective."

"What does Dad say about all this?"

"Not much. I think he's just hoping it goes away. Dex has been up my ass about the investigation, though."

"Of course he has," Ty quipped, not surprised. "He's always been about the image of the company. This situation is probably a PR nightmare."

"It doesn't bolster confidence, that's for sure."

"Has Dad lost any contracts because of this situation?"

"Dad hasn't shared that information with me. You

know how he is. Dad is a subscriber to old-school mi-
sogyny. He thinks women should stay in the kitchen and
out of men's work. Oh, and Uncle Shep is moving into the
carriage house. Mom is all in a tizzy about it. I caught
her scrubbing the stainless steel out of her pots and pans
the other day."

"Uncle Shep? Has he retired from the Navy?"

"Yep, and I guess he's ready to spend his retirement
fishing and doing whatever it is retired people do."

"Good for him. He's earned a little R and R." He recalled a memory. "Remember that summer Uncle Shep
was home before Yvette was born? Mom was pulling her
hair out with the triplets and dad was absent, as usual.
If it weren't for Uncle Shep I think Mom would've had
a nervous breakdown."

"Yeah, it was the best summer actually. Uncle Shep
made things bearable. Mom is too high-strung for her
own good. I swear someday her head is going to pop off
if someone leaves the bathroom without straightening
the bathroom towels."

Ty laughed. "You're always so harsh on Mom. Cut
her some slack. I can't imagine running a house with six
kids practically on her own while holding down a nursing
job. It's a wonder she didn't become a closet alcoholic."

"And relinquish some control? That would be a nightmare for Lilly Colton," Jordana returned with a snort.
"And you've always been a mama's boy so your opinion
is invalid. You don't have Mom always nitpicking at you
like she does me."

"I think you nitpick each other," he said.

That was a circular argument that Jordana didn't have
the energy or desire to continue. Ty would always side
with their mother, end of story. By this point in their lives,
she'd accepted that fact.

"You know Bridgette is home, right?" she said.

"Yeah, she mentioned something about coming home for a while to follow some kind of lead about a cancer cluster?"

"Yeah, in Braxville. It's pretty serious. She's staying at the house and Mom and Dad are always driving her nuts. I told her I'd help her look for a different place to stay while she's in town."

"All this talk of cancer makes me want to get a full checkup."

He wasn't joking. Jordana had no doubt Ty had already scheduled that checkup appointment but she didn't blame him. It was unsettling to hear that Braxville might be an epicenter of a cancer explosion. Maybe it wouldn't hurt to follow his lead.

"Hey, did you ever hear the rumor about Colton Construction being responsible for a few workers getting sick?"

Jordana did a double take. "No? What do you mean?"

"It's probably just people talking but I remember hearing something about Dad's company being the root cause of people getting sick."

"That's ridiculous. People will say anything when they're bitter and mean. Dad's made plenty of enemies in his time. He's not exactly the most personable guy in the world but he did an amazing job with the Ruby Row Center. You'd think people would stop spreading rumors when the man has actually done something great for Braxville. Besides, do you really think Dex would be out there pushing for more jobs if he thought Colton Construction was a liability?"

"That's true. Dex the Dealmaker loves money."

"Well, when running a business, at least one person should know how to network," Jordana said with a sigh, "because Dad would probably push away more people than gain them if it weren't for Dex."

Ty agreed. "Hopefully, it's all resolved soon. The stress can't be good for Dad's heart."

A chill settled in her bones. She didn't like to think of her dad being vulnerable to anything, much less the aging of his body, but the stress weighing on his shoulders was more evident each day. "He'll be fine," Jordana declared, refusing to think otherwise.

They arrived at the penthouse just as Clint arrived, as well.

Time to get this show started. Hopefully, Clint made a good impression on Ty, otherwise…things were going to get awkward.

Clint knew meeting the older brother was a big deal to Jordana so he wanted to be on his best behavior, but as it turned out Ty was a cool guy and he liked him immediately.

"Flight good?"

"As good as can be expected with only peanuts to chew on for the long flight," Ty grumbled. "According to my dad's business partner, Dex, they used to offer full-course meals on long flights. When did that stop? Jordana said something about deep-dish pizza. You know a good place?"

"Do I know a good place?" Clint repeated with a big grin. "I know of *the* place to get the best deep dish and I insist that you let me take you."

He caught the subtle roll of Jordana's eyes because she knew he was trying to make a good impression, but he also sensed that she appreciated his effort so he wasn't about to stop.

"Luigi's, owned and operated by the same family since

the 1930s, emigrated from Italy and brought all their culinary secrets with them. One bite from a Luigi's pizza and you'll wonder how you survived without it."

"Sounds like a moral imperative that I find out for myself if the claim is true," Ty said dryly. "But you honestly had me at family owned and operated. Any business that can survive working with family must be doing something right."

Jordana excused herself to freshen up before dinner and that gave Clint an opportunity to talk frankly with Ty.

"I really appreciate you coming out here to put Jordana's fears at ease. She's been wound up pretty tight about this whole situation."

"I agree with her," Ty said, surprising Clint. "Look, my sister has some killer instincts, and if she says something isn't right, I'd listen."

"It's not that I'm not listening, but the odds of all this being connected seem astronomical."

"Not really if you think about it. First and foremost, we're going to dig into your associates. Money is a big motivator for foul play. We will need to clear all the people closest to you before we can widen the circle."

"Jordana said the same. She's mentioned concerns about my business partner, Alex Locke, but I really can't see him doing something like this. We've known each other for years and created the company from scratch together. Aside from business partners, we're friends. He'd never do something like that to me."

Ty looked sorry to be the bearer of bad news. "In my experience, it's always the person you least expect who's screwing you over. Jordana said you also have an assistant?"

"Yeah, Jeana, but she's been my rock through this.

When you meet her, you'll understand, there's no way it could be her."

Ty nodded but kept his judgment to himself. Jordana reappeared from the bedroom and Ty clapped his hands together, ready to eat. "I can practically taste that melting cheese already. Let's do this. I can't think on an empty stomach."

"Bring your credit card—my brother can eat twice his weight in food. Mom used to always say that Ty was going to eat her out of house and home."

Ty puffed up, almost proud as he patted his stomach. "What can I say? I was a growing boy."

Clint chuckled as the two bantered back and forth as they went downstairs to get into the car, but his thoughts were stubbornly stuck on the realization that maybe he ought to stop downplaying everything that'd been happening.

Maybe he couldn't keep denying the fact that someone was actually trying to kill him.

The thought was a sobering one that not even the best deep-dish pizza in Chicago could budge.

Chapter 20

Having Ty in Chicago with Jordana lessened some of the homesickness that popped up unexpectedly, but as they dug deeper into Clint's business and associates, the strain of having someone over his shoulder all the time was starting to show.

"Ty is using the information found by the forensic accountant to dig deeper into who is embezzling from your company," Jordana said as they settled onto the sofa with their Thai takeout. "Whoever is behind this scheme is pretty sophisticated—"

"Can we not talk about the investigation tonight?" he asked with a touch of irritation. "We can talk about other things, right?"

She drew back, stung. "Of course but I thought you'd want to know what Ty has been doing. You are paying him to do a job—a pretty important job, in my opinion, which seems far more important than how much I don't care for the weather here in Chicago."

"What's not to like? The weather is temperate, practically California weather. Cool enough in the evenings for a light jacket but warm enough in the day for a short-sleeved shirt, or a dress," he said, trying to lighten the mood, but Jordana wasn't having it.

"I don't wear dresses," she said flatly. "And no, I don't care for the weather here and I miss Braxville. Why did I put my life on hold to help you when you're not willing to give just as much as I am to see your case solved?"

"It's not that black and white," he argued, realizing Jordana wasn't in the mood to play nice right now. "My memory is returning in fits and starts but I'm still struggling in the deep end of the pool having just learned to swim. I'm doing everything I can to keep the company moving smoothly while I recover."

"I get that but your life is more important than board meetings and new account acquisitions."

"Easy for you to say," he said. "You don't have the weight of everyone's livelihood sitting on your shoulders. If Broadlocke goes down because of all this, people will lose their jobs. I help put food on people's tables. I can't ignore my responsibility."

"But you're asking me to ignore mine?" she countered sharply. "I brought Ty here for a reason. I asked him to put you as a priority above his other cases because I care about you. Don't make me regret my decision to come here."

"I didn't force you to come," Clint said, rising to throw away his carton. "Don't turn this into some scenario where I'm the bad guy who dragged you away from Hicksville, Kansas."

Jordana's mouth dropped. This was a side of Clint she'd never seen: cold and detached.

She didn't like it one bit.

Jordana shook her head. "I don't know who you are right now, but I'm not interested in finding out. Good night," she said, leaving the sofa to toss her carton and retreat to the bedroom.

Once she was safely behind closed doors, she let the tears flow. She didn't believe in fairy-tale endings but it was shocking how much it hurt to hear Clint speak to her this way. She wanted to pack her suitcase and bail but she was wise enough to know that was hurt feelings talking. No one was perfect and people lost their tempers but she hadn't been ready to see that side of Clint yet. Was anyone ever ready to see the darker side of the person they were crazy about? No, but it happened just the same.

She didn't want to call Ty but she needed to vent. Picking up her cell, she rang up Bridgette.

"Hey, how's Chicago?" Bridgette asked as soon as she answered. "Please tell me you're eating your weight in amazing food. Chicago is such a foodie town."

"Yeah, there's a lot of good places to grub," she agreed, but Bridgette could tell by her tone that something was wrong.

"What's up? Everything okay?"

"No, everything is a mess actually," Jordana admitted, tears clogging her voice. "Clint and I just got into an argument. I know he's under a lot of strain, but I didn't sign up to be his emotional floor mat."

"What'd he say?"

Jordana gave Bridgette the abridged version of their earlier conversation, finishing with a sniffled and woeful, "And he hurt my feelings."

"Oh, honey, I'm sorry. Sometimes men are stupid."

And just like that Bridgette managed to make her laugh. "Yes, they are." She wiped at her eyes, chuckling at the irony that her younger sister seemed to have more wisdom than she did. "I just don't understand how he can be so stubborn about this whole situation. It's like he doesn't want to find out who is out there trying to kill him. Am I crazy for insisting that he make that his top priority?"

"Of course not, but you don't know what's going through his head. Maybe he's overwhelmed with everything and he has poor coping mechanisms. Everyone has their way of coping. Mom cleans like a maniac. Maybe Clint hides in denial."

"Yeah, I know, but his kind of coping mechanism is going to get him killed. Ty agrees that someone is out to get him, but Clint is treating the situation like it's nothing. Honestly, I couldn't care less about his business right now. I want Clint to be safe. Broadlocke Enterprises can suck an egg for all I care."

Bridgette laughed at Jordana's vehement reply. "He built that company from dirt, right?"

"Yeah, so?"

"You of all people should understand why he's being so stubborn. Look at Dad. Is he not the most stubborn person in the world? And wouldn't he do anything for Colton Construction?"

Bridgette had a solid point. "Are you saying I'm attracted to the same kind of man as our dad?" she asked, groaning. "How did that happen?"

"Genetics, social imprinting, take your pick. The fact is, you're going to have to work around him if you want to keep him safe for his own good, of course."

Jordana smiled. "Kinda like how Mom slips Dad his vegetables in things he won't taste?"

"Exactly. She knows if she serves up a plate of zucchini he's going to give a hard pass but if she puts it in his favorite bread? He's going to gobble it up and ask for another slice. You need to start working with what you've got instead of pushing against what you don't."

"Jesus, Bridge, when did you get so damn wise? Aren't I supposed to be the big sister?"

"While you were off being a hero serving our country, I was out making dumb mistakes. Wisdom doesn't come free."

"Ain't that the truth," Jordana commiserated. "Okay, so you're saying I need to do what I do and ignore Clint when he's being an ass."

"Pretty much."

Jordana sighed, knowing it was solid advice, but there was a sadness to the realization that the bubble had popped. "Does this mean we're officially out of the honeymoon phase? Damn, that was short. I thought we should get at least three months before we showed each other our bad sides."

"It sucks when the love goggles fall off," Bridgette agreed. "But you went to Chicago to do a job. So the job had side benefits. Doesn't change the original reason you left Braxville, so stick to the plan. If the benefits end, that's the way it goes."

She accepted Bridgette's counsel and thanked her for listening, but as she hung up, she crawled into the bed, still a bit sad. Had she thought Clint was The One? *Truthfully, yeah.* Was it most likely going to end as quickly as it began? *All signs point to yes.*

And that's why she fell asleep feeling as if the truth were her enemy.

Clint couldn't bring himself to apologize for snapping even though he felt like a jerk.

The truth was he was starting to chafe at the constant

presence in his life, the shadow of uncertainty that hovered above his head like an unwelcome thought.

Ty was doing a good job of staying out of sight, doing his work behind the scenes, but one of his team was planted within the head office for visuals and Ty had wired his office to catch any conversation that might be useful.

He wanted nothing more than to crawl into bed beside Jordana and pull her into his arms but he'd left things ugly and raw between them. Jordana wasn't the kind of woman to forgive and forget so easily.

Nor was she swayed by overt gestures.

It wasn't like he could buy a huge bouquet of roses and expect her to melt. That was one of the things he admired about her. She was strong, tough and smart. He knew she was right. The investigation needed his full attention but so did his business. There was only so much of him to go around. But Jordana meant so much to him. He needed to swallow his pride and apologize. As he rose to head to the bedroom, his cell lit up.

It was Alex.

"Hey, man, sorry to bug you so late but I'm a little concerned about something I need to talk to you about."

He paused with a frown. "Yeah? What's up?"

"What's with the security detail snooping around the office? I just had a run-in with a guy named Ty Colton, says he's on the payroll for security. I don't remember talking about anything like that. Is there something I should know?"

Clint swore beneath his breath. He'd hoped this case would be resolved before he had to talk to Alex but it seemed time wasn't his friend.

"Sorry about that. Yeah, I hired Colton's security team to watch my back after the situation in Braxville."

"You said it was a mugging. That could've happened to anyone, man. Don't tell me you've gotten paranoid all of a sudden," Alex said, half joking. "Do you need a night-light, too, buddy?"

"You get mugged and tell me how secure you feel at night, and yes, I would like a night-light," he quipped.

"Oh, hell, what am I talking about? You have a detective keeping you safe at night," Alex teased with a chuckle before continuing in a more serious tone. "Look, I'm all for you feeling safe but I think this is a little overboard. We have security. Nothing is going to happen to you at the office."

"Yeah, I know, but they thought it was a good idea, more of a precaution."

For reasons he hadn't fully examined, he hadn't shared the full details of his attack in Braxville with Alex. Mostly it was because he didn't want to seem weak or vulnerable in front of his business partner but there was something else that he didn't quite know that kept him from spilling the beans.

"Is there anything else I need to know about this security detail?" Alex asked.

"No, I'll probably send them home in a week or so. It's mostly to make Jordana feel more secure. You know how it is. Women worry." He cringed, knowing if Jordana had overheard him right now, he'd likely be dodging a plate whizzing past his face. "I'm sorry if they were disruptive in some way."

"No, no, I understand. Of course you have to placate her. I get it. Next time, a heads-up would be appreciated. I don't like being blindsided."

"Right, that's reasonable," Clint said. "Thanks for understanding."

"Yeah, no problem. I'm here for you, man. I mean it.

You can tell me anything. We started this company together and we're friends."

Clint chuckled. "Yeah, I know."

"All right, glad we got that settled. See you at the office tomorrow. It's your turn to bring the bagels."

"Got it."

Alex clicked off and Clint tossed his phone to the table with a long exhale. When would this all end? He wanted to get back to normal so he could put all this behind him. Maybe then, he could focus on Jordana like he wanted. Until then, he had to tread water and hope Ty or Jordana found answers soon.

Chapter 21

Clint was knee-deep in paperwork when Ty showed up at his office the following day. After his conversation with Alex last night, Clint was on edge about having Ty walking the halls. He gestured for Ty to close the door behind him so they could speak in private.

Ty dropped into the chair opposite Clint with a frown. "I heard your partner, Locke, isn't so keen on having my team poke around."

"Yeah, to be fair, if the shoe were on the other foot, I wouldn't much like it, either."

Ty shifted in the chair, all business. "Look, we need to talk about some of your inner circle. We've cleared most of the people on the payroll except a handful who work closest with you."

"And?"

"And we've found nothing to support that they might be involved with the embezzlement or the attack on your life."

"That's good news," he said.

"All it does it narrow the playing field. The people closest to you are the ones who stand to benefit if you aren't around. At some point we need to talk to Locke."

"I know but let's try and leave him out until we absolutely can't anymore."

"Okay, there are others we can talk to before Locke. Starting with your assistant, Jeana. It's time to question her."

He wanted to protest that Jeana would never do anything to hurt him—she practically adored him—but he knew it would be a waste of breath.

"Okay, I understand," Clint said on a sigh. "I'll let her know you'll be calling."

"Thanks." Ty paused before saying, "We did find some more information on the money. The transactions were tied to a terminal located within this building but narrowing down which computer was used takes time."

Clint's heart sank. It hurt to know that someone he worked with was stealing from him. He tried to create a good work environment and Broadlocke was considered top tier in the employment bracket for competitive wages.

And yet, someone was still stealing from him. Anger followed. "I want this person found. Who else is on your list aside from Jeana?"

Ty pulled a folded sheet of paper and carefully unfolded it before handing it to Clint. "That's the short list we compiled. Everyone on that list needs to be cleared."

Clint perused the list. Some names were familiar but others were hazy, as if he should know them, but his memory was still glitching. Of course Alex and Jeana were at the top.

"Another theory we're working on is, do you have

any disgruntled employees that come to mind who might feel justified in helping themselves to the piggy bank?"

A name jumped to his memory, Derrick Rochester, an analyst who used to be in charge of the old computer system before they upgraded. Rochester hadn't been happy about the change, loudly protesting. In the end, Clint thought a different place might be a better fit and he was let go.

"Sounds like a good foundation for motive," Ty said, jotting the name down along with contact information. "Anyone else?"

"We like to pride ourselves in being a good place to work," Clint answered, searching his memory. "We don't have a lot of people who don't stay. We hire good people and good people stay."

"Fair enough. We'll look into Rochester and see if he's keeping his nose clean."

Clint nodded, unsettled by the conversation. He'd always been a straightforward guy. He tried to be fair and consistent, but there would always be someone who thought you were the worst no matter what you did.

Was that the case? Was there someone out there hating him so much that they wanted him dead?

"What about past lovers?" Ty asked. "Sometimes matters of the heart get messy."

"There's only one woman I dated in the recent past, Iris Yearly, and she's already moved on to someone else. I doubt she cares about what I'm doing enough to cultivate this kind of scheme."

"We should check it out, just in case. When it comes to emotion, things are never as black and white as we want them to be."

He knew that to be true. This situation with Jordana had him twisted in knots. Clint nodded and jotted down

Iris's contact information. God, he hoped it wasn't Iris. He exhaled a long breath. He wanted this nightmare to end. "Do you need anything else?"

"No, I think this will keep us busy for a few days."

"Good." Clint wanted to focus on work; that was something he understood. He had a major meeting with a new client and if they landed their account it could mean a lot to their company. He didn't want to let anyone down and he still felt insecure about his memory. There were patches, blank spots, in his memory that cropped up at unexpected moments and he sweated the possibility of losing something vital at a crucial moment.

It was why he'd been staying late at the office. It could also be that he wasn't entirely proud of his mumbled apology for being a difficult ass. Sure, Jordana had accepted his weak defense but he hadn't let himself off the hook because he knew she'd deserved some groveling on his part. The thing was, he wanted to be able to show Jordana that they were both safe from any real threats, but he couldn't do that unless he could prove it.

While Jordana worked with Ty, he poured over past accounts, refreshing his memory, reading mountains of memos, texts and emails so that his recall was up to date.

But all that "homework" took a toll on his time with Jordana, which he hated, but he couldn't see a way around it. He'd much rather spend his time curled around her luscious body, listening to her laugh, making her sweat, but he couldn't risk losing everything because of his memory loss. It was a full-time job keeping that information under wraps, particularly from Alex. If it weren't for Jeana, he never would've been able to pull it off.

Speaking of Jeana, he hoped and prayed Ty was able to clear her. It would stab him in the heart if Jeana were found to be the one behind all this drama.

Also, if it was Jeana, he was in a whole lot of trouble because she knew everything.

She also knew when would be the best time to strike again.

He was living on the edge of a sword but he didn't know who was doing the swinging.

Jordana was restless back at the penthouse. She felt like a caged bird in a pretty prison but she couldn't leave unless she knew Clint was safe. She wasn't the type to go shopping or sightseeing. She preferred having a job. So when Ty showed up at the penthouse and invited her to come along to question a former employee, Derrick Rochester, she couldn't dress fast enough.

Meeting Ty downstairs in the lobby, she grinned when he ushered her into an awaiting rented car. "You have no idea how you are saving my sanity right now," she said.

"I figured you were going stir-crazy when Clint said you were staying behind at his place."

"You got that right," she replied. "I'm beginning to question if it was a good idea to come to Chicago. I'm not being all that useful and I can't just sit at home like a good little puppy waiting for its master to come home."

"Which is basically what everyone was thinking when you decided to leave with Clint. He seems like a great guy, don't get me wrong, but everyone who knows you… well, this kind of gig just isn't your thing."

She knew he was talking about the completely different world Clint inhabited in comparison to her own. "I know," Jordana said, shaking her head. "I care about him a lot, maybe I even love him, but I don't know how this works out in the long run. I've been thinking, maybe I should go back to Braxville."

"Is that what you want?"

"I don't know what I want. I just know that I'm not doing any good here. He doesn't want to work on the case with me and he's so distracted with the business that he doesn't have time for me on a personal level so why the hell am I staying?"

"What do you mean he doesn't want to talk about the case?"

"He says he's overwhelmed and just needs a break when he comes home, which I can understand, but sometimes I feel he doesn't give sufficient weight to the fact that there's someone out there trying to kill him."

"If it makes you feel any better, I don't think he's trying to ignore that fact. I think he's trying to keep a lot of balls up in the air and a few keep dropping. I feel bad for the guy, honestly."

"Yeah?"

"I do. He's trying to balance a new relationship in spite of a bunch of different and equally time-consuming situations. I think anyone would be overwhelmed."

Jordana digested her brother's comment, nodding. "Yeah, that makes sense, but even so, it does draw attention to the red flags that are waving all over the place."

"Such as?"

"Such as, I don't belong in his world. I don't fit. I'm not ever going to be some society girl or a 'lady who lunches' and I don't see myself joining the Chicago PD. I like the pace of Braxville and maybe that's not ambitious enough for some people but I liked my job back home. Hell, I miss home. I miss my bed. I miss my judgy cat."

"Ugh, that cat. He *is* judgy," Ty agreed.

"But I don't want to leave unless I know Ty is in good hands."

"Do you want to leave Clint behind?"

"Not really," she admitted with misery. "But I don't think I can stay, either."

"Why not?"

"Because if I stay, I'll become more resentful and eventually it'll just tear us apart. I'd rather leave before we hate each other."

He chuckled. "Maybe it won't come to that."

"No, it will. I can't stay," she realized, her sinuses clogging with the sadness of that conclusion. "Maybe it's true that if you truly love someone you have to let them go. Staying would be a disaster for us both."

"I want you to be happy, sis. If you think leaving is the best for both of you, I know I won't be able to change your mind. All I can do is promise that I'll keep your man safe while you're gone."

Jordana wiped at her eyes. "Thank you."

"When are you going to tell him?"

"Probably tonight, after I make my flight plans. I don't want to give him the chance to change my mind."

"For what it's worth, I think he's a good man. I like the way you light up around him. I've never seen you so happy...or so sad. I think it's real between you."

She smiled, appreciating her big brother's support. "I think it's real, too."

But staying would be a mistake. As much as she loved Clint, she wasn't doing him any good here and she was needed in Braxville.

Sometimes being an adult meant making hard choices.

Leaving Clint behind before she knew who was behind his attack was a thorn in her side but she knew she was leaving Clint in good hands.

Ty would do whatever was necessary to catch the person responsible.

She wasn't looking forward to that conversation when she told Clint she was leaving.

Until then, she was happy to distract herself with a little old-fashioned investigative legwork.

Chapter 22

"I don't want you to leave," Clint said, facing off with Jordana, even as she stood with her bags packed and her Uber waiting downstairs. "C'mon, Jordana, talk to me. What's this about?"

"It's about me being in the wrong place for the wrong reasons," she said, wiping at her eyes.

Clint was at a loss. One minute things were great and the next Jordana was bailing? "Is this about our argument the other night?"

"Yes, but no."

"I should've apologized better. I knew you deserved a better apology but I got caught up in work—that's no excuse, I'm sorry. I was rude and insensitive," he said, trying to make things right.

But Jordana shook her head. "It's not that. I'm not so petty as to decide this over one fight. The fight was just what opened my eyes to what is happening here. I'm dying not being able to be useful. I'm not the kind of person who can spend hours shopping and being frivolous with my time. I like to have a job. I'll never have that here and it doesn't matter how much I love you—"

His heart leaped at her admission. "You love me?"

She pressed her lips together as if pained, admitting, "Yes, I do. Maybe it's crazy to fall for someone as quickly as I did but, Clint, I do love you, whether it was too fast or not. However, sometimes love just isn't enough. You and I are old enough to know that it takes more than just feelings to make things work. The logistics between us are a nightmare."

"I'll fix it," he promised. "Give me a chance to fix things."

"It's not something you can fix or you should fix. You belong here. I belong in Braxville. C'mon, we both knew that this was a fairy tale that wouldn't have a happy ending. I should've listened to everyone who told me that it was a mistake to come here. I'm just coming to my senses and righting the ship."

"So, I'm a mistake? Your feelings for me are a mistake?" he asked, stung.

Jordana looked exasperated and sad at the same time. "Of course not, but maybe a little? I'm sorry, I know I'm not making much sense. All I know is that I can't stay but I'm leaving you in good hands. Ty will figure out who's threatening you, and your life can get back to normal. I'm not a part of that normal life. If you stop to think about it, you know I'm right."

"Bullshit, Jordana, you're running away from your feelings because you're not ready to admit that I'm the game-changer in your life. You don't like surprises or things you can't control. I'm sorry I threw your life into a tailspin but I'm not sorry for the way I feel—and you shouldn't be, either."

She didn't argue his point. "My Uber is waiting. I have to go if I'm going to catch my flight."

"Screw your Uber. You're not leaving."

"I am leaving," Jordana said, grabbing her suitcase and carry-on. "Don't make this harder than it already is."

"Please, don't go."

Tears welled in her eyes but she didn't waver. "You'll realize this is best when you've had some distance."

"I love you, Jordana."

"You'll get over it," Jordana said, her voice strangled. "Goodbye, Clint."

And he watched her leave. His heart cracked in two but his feet remained rooted to the carpet. He should run after her, beg her to stay, but he couldn't do it.

Wouldn't do it.

If she wanted to go, he couldn't tie her to a chair and make her stay.

Was it his pride? Maybe.

But maybe it was because he didn't know how to convince her that he wanted her more than anything else if she didn't already know it. Or deep down, he knew she was right at a certain level, in that place where he didn't want to acknowledge or see.

Chicago wasn't her town, wasn't her vibe. He'd seen her slowly withdraw, and when she'd tried to reach out to him, he'd been too focused on work to make the effort.

Hell, maybe love wasn't in the cards for him. If it wasn't going to happen with Jordana, he didn't want it with anyone else.

Clint cursed under his breath and wiped at the tears on his cheeks. *Screw it, if she wants to leave, that's her choice.*

He had plenty to keep him busy.

Even though it hurt, Clint shoved Jordana from his mind. He had bigger problems than his fractured love life.

Time to focus on what mattered.

Jordana cried the entire Uber ride to O'Hare. Barely managed to wipe her tears away long enough to board her flight and then quietly sobbed through most of the two-hour flight back to Kansas.

By the time she reached her house, it was late and she was emotionally exhausted.

Falling into her bed, she took comfort in the familiarity but then caught a lingering whiff of Clint in her bedding and she started crying all over again.

At some point, she fell asleep, but by morning, she felt run over by a truck. Still, routine offered some semblance of calm as she showered, dressed and headed to the station.

Reese looked up, surprised to see her.

"What are you doing here?" he asked. "You're supposed to be in Chicago."

"I'm back and ready to jump into my caseload," she answered with false cheerfulness. "Turns out the Windy City wasn't for me. I'm excited to get back to work. Any leads on the Fenton case?"

She didn't want to talk about Clint or Chicago, a vibe that Reese caught right away and followed her lead for the time being. She was sure he'd have plenty of questions later but she appreciated the fact that he knew her well enough to leave it alone.

"Maybe. So forensics came back on both the bodies. They tested positive for chromated copper arsenic, an unusual chemical to be found on bodies that are twenty-plus years dead."

"Arsenic of the deadly sort is found usually in soft tissue but there wasn't any soft tissue left," she said.

"Exactly. So that begs the question, why was it found on the bones?"

"Unless it was an environmental property within the surroundings where the victims were found," she supposed.

"That's what I was thinking. I did a little digging and it turns out that chromated copper arsenic is a pesticide/ preservative used to prevent rotting in lumber that's going to be used outside. CCA is usually found in pressure-treated wood."

Jordana mused over the information, apprehension replacing her previous determination to focus on nothing but work. She had a bad feeling about this new development.

"Tell me more about CCA. Is this a normal building material?"

"Maybe back when the warehouse was built but not since the EPA put the kibosh on CCA-treated wood in 2003." He looked to Jordana. "Do you know when that building was built? If it was built in the 1970s up until 2003, then it makes sense that it might have CCA-treated wood."

"I don't know when that building was built," she murmured, worrying her bottom lip. "I could ask my dad. He should know."

"Do you want me to ask him? Just to give you some separation from your family with the case?"

Her dad would not appreciate Reese poking around his business and it was not likely to end with her dad's cooperation without a warrant. She sighed. "No, I'll ask him. My dad can be difficult at times."

She returned to the bodies. "Okay, let's assume that

the bodies were close to CCA-treated wood and that's why the chemical compound showed up in the lab. It doesn't give us much information on who killed them."

"No, but most killers don't leave calling cards," Reese quipped.

Jordana allowed a short smile but she didn't feel like joking around. Her heart was heavy and now her mind was cluttered. There was something about that CCA showing up that bothered her but she couldn't quite put her finger on why. "So CCA-treated wood was a commonly used building material until 2003?"

"From what I can tell."

"So why'd the EPA ban the use of it after 2003?"

"It's sick. Chromated copper arsenic, as it turns out, is dangerous to humans. Like, as in real bad. Of course, it took some people dropping like flies for the EPA to figure out that maybe humans shouldn't be around that poison before they dropped the ban hammer. Hey, as we all know, government agencies run slow as molasses in winter."

She agreed, still thinking. Did her dad know about the chromated copper arsenic in that warehouse? She couldn't imagine that he had. Her dad liked to do things by the book. If he found out that the materials being used were harmful, he'd take care of it. Her dad was a lot of things but he wasn't a monster.

"So, everything okay?" Reese asked, tentatively broaching the subject she wanted to avoid. "I didn't expect to see you back so soon."

"It just didn't work out. Turns out I was more of a distraction than a help so my brother Ty is there running down leads and I came back here where I'm useful."

"Oh, so everything's cool with you and Broderick?"

"Um, I'd rather not talk about it, honestly. I just want

to focus on work," she answered, struggling to keep the tears at bay. Reese nodded, letting it go, and she was grateful. "Hey, so, does it matter when that warehouse was built? It's not like chromated copper arsenic killed Fenton and the other victim, right?"

"Yeah, I guess not. I was just curious. Seemed an interesting find on the forensics."

Jordana breathed a secret sigh of relief. She didn't want to talk to her dad about the warehouse even though it was inevitable at some point. He owned the building where two bodies were found. She'd been the one to stop construction, which hadn't been the greatest conversation she'd ever had with her dad.

And as long as the investigation was ongoing, she couldn't let construction resume, which was putting a strain on her dad's budget, but she didn't have a choice. It was her job.

Now was a complicated time in her family's life with Uncle Shep coming home and Bridgette back in town.

Honestly, sometimes she understood why her mother was always scrubbing the kitchen.

A clean kitchen was something she could control.

Maybe she ought to give her kitchen a good scrubbing. Lord knows, she could use the outlet.

Chapter 23

Clint stared morosely into his Scotch, asking Ty, "Why'd she leave?" but he knew Ty didn't have any answer that was different from the one Jordana had given any more than his fourth Scotch had the answer. "I don't understand. We had something good and she just up and left me behind like I was nothing to her."

Now he was repeating himself. He'd turned into the weepy kind of drunk he hated but his heart wouldn't accept the truth as it stared him in the face. He wanted a different answer, something that made him feel better but there wasn't anything that would make him feel any different and he knew it.

"I think you've had enough, buddy," Ty said, signaling to the bartender for the tab, but Clint wasn't ready to leave. He wanted to get hammered and forget that the woman he was crazy about had left him. But Ty wasn't taking no for an answer. "You'll thank me in the morning," he promised, helping Clint off the stool. "Besides, no one needs to see you like this."

Ty made a fair point. He was the boss. People depended on him. He signed the checks. Being sloppy drunk wasn't a good look. If only his heart didn't feel like it was being torn in two by dueling rottweilers.

"Fine, we'll go but only if you promise to call Jordana for me and put in a good word. Maybe she's not mad anymore," he said, his mind swimming. "I mean, how long does your sister stay mad?"

"She didn't leave because she was mad," Ty said, maneuvering him out the pub door and into the awaiting Uber. He slid in beside Clint and shut the door. "She left because she wasn't getting any traction here and you didn't exactly help her feel like she was needed."

"What are you talking about? I need her. I need her like nothing I've ever needed before in my life. Do you even know how hard it is for me to admit that?"

Ty chuckled. "Yeah, I can guess, but Jordana needs a job. She's always been that way. Maybe this was for the best."

"Stop saying that," he growled. "Does it look like it was for the best? Do *I* look like I'm at my best? You don't even have to answer—I can tell by your face that I'm a mess. I know it, you don't have to lie."

"Okay, I won't lie," Ty said. "You are a mess but my sister's not one to stick around to prop up broken men. Figure it out, man."

"I didn't say I was broken," Clint muttered, drawing away only to smack his head on the glass by accident. He cursed loudly as he rubbed his forehead. "This car is too small. Why are we riding in a shoebox?" To the driver, he said, "No offense, my man, I'm sure it's great," and returning to Ty to whisper in a not so whispery voice,

"Seriously though, what the hell? I have a car service with adult-size cars at my disposal. Why are we riding in a toy car?"

Ty laughed. "You are messed up. Shut up and enjoy the ride. You're lucky I like you enough to get you safely home. I promised Jordana I'd look out for you but I'm not sure that extended to drunken binges after-hours."

"I miss her," Clint admitted in a sad voice. "I miss the smell of her hair, the taste—"

"Whoa, hold up, that's my sister, remember? I'm going to try and pretend that I don't know how close you two were, okay?"

"Right, right," he said, apologizing. "I've never had a sister. Or a brother. My parents weren't the prolific type. I'm not even sure how they made me. Separate beds my entire childhood," he shared in a slurred whisper. "Never the two shall meet. Seriously, how'd they make a kid if they didn't share a bed? It's a mystery, right?"

Ty grinned because he was being an idiot but Clint didn't care. He was sloppy drunk, no sense in denying it. But that's what happened when you had to numb the pain of losing someone. "Tell me something about Jordana that I don't know," he said, almost desperate to hear anything about her.

"Like what?"

"I don't know…what was her favorite cereal as a kid?"

Ty did a double take. "Cereal? Hell, I don't know. She wasn't much of a cereal eater that I can recall. She was always bitching about how everyone left an empty box in the pantry. Now that I think about it, she liked Cream of Wheat. Not cereal per se, but a breakfast meal. But she liked it lumpy. Out of all us kids, she was the only one who liked her Cream of Wheat with big ol' lumps in it. No one liked it when Jordana made it for everyone, which I think she did on purpose so she could eat the whole pot herself."

"That's my crafty girl," Clint said, happy and proud for no particular reason, only that it was a story about Jordana. "She's a go-getter."

"She is," Ty agreed. "One time for a science fair project she proved that ants' stomachs were transparent by collecting a handful of ants and then feeding them colored sugar water. Bugs never bothered Jordana—she was a bit of a tomboy. Afterward, she released the ants back into the ant hill where she'd collected them but the colony rejected the ants because of their colored abdomens and tore them apart. It was brutal. She was more fascinated by the ants' reaction than the results of her science fair project."

"No wonder she went into detective work," Clint said, impressed and a little scared of twelve-year-old Jordana. "Ants' stomachs are transparent?"

"Yeah, well, at least the ants she collected. Not sure about the specific species and whatnot. Too many years between now and then. I remember our mom being freaked out about the ants being in the house. She found it macabre and disgusting at the same time."

"I think it's cool," Clint said.

Ty nodded. "Me, too."

They arrived at the penthouse and Ty dutifully made sure that Clint made it inside before telling him to hit the bed and he'd call in the morning.

Ty left Clint for his hotel room in spite of Clint's offer of the spare bedroom to crash in.

"You probably snore and I'm a light sleeper," Ty joked. "I'll talk to you tomorrow. Sleep it off, buddy."

But it was Clint who slept in the guest bedroom. There was no way the ghosts in his bed would allow any sleep.

Some battles you just couldn't win.

* * *

As much as Jordana tried to get out of a family dinner, Bridgette's pitiful begging forced her hand.

"Please don't leave me alone with our parents. All they want to talk about is why I haven't started dating yet, and no matter how many times I tell them I'm simply not ready, they don't seem to hear me. I'm going to need backup."

"There's no time limit on grief," Jordana said, being supportive. "I think it's a testament to how much you loved Henry that you're reluctant to step back into the dating pool."

"It's like people expect me to just move on and that's not happening. I planned to spend a life with him. Now that he's gone, I don't know how to pick up the pieces again without feeling guilty for snatching some happiness."

"Never feel guilty for happiness," Jordana admonished. "Henry loved you so much. He'd never want you to wallow in sadness for the rest of your life."

"No, he would've told me to move on," Bridgette agreed with a watery laugh. "Henry was laughter personified. The man never met a person he couldn't make a friend. It's not fair that he's gone and terrible people are walking around fresh as a daisy."

"Life isn't fair," Jordana agreed sadly. "Yes, I'll be there tonight and be your backup if our parents start in on you."

"Thank you, sis," Bridgette said with a sigh of relief. "I owe you one."

Jordana chuckled. "You still owe me for that time I didn't tell Mom and Dad you snuck out your freshman year to be with your boyfriend at the time who was a senior. Your ass would've been toast."

"Oh, my goodness, I forgot about that." Bridgette laughed. "What was I thinking? That could've ended badly."

"Yeah, and I didn't sleep all night until you slipped in at five in the morning. I wanted to ring your neck. I had finals the next day and I was exhausted from worrying about you."

Amusement colored Bridgette's voice as she retorted, "It's not my fault you never took any chances or risks in high school. You were so straitlaced. No one was surprised when you decided to go into the military right out of high school. Why didn't you go career military?"

"I liked the structure and the strong sense of duty, but in the end, I just couldn't see myself toe the line under someone else's command until I retired. As much as I wished I had Uncle Shep's resolve, I knew it wasn't going to be for me in the long run. I don't regret a single moment in service, though."

"Makes sense. For all your determination to follow rules, you have a rebel streak buried inside you. I see it now and then and I fully support seeing it more often." She paused a minute before asking, "Have you talked to Clint since coming home?"

"No, and I don't plan to," she answered, losing her smile. Clint was the hot stove that she couldn't quite touch yet. "Ty gives me updates so I know what's happening with the investigation, but other than that, I steer clear."

"Do you miss him?"

"Yes." That single word wasn't big enough to convey what she felt in her heart but it was all she had. "More than I thought possible."

"Then swallow your pride and *call* him," Bridgette said.

"No, it's better this way. A clean cut. We can both

move on," she said, holding the line. "Trust me, chasing after something that's doomed from the start is a really bad idea."

"I think the reason you're running away is because you're scared of the big feelings you have. You're always the one in control, but when you fall in love, the things you thought you could control go out the window."

"I've been in love before," she corrected her sister, but it hadn't felt like this. From the start Clint made her feel something different. Her feelings had been wild and untamed, definitely something she wasn't used to, but she wasn't running. "Trust me, he's much better off finding a woman who's content to be arm candy. You know that's just not me."

"He fell in love with you," Bridgette insisted, refusing to let it go. That was the thing about family—particularly sisters—when they had a bone, they never let it go. "If you're hurting, he must be, too. Think about that."

She didn't want to think about Clint at all. She just wanted him to be safe. "Can we change the subject?" Jordana asked. "I'm not in the right frame of mind to have this conversation. Besides, I'm going to need your backup with Dad. I know he's going to ask me again when I can let him resume construction and I don't have the answer he wants."

"Yeah, that's a tough one."

"Gee, thanks, you think?"

"I'm sorry. You're right. We both need to have each other's backs. It's going to be a rough one. Do you want me or you to pick up the wine?"

"I'll do it."

"Cool. See you at six."

"I'll be there with bells on—with alcohol in both hands."

"You're the best big sister," Bridgette said.

"I'm your only big sister."

"That's what makes you the best."

They ended the conversation on a shared chuckle but Bridgette's advice to call Clint stuck in her head. Closure was important for them both. Calling him would only re-open wounds that were trying to heal.

But she missed the sound of his voice.

The way that cute dimple popped out when he grinned.

And the way it felt to fall asleep in his arms, safe and secure that all was right in the world for at least that moment.

No, she wouldn't call.

Even if she thought about it every day.

Chapter 24

Jordana's first response to her mom's invitation of dinner was to make an excuse to avoid a sit-down with her parents given the uncertain situation facing the investigation, but she chickened out and caved. Mostly for Bridgette, so she wasn't left sitting through an awkward dinner alone. But Jordana could've timed her watch to her dad's launch into the "nonsense" holding up his timeline and she wished she'd followed her first impulse, sister or not.

"Do you realize how much money I'm losing each day you hold up demolition on the warehouse? I've got investors that are chewing on my ass wanting answers and I don't have any to give them."

Jordana shared a glance with Bridgette before answering carefully, "You know I can't talk about an open investigation, Dad. We're moving as fast as we can, that's all I can say."

"I don't understand why you've got to keep the demo

shut down. You've got the bodies. Why do you need the site any longer?" her dad persisted, ignoring the pointed look from his wife. "It's total bureaucratic red tape and it's costing me millions. I could lose this bid if it keeps up. You want that to happen? You enjoying the food on this table? Well, if I lose this bid, you can bet things are going to change around here."

"Dad, it's not Jordana's fault two bodies were found in your warehouse," Bridgette piped in. "Just let her do her job."

Their dad swiveled his gaze to Bridgette, pointing his fork at her, "And you, missy, you're no better in all this. What's with all the questions about chemicals with my business. If I didn't know better, I'd say my whole family was trying to bankrupt me."

"Fitz!" Lilly gasped, appalled. "Stop it. We're not talking business at the dinner table."

"Well, Lilly, my business is under attack," he shot back, not willing to back down. "Dex told me the other day that Bridgette's office is poking around in our supply chain, asking questions about history that has nothing to do with today. I never thought I'd see the day when my own family had a knife to my throat."

"Daddy, that's not what's happening," Bridgette insisted. "It's standard procedure. You know I'm here because of the cancer cluster. Every business is under scrutiny, not just yours. I promise you it's not personal. Besides, why are you worried? I'm sure you've done nothing that's going to turn up bad."

"That's not the point. Of course I'm not worried about that—I'm worried about losing this contract, which my business sorely needs. Construction jobs are down, the economy is depressed and I had to fight tooth and nail to win the bid. The last thing I need is a cloud of suspicion hanging over my head scaring off future investors. You're only as good as your last job and I don't want the Ruby Row Center to be the last job Colton Construction gets to call finished."

"It won't be," Bridgette assured their dad, but Jordana shifted against the feeling that their dad wasn't being entirely honest.

"Dad…when was the warehouse built?" she asked, remembering her earlier conversation with Reese.

He looked up from his plate, annoyed. "What?"

"I'm just wondering…when was the warehouse built?"

Her dad waved away the question. "What does that matter?"

"I was just curious." She couldn't share that CCA was found on the remains without getting into the details of the investigation. "I thought you might know."

"I don't know, mid-1970s," he answered gruffly. "Somewhere around there."

She breathed a secret sigh of relief. If the EPA hadn't banned the use of CCA-treated wood until 2003, her father was in the clear as far as the chemical showing up on the bodies.

"I don't want another word about business," Lilly declared, putting her foot down in a firm tone. "I want to enjoy a nice dinner without all the shouting and bad energy. Am I clear?"

But without work to focus on, Lilly was quick to jump to Bridgette. "Darling, we're so happy to have you home again. I know it's been hard without Henry. How are you doing?"

"I'm fine, Mom," Bridgette answered with a bright smile, but her eyes told a different story. "Just keeping focused on my career. This assignment was a huge coup for my promotion. It was coincidental that it landed in

Braxville but I'm happy to be home for a bit. Nice change of pace."

"And we're so happy to have you home. Oh, I ran into that nice boy you used to date, Vincent Hogan, the other day. He works at the Feed 'N Seed now. Runs it for his dad. Very nice young man. You should see if he's free for lunch sometime. I always thought you made a nice couple."

Jordana was ready to jump in to deflect their mom's direction but it was Fitz who shut her down first. "Lilly, give it a rest. Stop trying to play matchmaker all the time," he growled with irritation. "The girl can find her own dates. She doesn't need you throwing eligible bachelors at her."

Lilly's mouth pressed together as she shot daggers at her husband. The tension between them was uncomfortable. Jordana felt for Bridgette being stuck in this house with the two of them. "I'm just making conversation, Fitz," she replied stiffly.

"It's okay, Mom," Bridgette assured Lilly, trying to salvage their ruined dinner. "Vince was always very nice but we had nothing in common. We were better as friends."

"Being friends first is important," Lilly said, slipping one last comment in before moving on. "Anyway, it might be nice to catch up. As friends, of course."

"Maybe. If I have time," Bridgette said with a smile for Lilly's sake.

Mollified, Lilly rose, saying, "I made pie from apples picked at Applegate Orchards. Frannie says this batch is probably the best they've had in years. Well, you know they had that worm infestation that one year. Terrible stuff. But they're all good now." She smiled, hands on hips. "So, who wants a slice?"

Fitz wiped his mouth with his napkin and rose without answering. When he left the room, Jordana tried not to see the pain in her mom's eyes. Why was her dad wound so tightly?

"I'll have some, Mom," she said, prompting Bridgette to join in.

"I can't turn down pie."

Lilly nodded, her smile strained but appreciative. "Two slices coming up." She disappeared into the kitchen.

It wasn't until her mom was clear of the dining room that Jordana looked to Bridgette in question. "What bit Dad in the butt?"

"I think this demo situation is hitting him harder than we realized. I've never seen him strung so tight, which is saying a lot."

Jordana nodded. "I'm working as fast as I can," she promised, but in light of her dad's meltdown, she couldn't help but feel the pressure.

And no amount of apple pie was going to fix that.

Clint was doing everything he could to distract himself from Jordana's absence but seeing as he wasn't sleeping in his bed—and the guest bed wasn't quite as comfortable—he had a crick in his neck that didn't help his surly mood.

He eyed the phone as if it were a traitor for not ringing with Jordana on the other end. How could she just walk away as if what they'd been to each other was nothing?

Was it so easy for her to slip back into her routine as if he'd been nothing more than a momentary distraction, a blip on her emotional radar that warranted little response?

Jeana walked in, the picture of efficiency with a permanent pleasant smile etched on her face. Suspicion narrowed his gaze. Could Jeana be the one poised to stab the knife in his back? Clint was still doing background checks so he didn't have an answer. For now, he was supposed to act like it was business as usual.

"Good news, Nortec is ready to negotiate their newest tech contract and Broadlocke was their first choice. Should I set up a meeting?"

He grunted in answer. "Make sure you cc Alex. I want him there, too. Alex knows Nortec's CEO, Byron Zucker, and it could help to have a friendly face across the table."

"Certainly. I'll make sure Mr. Locke is present. I picked up your dry cleaning and hired your new cleaning service as requested."

He couldn't remember asking for a new service. "When did I ask for that?"

"Oh, right before you left, sir. Seems the prior cleaning crew wasn't up to your standards. This new service comes highly recommended."

How hard was it to clean up after a bachelor who was rarely home? And what the hell kind of bad job had the previous service done in his eyes? His memory had returned for the most part but some lingering patchy spots made him feel like an old man losing his marbles. He nodded at Jeana with a short smile. "Thank you, Jeana."

She nodded, jotting some notes in her folder before snapping it shut and peering at him with concern. "May I speak freely, sir?"

Clint leaned back, curious. "Of course. Is something bothering you?"

"Not at all. I'm more concerned about you, sir. You've been…preoccupied since Miss Colton returned to Kansas. I wondered, if I might be so bold to suggest, that you try and smooth things over with her."

A wry smile curved his lips. "I appreciate your concern but that ship has sailed. I'm sorry I've been preoccupied. I'm working on it. I'll try harder."

"Oh, sir, I don't mean to imply that you've been less efficient. However, you do seem sad."

"Jeana…was I good boss? I mean, I'm starting to remember things that make me think that maybe I was a jerk. If I was, I apologize. You're an asset to my team and I don't know what I'd do without you."

Her pale cheeks flooded with color as she ducked her head, flustered and pleased at the same time. "Thank you, sir. That's the nicest thing you've ever said to me."

"You see, right there, that comment… Was I horrible? Please be honest. I need to know what public opinion of me is like around here."

He could tell she was choosing her words carefully as she shared, "Well, sir, you were certainly a boss who knew how he wanted things done and you were fairly rigid in how you would expect people to do them. I'm sure some've chafed under that kind of leadership, but to be fair, you're very good at what you do and with that skill takes a certain level of confidence, which can be off-putting for some."

"But not for you?"

"Oh, goodness, no, I appreciate a firm hand. I like guidelines and structure. You have always provided both."

There was something about the way she looked at him, both adoringly and shy, that made him wonder if Jeana had a secret crush on him. From what he knew of Jeana, she would never act on it even if she went to bed with a life-size pillow with his face plastered on it.

Unrequited love could be dangerous.

He regarded Jeana with quiet speculation. "Jeana, may I ask you a personal question that may sound out of line?"

Jeana's expression faltered but she nodded. "If you think it will help, of course."

"My memory is still spotty in some places... Did we ever...what I mean to ask is...well, I don't remember if we ever...had..."

Jeana's eyes widened as she caught where he was fishing. She blushed harder and shook her head vehemently. "No, sir, never! You've always been the picture of a gentleman. Never improper with any of your employees. I can say with authority that your moral character is beyond reproach."

He breathed a short sigh of relief. God, it was shocking how worried he was about her answer. "Good, good," he said, tapping the top of his desk lightly. "Very happy to hear that. Thank you, Jeana. I appreciate your candor."

"Will that be all, sir?" she asked, lifting her chin, returning to the efficient assistant within a blink, as if she clung to that persona as a life raft when the seas turned choppy.

"Yes, thank you."

Jeana smiled and nodded, turning on her heel, click-clicking out of his office with short efficient steps filled with purpose.

Jeana was an odd duck but was she a killer?

Either she was the world's best actress or Jeana was exactly as she seemed—a stellar assistant with a possibly mild but ultimately harmless crush on her boss.

Being wrong could prove to be a fatal mistake.

Chapter 25

"A blind date? Are you insane?" Jordana asked, staring at Reese as if he'd grown a second head. After that disastrous dinner with her parents, the fire to solve the warehouse murders was burning bright, but Reese was too interested in setting her up with a buddy to be serious for a minute.

"You need to get out there, shake things up a bit," Reese said, undeterred.

Good grief. Jordana made a concentrated effort to return the conversation to solid ground. "Oh, I talked to my dad about the warehouse, and it was built in the 1970s. He couldn't remember the exact date but it doesn't matter because the EPA didn't ban CCA until 2003 so the point is moot."

"C'mon, Jordana. The best way to get over a guy is to get onto a new guy," Reese said, stubbornly refusing to drop it. "His name is Blaine and I think you'd dig him."

"First of all, gross. Second of all, I would never agree to a blind date with a guy named Blaine. Where'd you meet him? The country club?" She'd had her fill of wealthy men.

"Does Braxville have a country club?" Reese asked, momentarily distracted.

"Yes, of course we have a country club. Even people in Braxville like to golf," she answered, exasperated, gesturing back to the case on her desk. "Can we please talk about the case? We need to focus. I think we should go over what we know, a recap of the facts to refresh our memories. Sound good?"

He groaned. "No, it does not sound good. You might've taken a break but while you were gone I did nothing but eat, sleep and dream about these bodies and that damn warehouse. Maybe I need a break this time."

"Well, playing matchmaker isn't going to help you relax. You should stick to something you're good at." She paused to question, "What exactly are you good at?"

"Ha. Ha. Very funny." Sighing, he swiveled back to his desk and pulled his research file. "Fine. Here's what we know so far—two bodies, one male, one female. The male, approximate age mid- to early fifties, and the female, mid- to late twenties. Both suffered blunt force trauma to the head, which suggests foul play. The male, Fenton Crane, was a private investigator related to your John Doe, later identified as Clint Broderick, and the female, Olivia Harrison from Kansas City, was reported missing by her mother, Rita Harrison, but never found. Dental records were used to positively identify both."

Jordana rubbed her forehead. It was impossible to untangle her family's connection to all the players in this case. Gwen Harrison, Olivia's daughter, showed up in

Braxville looking for answers and instead fell in love with Jordana's younger brother, Brooks.

Not the most convenient love match but she supposed you couldn't help who you fell in love with. Tiptoeing around all the conflicts of interest in this case was turning into a tap-dancing competition.

"And Fenton was hired by Rita to look for her daughter, Olivia, which unbeknownst to her had been walled up in an abandoned warehouse owned by my father."

"Yep."

"And it would seem that Fenton met the same fate as Olivia, possibly by the same perp, seeing as both died from blunt force trauma."

"The evidence would suggest as much."

"The question that keeps bouncing around in my head is why someone would kill a young mother?"

"Statistically, probably the father of her child, but seeing as Olivia was tight-lipped about who she was seeing, I don't know how we'd figure that out. Rita is too old now to remember much detail from back then."

That was true. They'd questioned Rita Harrison about the disappearance of her daughter, Olivia, but twenty-plus years was a long time to hold on to small details that could make or break a case.

The sad fact—and one she wasn't ready to embrace— was cold cases with murdered women were hard to solve without DNA left behind at the scene. Forensics hadn't pulled anything from the body aside from the chemical CCA and those bones weren't doing much talking.

"We've taken DNA samples from Gwen and put it into the database, but unless the DNA of the father pops up somewhere, we're poking around in the dark," Reese said.

"It bothers me that whoever killed these people has been walking around scot-free. It's not right," Jordana said. "I hate injustice. There's too much of it in the world. Sometimes it's overwhelming. Are we making a difference at all?"

Reese's gaze met hers with conviction. "Of course we are. Little things add up to big things. Sure, maybe we're not the FBI or some bigger municipality but we make a difference here, in Braxville. People look to us to keep them safe and that's what we do every day to the best of our ability."

"But that's just it, Reese… I'd say Fenton Crane and Olivia Harrison might disagree that Braxville is a safe place. Right now people are looking for answers, not so much because they care about the case but because they need to feel safe again. If we can't solve who killed those people, we're going to lose the faith of people we are about."

"We're going to do our best," Reese maintained, refusing to let Jordana's pessimism leach into his belief. "Jordana, you're one of the most stubborn, most dedicated, officers I know. It's the reason you're lead detective on this case. The captain believes in you but so does everyone in this station."

"I appreciate the vote of support but let's be honest— the reason I'm in front of this case is because we're short-staffed. You and I both know, the conflicts of interest are so complicated and entangled that there's no way I should be lead detective."

"Don't look a gift horse in the mouth," Reese warned with a half smile. "I'll be honest, I didn't think you should be involved at first but you're incapable of being shifty. Your need to seek justice is part of your spine. I do not doubt that you'd haul in your own father if it turned out he was involved."

A shiver slithered down her spine at Reese's supportive statement. She murmured her thanks but in her mind's eye she saw her dad's obvious agitation from dinner and that chill turned to a cold freeze.

What if her dad knew more than he was letting on?

And if her dad was guilty, could she put handcuffs on her father and take him to jail?

She swallowed the sudden lump in her throat.

Please don't make me cross that bridge.

Alex strode into Clint's office, a storm crossing his features that didn't bode well. "Do you want to tell me why a security agency is snooping around my personal affairs? Is there something I should know?"

Ty was making discreet inquiries but it was just a matter of time before Alex found out. That time was now.

"I hired Ty Colton for personal security. He's just doing his due diligence. It's a formality. I'm sure you're fine. Once he can scratch you off the list, it'll be like it never happened."

"I don't appreciate being watched," Alex growled. "You should've given me a heads-up that my privacy was going to be compromised."

He could understand Alex's ire but he couldn't tell Ty to back off. "If you can do me this favor, I'll owe you one."

"This is more than just buying someone a beer for a favor. He was asking questions that implied I might be a criminal or something. I'm a cofounder of this company. I'm not going to stand by and let some jerk-off disrespect me like that. I'm insulted that you would even suggest such a thing."

"C'mon, Alex. No one is asking you to stand naked in front of a stranger so he can give you a cavity search. I think you're overreacting a little bit."

Alex's nostrils flared. "Easy for you to say. It's not happening to you."

Clint knew Alex wasn't going to let this go unless he gave him some backstory but he was taking a risk sharing the full details of his time in Braxville before Ty could clear Alex. He supposed in the interest of keeping the peace, he had to try.

"Sit down for a minute," he said, gesturing toward the open seat. When Alex dropped into the chair, his expression still hard, Clint said, "I wasn't entirely honest about my time in Braxville."

"What do you mean?"

"I mean, something happened to me while I was there that I tried to keep under wraps for the company's sake."

"What happened?" Alex asked, frowning with confusion. "I thought you went to Kansas to talk about your estranged uncle, the one they found walled up in a warehouse."

"Yeah, I did, but before I could talk to the detective, I was waylaid. Someone bashed me in the head and left me for dead. It was pure dumb luck that someone saw me crumpled on the side of the road."

"You were attacked?" Alex repeated, dumbfounded. "What the hell, man? Why didn't you tell me this earlier? I could've put a security detail together."

"I wanted to handle it privately. I didn't want anyone to lose confidence in my abilities to run the company. You know how scared investors can get when something upsets the status quo. I didn't want you to worry about me when you had to work on landing Nortec."

Alex waved away Clint's answer. "You're my best friend, not just my business partner. If someone was harassing you, you should've told me. I hate that you thought you had to shoulder that alone. Are you okay?"

"Yeah, all good. I was bruised and battered for a short while but I recovered and now I just want to make sure whoever attacked me isn't looking to finish the job the next time."

"Wait, you think this was more than just a random attack?"

"Honestly, I don't know, but in this case, I'd say it's better to be safe than sorry, right?"

"Sure, sure," Alex agreed, nodding. "Hey, I'm sorry I came in so hot. I didn't realize what you were going through."

"I know, it's okay. I wanted to tell you but I also wanted everything to go back to normal. Business as usual. It's bad enough that I have to deal with the aftermath. I don't want to deal with my business landing on shaky ground because of it."

"*Our* business," Alex corrected him with a wink.

"You know what I mean," Clint said. "Of course it's our business."

Alex accepted Clint's correction and said, "Okay, well, I think it's safe to say I'm not a threat. We've been in business together for too long. If I was going to kill you, it would've happened before now."

They chuckled together. Clint adding, "Yeah, a lot of water under that bridge."

"Damn straight. Remember when we were first starting and you didn't want to take that contract with Greger Corp? It would've been our first big contract and we needed the money, bad."

"Yeah, because when you get in bed with dogs, you end up with fleas," he said. "Besides, we ended up getting a better contract with a better class of people right after."

"Lucky break. Aaron Greger might not have been the kind of guy you wanted to share a dinner table with but that account would've put us on the map far earlier than we had on our own."

But Clint had dug his heels in and threatened to walk if Alex continued to chase after that contract and eventually Alex caved, which probably saved their friendship.

"See? If we could come out the other side after that major blowup, we can handle anything," Alex said.

Clint smiled, nodding. "Yeah, everything else feels like smooth sailing."

"We work well together," Alex said. "I mean, I wish you'd let us take some more risks, but you know, that's an old argument that we'll probably never resolve."

"You're already a wealthy man." Clint chuckled, shaking his head. "What's a little more in the bank going to do for us?"

"More is always better."

"Not always."

"And that's where we agree to disagree," Alex said, rising. "About that security detail…would you mind sending them in a different direction? I don't usually let someone that far up my ass unless they're paying for dinner first."

"I'll talk to Ty," Clint agreed, waving him off. "Get out of here and do some work, you heathen."

Alex laughed. "Takes one to know one, brother." He left Clint's office.

But once Alex was gone, Clint wondered if he'd just made a big mistake sharing that intel with his oldest friend. He didn't know who he could trust.

Damn, he missed Jordana. She was the one person he knew had his back.

If only his pride would allow him to beg for her return.

Chapter 26

Jordana did anything she could to remain busy, even if it meant doing busywork at home that only a lunatic would jump feetfirst into—such as organizing her spice rack by alphabetical order. Her justification was that she didn't want to search for what she was looking for when cooking. She wanted to be able to go straight to the spice in question. Quick and efficient.

But then that job turned into a consolidation of spices, making sure that she didn't have duplicates, checking expiration dates and making a list of replacement spices as well as adding new ones. Her small project had turned into a major ordeal but she was happy to keep her mind occupied with anything other than fighting her urge to pick up the phone and call Clint just to hear his voice again.

As if summoned by her subconscious, her cell rang and she nearly ran to it, hoping against hope that it was Clint calling her.

When she saw it was Ty, her hope turned to dread.

"Hey, Ty, are you calling me with good or bad news?" she asked.

"Depends on your outlook. It could be considered good news but then it could also be very bad news."

"You know I hate ambiguous answers," she said with a groan. "Spit it out."

"I found the embezzler, if not who attacked Clint."

Her heart stopped. "Yeah? Who is it?" Someone he knew? Someone in his business circles? A past lover? The suspense was killing her. "C'mon, don't drag it out."

"Alex Locke is the one siphoning from the business accounts and he's been doing it for a long time. I'm talking millions. The guy has been living large on Broadlocke's purse."

Jordana let out a breath of disappointment. Clint was going to be crushed. "Have you told Clint yet?"

"No, not yet. I was going to do that this afternoon but I wanted to tell you first."

"Don't tell him yet. I'll deliver the bad news. He should hear it from a friendly face."

"Do you think that's a good idea? You left for a reason. I'm not sure you ought to rip open that wound all over again. Not just for you but for him, too."

"What do you mean?"

"The guy's been a mess since you left. He's only just now starting to pull it together. I'm not sure it's a good idea for you to come out here when he's finally doing better."

"I wouldn't be coming to reignite anything romantic. I just know that this news is going to devastate him. He should hear it from someone he knows has his best interests at heart."

Ty sighed, knowing that Jordana wasn't going to listen. "Fine. That works out. I have to cut things short here, anyway. I've got another case that's blowing up and needs my attention. My flight leaves tonight. How soon can you get here?"

She checked her watch and then her gaze met the spice mess on her counters. Forget the spice project. It could wait. "I'll take the next flight out."

Ty offered to put her flight on his expense account and Jordana let him. She wasn't going to let pride get in the way of getting to Chicago. Following a quick message to Reese explaining the situation, she quickly packed, smothering the little voice in the back of her head that cautioned against doing this. Ty was probably right but she couldn't bring herself to stay back. Clint needed her. She wasn't going to let him face this terrible news alone. Reese would be able to handle anything on the warehouse murders until she returned but Clint was in grave danger and needed her.

But what if, when she arrived, she was the last person Clint wanted to see? It wasn't as if she expected him to welcome her with open arms but she hoped he wasn't hostile. People with broken hearts were unpredictable in their reactions. It would crush her if Clint said awful things and pushed her way.

Judging by what Ty said, Clint had been suffering. She hated that she was the cause of that pain, but ultimately, it'd been best for them both. At least, that's what she told herself when she white-knuckled her urge to pick up the phone and apologize for running away.

The heart could justify just about anything. Such as making a trip to Chicago to deliver bad news.

Ah, for crying out loud, who was she trying to convince? She missed him. She missed Clint in a way that defied logic, the pain of his absence like a physical thing.

Trying to ignore the pain of his absence was like trying to ignore a knife in her side.

So, it was probably really shortsighted of her to jump onto a plane to see the man she was trying to put in her rearview mirror. These circumstances weren't ordinary, though, she reminded herself. It wasn't as if she were traipsing off to see an ex-boyfriend for funsies or just to see if the spark was still there because she saw him on Facebook and he looked pretty good.

That was what her friend Layla did. Left her life in Braxville to go see an old boyfriend who had relocated to Washington state. For her, it worked out. Layla and her guy were living happily in that soggy state as if the years apart meant nothing.

But that was a fairy-tale ending that wasn't going to work out for Jordana and she wasn't expecting it to.

What was she expecting? First things first, she needed to make sure Clint was safe. Then they'd navigate the choppy waters of getting justice.

Of course Alex should go to jail but white-collar crime was usually given a slap on the wrist. Pay restitution, do some community service.

But if Alex was behind the attacks on Clint's life? That was a whole different story. Alex was in deep trouble if that was the case. Honestly, Jordana wasn't sure which scenario she hoped for more. A friend can forgive a lapse in judgment fueled by greed. It's a lot harder to forgive attempted murder.

Jeana entered his office to announce, "Miss Colton is here to see you," and if he hadn't looked up in shock to find Jordana walk in, he would've sworn he'd misheard her. But there she was. Looking as beautiful as ever with her kissed-by-the-Kansas-sun skin, her eyes bright and those long legs that he remembered quite clearly kissing the length to find the promised land, and striding into his office with purpose. An Amazon warrior queen—that's what she looked like. That is, if an Amazon warrior queen was licensed to carry a gun instead of throwing a spear.

He blinked, half-afraid he was imagining Jordana, but when Jeana quietly closed the door behind her, leaving them alone, he knew he wasn't dreaming. Jordana was here.

And he couldn't play it cool. He was overjoyed. "You came back?" he asked. "Is everything okay?"

"I came to deliver you the news personally about who's been embezzling from your company," she said, her expression chagrined. "I wanted you to hear it from a friendly face."

"That doesn't bode well," he said, losing some of his joy. He held his breath, afraid of her answer. "Why didn't Ty tell me?"

"He was going to but I told him I'd do it. Seemed appropriate that since we started this journey together, I should be here with you when it ends."

"Don't say it like that—sounds like I'm dying or something."

She chuckled. "Sorry about that."

"At any rate, I'm glad you're here," he said, coming toward her. The tremulous smile on her lips told him she missed him, too. He wanted to fold her into his arms but there was also something about her body language that told him she wasn't there to pick up where they left off. He folded his arms across his chest, ready for the bad news. "All right, hit me, who's been stealing from me?"

"Ty found evidence that… Alex Locke has been stealing from the company for years. I'm so sorry."

He wasn't prepared for that punch to the chest. He'd

half expected it to be a disgruntled employee looking to get even or a current lower-level employee with a grudge.

But Alex? Why? That couldn't be true. "Alex has no reason to steal from me. Ty is wrong."

"He's not wrong. Ty is very good at what he does. Ty sent me the documents." Jordana pulled her phone from her purse and queued up the files for him to see.

He accepted the phone in disbelief. Scanning the documents, he saw what he couldn't bring himself to believe. *Alex?* "I don't understand," he said. "Alex does not need to steal from the company. His net worth—"

"Is all on paper. Alex Locke is cash poor and he's teetering on the edge of bankruptcy. I'm sure he thought he didn't have a choice."

"He could've asked me for a loan if he was struggling." Clint, still reeling, was having a hard time wrapping his head around this information. "He's my oldest friend. I would've helped him out."

"Pride is a powerful thing," Jordana said sadly. Drawing a deep breath, she continued. "But now that we know, we need to alert Chicago authorities. They need to take over from this point."

"Turn him in? No, I don't want to do that. The bad press will kill this company. No, I'll handle it privately."

"I know you have to think about your company but you need to let the authorities in because there's a chance that Alex was the one who tried to kill you."

"No, I don't believe that at all. Sure, money problems I can understand. Bad judgment, whatever. But Alex would never try to kill me. That's absurd."

"I know how it feels to want something not to be true but the evidence is right here. Alex is the thief but he could also be the one who is trying to kill you. You can't take that chance. Once he figures out that you know, he might get desperate. Desperate people do stupid things. Don't let your friendship blind you."

"I need a minute to process," Clint said, leaning against his desk. He couldn't deny he was seeing the paper trail leading straight to Alex's doorstep but he couldn't accept that Alex had tried to kill him. "What does Alex have to gain if I'm dead?"

"Sole ownership of Broadlocke?" Jordana guessed as if it were a no-brainer. "He has money problems. Think of how it would benefit him to have you gone. Maybe he's tired of running plans by you or having to share the responsibility of decisions. I don't know, people do terrible things for less reasons."

Clint had a hard time accepting that Alex would do this to him but a niggling sense that Alex often chafed against Clint's decisions gave Jordana's theory a little more weight. Sure, he and Alex didn't always agree on which accounts to take, but in the end, they always managed to make it work.

Betrayal tasted bitter in his mouth. Jordana's expression softened, and she reached out to him, placing a hand gently on his, offering a simple, "I'm sorry," but he couldn't produce an appropriate response because his throat was choked up. Finally, he managed, "Meet me at the penthouse. I need to talk to Alex," but Jordana wasn't having it.

"No, that's a bad idea," Jordana protested, but his mind was made up. He and Alex had started this business from the ground up. He deserved answers and he wanted the man to look him in the eye when he gave them. But he should've known Jordana wasn't going to hang back. "If you're hell-bent on making a stupid decision, I'm not letting you go in without backup."

He already knew he loved her but in that moment, eyes

shining with grim acceptance, willing to face an uncertainty with him, he loved her that much harder.

When this was all said and done…he was going to make things right with Jordana.

Chapter 27

Jordana knew there was a high probability of things turning bad once Clint confronted Alex. She'd seen too many instances where people got hurt. And against her better judgment, she didn't alert the authorities as she wanted to. Clint wanted to handle this himself. Jordana wouldn't dream of letting him walk into the lion's den alone, even if it meant things could go seriously sidewise.

Alex, similar to Clint, lived in a posh building on the top floor, but the immediate difference between Clint's place and Alex's was stark. For one, it looked as if Alex had been burglarized and just forgot to call police and report it. What little furniture remained in the room lay toppled as if someone had thrown them in a rage. One chair rested on its back with a broken leg. A wall mirror was shattered as if it'd been punched. Beyond that, the place was relatively bare but there was evidence on the walls that art or decor had once hung there. There was an air of sadness and ruin that was hard to miss.

"What the hell, man?"

By the look on Clint's face, it'd been a while since he'd been to his friend's place and the last time he was there it hadn't looked like this.

"Hey, uh, what are you doing here?" Alex asked, his gaze darting from Jordana to Clint, trying not to squirm. "I wasn't expecting guests tonight."

"Or ever, if your place is any judge. What's going on?"

Alex ran a hand through his hair, irritated. "It's been a rough night. How about we talk about this in the morning. I've been getting ready to remodel, is all."

But Clint was already piecing together the puzzle. "You've been selling your stuff. Why?"

"No!" Alex barked a short, nervous laugh. "Why the hell would I sell? No, I mean, I got rid of a few things because I'm going in a different direction. You know me, I bore easily. Probably why I can't keep a girlfriend for longer than six months."

The attempt at a joke fell flat. Jordana shifted against the tension in the room. Clint held Alex's stare as he said, "I know you've been embezzling from the company. Upward of millions." He took another glance around. "Judging by the sparse furnishings, I'm guessing you've had money problems for a while. What is it? Drugs? Gambling? What's your vice, man? Something made you take that leap. What was it?"

"I don't know what you're talking about," Alex said, becoming defensive. "Is this what that crap private investigator told you? He's messing with you. Probably trying to get some more billable hours by sending you on a wild-goose chase. It's all crap, man. I would never steal from the company. That would be like stealing from myself."

"Or stealing from me," Clint replied, unfazed by Alex's denial. The paper trail was hard to ignore. "You've got five seconds to come clean before I call the Chicago PD and report you. Help me understand what the hell you were thinking."

Alex sent a sharp look Jordana's way. "This is probably her doing. She's got her brother sending you bad intel for some reason. Maybe you ought to look a little more deeply into her background before you start pointing fingers."

"Leave Jordana out of this. Right now, she's the only thing standing between you and my fists because I'm seeing red. Start talking."

Jordana's muscles tensed. If things were going to go down, this was the moment. Razor wire separated them from all hell breaking loose and calm, rational thought. A tic spasmed Alex's right eye. The air practically bristled with taut energy. Clint held Alex's stare. "Don't make me report you," he warned.

Finally, Alex crumpled under the pressure, releasing a pent-up breath as he walked away from Clint to drop onto the sofa, the picture of a broken man who couldn't run any longer.

"It started innocently enough," Alex started. "A game here and there to win over clients, networking to bring in new business. A few wins, a few losses, no big deal. It was all business."

"You're addicted to gambling," Jordana finished for him.

Alex didn't want to admit it but he grudgingly nodded. "Not sure how it happened, but before I knew it, I was up to my eyeballs in debt to some shady people. The only way I could pay them off was to dip a little in the company books but I fully planned to pay it all back."

"Except you didn't," Jordana said.

"No, I didn't," he said bitterly. "And then I had to borrow more. I had to keep up the flow or else I'd sink. It was like trying to swim in quicksand. I could never get a foothold and I was barely keeping my head above water."

"Why didn't you come to me for help?" Clint asked. "You have a problem. I would've helped you before it got to this point."

"Hey, I don't need Clint Broderick coming in to save the day, all right?" Some of that earlier bristling returned. "I can save myself. And I did. I was doing good for a while. My luck was turning around, I could feel it."

"Spoken like a true addict," Jordana said. "It's always the next game, or the one after that, that's going to make everything right again."

Alex didn't appreciate her input but he knew enough to keep his tongue in his head. Clint rubbed his forehead. "So how deep are you?"

"Uh, a million."

Clint swore under his breath. "Jesus, Alex, what have you done?"

"Look, I know it was stupid. I couldn't seem to stop myself. I'm underwater, man. There's no stopping what's happening at this point."

Jordana's ears pricked at something in Alex's statement. Taking a chance on her gut, she said, "So, when did you hire the hit man to take Clint out?"

Clint looked sharply to Jordana but then slewed his gaze at Alex, awaiting an answer. Jordana knew Clint wanted Alex to deny that part, to prove that he wasn't a murderer, just a thief. But when Alex's eyes watered and he choked on his admission, Jordana knew with a sinking heart her gut hadn't been wrong.

"Man, I'm so sorry. I wasn't thinking! I was desperate, out of my head, scared. I was messed up. I wanted to take it back but it was too late."

"What was too late?" Jordana asked.

"The hit was paid. I couldn't take it back without it coming back on me. I didn't know how these things worked, and when I called to cancel I got a message that there were no refunds, and if I tried to do anything to cancel the hit, I'd be next."

"Who is this person?" Jordana asked, immediately grabbing her phone to call Chicago PD. "We have to call the police."

"No! They'll kill me for ratting them out. Besides, I don't have a name, just a number, and it's a burner phone. It's not like you can just flip through Yelp and find a contract killer. There are channels you got to go through and they don't mess around."

"You hired someone to kill me?" The pain in Clint's voice tore at Jordana. "How could you? We were friends. You were my *best* friend. Stealing money I can understand but to want me dead?"

Alex buried his head in his hands in shame. "I'd do anything to take it back, man. I regretted it the minute I set the plan in motion. When I heard that you'd been attacked in Braxville but you thought it was a robbery gone wrong, I was relieved. I thought maybe the hit man might've thought he got the job done and moved on. But I got a message saying, *Attempt two*, and then your car got hit. That's how I knew that it wasn't over yet. I've been trying to think of a way out of this but I'm spun out of ideas. I'm so sorry, man."

"I need everything you have on this contract," Jordana said to Alex, disgusted by the man's weakness. "I can run a trace on the phone and see who it leads to."

"It's a burner phone. You're not going to find anyone," Alex insisted. "Look, you should do yourself a favor and take a vacation while I sort this out. I'll figure out how to fix this, but in the meantime, get out of town."

"Sorry if I don't take advice from you right now," Clint said coldly. "If you'd come to me before you started this, maybe we could've fixed it together. It's too late now."

"What are you going to do?"

"The only choice you've left me," Clint answered, his phone going to his ear. "I'd like to make a report of embezzlement and attempted murder."

Alex broke down and sobbed. There was nothing more to be said.

Clint's lips were numb as he watched Chicago's finest take his best friend into custody. He still couldn't wrap his head around the fact that Alex had screwed him over for money.

"I didn't see this coming," he admitted to Jordana, his voice hoarse from trapped tears he couldn't cry. Alex didn't deserve his tears. "He was willing to see me dead over money. How could he betray me like this?"

Clint knew Jordana didn't have the answers but her pained expression told him that she wished she did.

One of the officers broke away to ensure Clint was going to come to the station to make a statement.

"First thing in the morning," Jordana jumped in, sliding her hand through his, explaining to the officer, "It's been an overwhelming night."

"Of course." The uniform nodded and handed Clint a contact card. "Ask for Detective Milton."

Clint nodded and the officers took Alex away. Clint locked up Alex's apartment and they walked out of the building. Jordana started to hail a taxi but he stopped her. "Can we just walk for a minute? I need to clear my head."

She nodded and wrapped her arm around his. "Walking is good."

They fell into an easy step together with no particular destination in mind. Clint couldn't go home with everything swirling around in his head. He needed an outlet or he would lose his mind.

As it was, his heart was howling.

"We met freshman year in college," he shared, needing to talk. "He was the fast-talking, smart-ass kid with the jokes. People just flocked to him. I was the exact opposite. Somehow we fit together."

"Opposites attract, even in friendships," Jordana said.

"I should've seen this coming. Even in college, Alex had always been looking for shortcuts. He almost got busted for stealing tests. Skated past that collision by the skin of his teeth. At the time we laughed about it. Now, it seems cheating the system for his gain was ingrained in his DNA."

"Some people change, some people don't. You couldn't have known that Alex had a character flaw that big."

"Couldn't I, though? I missed that red flag even though it was waving in front of my face. My blindness nearly got me killed. I trusted the wrong person with everything I had. What if Alex had bankrupted Broadlocke? What, then? It's just stupid luck that we haven't gone under now that I know Alex has been sucking off the books like a damn vampire."

"You'll be able to fix this. What's most important now is finding who this hit man is before he tries to finish the contract." She shivered, glancing around. "I'm not sure it's a great idea to be wandering around in the open. You never know if you've got a target on your back. You should come back to Braxville with me. It's not safe here."

"It's not safe anywhere," he reminded her.

"Yes, but the odds of the hit man getting to you are significantly lower if you're where I can protect you."

"I'm not going to run and hide."

"Don't look at it that way," she said, frustrated by his refusal. "This is about more than your male pride."

"I don't want to argue with you." But he wasn't going to let anyone run him out of town.

"You're impossible," Jordana growled, but her eyes were soft with concern. "At the very least, we should get you inside. Let's get you home."

He supposed Jordana was right but he didn't relish the idea of spending the night alone. He stopped, turning to meet her gaze. "Stay with me tonight."

Jordana winced in a subtle movement as she shook her head. "I'm not sure that's a good idea. I have my hotel room."

"Forget the hotel. Stay with me."

"I've already paid," she said, fishing for reasons.

"I don't care. I'll give you the cash. I just don't want to be alone right now."

"I don't want your money. I want you to be safe."

"I need you, Jordana," Clint said with a catch in his voice. God, he'd never needed anyone more than he needed her right now. "I don't know what to think anymore. I need someone I know I can trust with me tonight. You're the only person I trust in this entire world."

Jordana softened and relented. "Just tonight," she warned when his relieved smile widened too far. "We already know how this doesn't work out. I don't want a repeat of before. I'm not staying in Chicago."

He'd take those terms. "Just tonight," he agreed, closing his eyes before pressing a kiss to her forehead, repeating in a cracked murmur, "Just tonight."

It was a devil's bargain. One night of comfort would only soothe temporarily but the heartbreak of watching her leave again would only twist the knife deeper into his heart.

It is what it is. He'd take what he could get.

Chapter 28

It was a wordless exchange, an offer without sound. Jordana knew accepting his offer would mean one thing—she wasn't sleeping anywhere but beside him. And she was shaking with the desire that heated her blood. It was one thing to pretend she was over Clint when she had work to distract her. It was completely another to be in his arms, his body pressed against hers, as her heart awakened with a painful jolt.

"Clint," she said with a soft cry as he hoisted her onto his hips, carrying her to the bedroom. Memories washed over her from her time there, both good and bad. He laid her down gently as he quickly stripped, his eyes centered on her as if he were afraid she might disappear if he blinked. She let her gaze wander the exquisite planes and valleys of the man she adored with all her heart but would never get to keep, and reached out to him, almost desperately. "I've missed you," she whispered a confession as he helped her out of her clothes.

"Baby, you have no idea how much I've missed you," he returned in a feverish tone. He lavished attention on her bare breasts, taking care to gently drag his teeth against the sensitive nipples, causing them to pearl into hardened tips that he sucked into his greedy, hot mouth.

Jordana gasped as his tongue rasped along the tender skin, suckling at her breast as his hand slid down her belly to find the softness of her mound. She curled around him, cradling his head, before he released her breasts to travel where his hand rested. He inhaled her scent, driving himself wild. His groan of appreciation sent goose bumps of awareness rioting through her nerve endings, awakening a hungry beast inside her.

He parted her legs, pressing sweet kisses down her inner thighs until he settled on the swollen bud between her folds. Her sharp gasp as her hands curled into the bedding was the encouragement he enjoyed. "That's it, baby," he murmured against his damp skin, "come for me, sweetheart."

She cried his name as pleasure washed over her in a crashing cataclysm that left her toes curled and her womb clenching as everything spasmed in beautiful unison. Jordana fell back, damp and spent, breathing hard as the final waves of pleasure continued to ebb around her. Clint climbed her body to plant a deep, soul-searching kiss on her awaiting lips.

This was heaven and hell. Heaven to know that perfection existed within another's arms; hell to realize it would never work between them.

Tears sprang to her eyes and Clint seemed to understand, wrapping his arms around her, rolling to his back so he could gaze up at her. "You're so beautiful," he murmured. "I love you, Jordana."

"I love you, too," she said, choking on her tears. His

hardened length burned beneath her, hard and insistent. Jordana was desperate to feel him inside her, to merge with him in the most primal way possible. Positioning him at her entrance, she slowly descended on his hot staff, taking each inch with deliberate intention, sinking into the pleasure of being filled by the man who owned her heart.

He groaned as her wet heat enveloped him on all sides, gripping his length as he bracketed her hips, guiding her as she rode him, finding her pleasure as he took his.

"Jordana." He gasped her name like a prayer, his fingers curling into her flesh, creating delicious disharmonious sensations to compete with her nerve endings. She found the rhythm that suited her best, moaning as she neared her climax. Sweat broke out across her hairline, her breasts swelling, nipples hard. She shuddered as heat washed over her, pleasure rippling up and down her body as she crashed into an orgasm that exploded from a deep place inside.

Stars alive, I'll never meet anyone like you. Falling to his side, limp and out of breath, Clint threw one leg over his shoulder, bending her in half as he impaled her again on his length. His name escaped on a cry as Clint thrust against her with a fervor that spoke of a man running from grief, heartache and betrayal. All she could do was be his vessel, his conduit to some sort of relief.

But even as he neared his climax, Jordana felt the beginnings of a new orgasm rumbling through her nerve endings, tingling and ringing as loudly as a bell atop the church tower. There was no escaping the pleasure as it gripped her around the throat, sending sweet surrender cascading through her body, wave after wave until they were both drenched in sweat and breathing hard as they recovered.

Moonlit skies filled the bedroom window, bathing their naked, glistening bodies in a pale glow.

She met his gaze, her fingers finding his, curling together. In this moment, perfection was a tangible thing, a tangle of arms, legs and souls. She'd never been one to spout poetry or over-the-top proclamations, but she suddenly understood the impulse. Clint was unlike anyone she'd ever met. He was not replaceable. How cruel was fate to introduce them, only to tear them apart?

Just as she couldn't ask him to leave everything he knew where he was established, he shouldn't ask her to do the same. They lived in different worlds and neither were compatible.

Fresh tears welled in her eyes. Clint pulled her into his embrace with a murmured, "Shhh," as if to say he understood but now wasn't the time to talk about it. Jordana nodded and settled against his chest, her naked body fitting so well against his.

If tonight was all they had, why ruin it with the reality of tomorrow?

Her eyes drifted shut on a sigh.

Clint knew the minute Jordana fell asleep. Her breathing slowed as her body relaxed, followed by light snoring that he found incredibly endearing, though she would likely disagree.

A smile found him even though he knew she was fully planning to leave him again. It was no use to try and convince her to stay. It'd been wrong of him to drag her to Chicago in the first place. She was a beautiful wildflower that only grew in the country. Chicago, with its cement forests and cacophony of human life, had been slowly killing her. But he wanted to ask her to stay. He wanted to sleep beside her every night, listen to the minutia of her day and argue about stupid stuff, like whose turn it was to wash the dishes.

The reality that Alex had betrayed him in the worst possible way left him with the realization that Jordana was the sole person he trusted completely, and she was going to get on a plane and leave him behind. Fate and circumstance were nasty bedfellows. And he had to find a way to stop beating himself up for missing the red flags that'd been waving in front of his nose.

Loved ones are always our blind spots. He loved Alex like a brother. The fact that that street had been one-way hurt more than he wanted to admit.

He tightened his arms around Jordana, needing her warmth to permeate the winter chill on his heart. Only Jordana made him feel like happiness was possible, that trust was rebuildable. Not with Alex, of course, but with others. He had details to work out with the lawyers, business entanglements to sort out, protections to put in place as they went forward without Alex.

Attempted murder coupled with the embezzlement came with a hefty sentence. Alex would likely go away for a very long time. Tears stung his eyes. Betrayal was a bitter taste on the tongue. Tomorrow he'd have to give a statement to the police. He'd have to tell in great detail everything that'd happened since his assault in Braxville. Word would likely get out quickly that Alex Locke of Broadlocke Enterprises had been busted. Company morale would be shattered. Investor confidence would be tested.

He had to have a plan to save his business before Alex's actions completely tanked a dream that took years of grueling work in the trenches to create.

Fresh anger flooded Clint. What the hell was Alex thinking? Was he thinking at all? Like Jordana said, addicts didn't think about the people they were hurting, only the fix. He knew more heartache was coming when he had to face Alex in court, to stare in the eyes of the man he'd thought had his back only to find out that same man was his enemy.

A sigh rattled out of his chest and Jordana stirred with a faint whimper. He pressed a soft kiss on her exposed neck and she settled. Was there a way to convince this strong, independent woman that their lives could intertwine without sacrificing either of their interests? She'd want a plan; he didn't have one. Saying "But I love you" wasn't going to cut it. Ignoring the selfish part of himself that wanted to do whatever was necessary to keep her with him was a struggle.

But he'd never ask her to stay when she wanted to leave. He'd respect her wishes but nothing could stop him from wanting her. Until then, he'd just have to savor the moment until it was gone.

Chapter 29

Morning came and, with it, the sad acceptance that she had to go back to Braxville.

She woke before Clint, giving her the chance to watch him sleep. He had a classically handsome face with a hint of ruggedness. His chest rose and fell with each heavy breath. Muscles that had no business residing behind a button-down shirt and jacket made her hunger for something other than food.

His eyes slowly fluttered open, a smile following as he reached for her. "I'll never tire of waking to this face," he said with a sexy sleep-roughened voice.

Jordana didn't want to talk. She wanted to spend this last morning with Clint, loving him without words.

She slid her hand down his stomach to find his erection, already hard and ready even if he was barely awake. Smiling, she burrowed under the blankets to take him into her mouth.

He groaned, his hips thrusting gently against her mouth. Jordana worked him until he was ready to burst. Clint threw the covers aside and fell back against the bedding with a harsh moan, his muscles tensing as he neared his climax.

A raw sense of power rippled through Jordana as she held this powerful man between heaven and hell. She teased him, pushing him to the brink, only to slow down before starting again.

"Oh, God," he moaned.

Finally, she pushed him to the edge. Clint stiffened, going rigid as he came. It was primal and raw.

She rose, her hair a mess but a smile wreathing her lips. Clint looked more in love with her than ever. That expression was the sweetest memory she'd take with her. Jordana kissed him, then rose to drink some water. She took her fill and handed Clint the bottle. He guzzled the bottle, finishing it. He fell back on the bed, inviting her to return to his side, but Jordana had to get to the airport.

"If I climb back into that bed, I won't leave." At Clint's raised brow, she clarified, "And I have a plane to catch."

His expression dimmed and she hated to be the one to ruin the moment. "You know, if you're ever in Kansas… you can always look me up."

It was an attempt at brevity but they weren't friends with benefits, happy to leave each other behind until the next time. Their lives were so complicated there was no easy answer for either of them.

"Is there anything I could say that would make you want to stay with me?" he asked plainly.

"It isn't a question of wanting to be with you," she answered. "It's just that we tried it already and your world isn't compatible with mine."

"Maybe we didn't try hard enough."

"Maybe we ignored what we should've seen from the start."

"Which is?"

She gazed at him with love and sadness. "That I'm a police detective for a small town who loves her job and you're a wealthy business owner who has to wine and dine clients for future contracts. You need someone on your arm who will help you achieve that. I'm not that person."

"You make it sound like I'm the kind of guy who uses a woman for an advertisement. I've never been the type to chase after a trophy wife. If I'd wanted that kind of partner, I would've stayed with Iris."

"Maybe that's the person you need."

"Don't patronize me, Jordana," he said, his temper flaring. He rose from the bed and pulled on his loungers. "I understand your world. Maybe you're right that I wouldn't fit in a small town and you don't fit in a city but you never asked me if I could try and make it work, either."

Jordana frowned. "Why would I ask you a question that I already know the answer?" she asked in confusion, hating that the morning was turning sour. She tried to smooth things with an apology. "I shouldn't have said that about Iris. I didn't mean to patronize you. Sometimes my mouth gets away from me." She peeped a sidewise glance at Clint. "Sort of like this morning…"

The sexy reminder softened the hard edges of his expression. "You might be the devil," he growled, walking toward her. He pulled her into his arms for a tender kiss that belied his rough touch. "But I like whatever you are."

Jordana threw her head back to give him better access to her neck. He nibbled and kissed until he returned to her lips, announcing with an impish grin, "We should shower," then shocked her when he scooped her up, carrying her to the bathroom.

She knew what was going to happen the minute they were both naked. And she wasn't complaining. She still had plenty of time to catch her flight. Or she could reschedule. Either way, Clint was doing his best to make her forget all about Braxville.

For now.

Clint knew that no matter how many epic orgasms he gave Jordana, she was determined to be on that plane back to Braxille, but he gave it the good ol' college try. In the end, all he managed to convince her to do was share a late breakfast with him at his favorite restaurant after she confessed her secret love of eggs Benedict.

His favorite breakfast place was world-renowned for their eggs Benedict, and if that's what his woman wanted, that's what she was going to get.

Once seated, he said, "So tell me about the case with my uncle. Have you found out anything new?"

Pleased to talk about anything other than boarding that plane, Jordana nodded with a smile. "Actually, yes, but I'm not sure if it was a lead or anything. The bodies were found with an odd chemical on the bones, CCA, which stands for chromated copper arsenic. It was a common enough chemical treatment in the '70s but the EPA banned its use in 2003."

"When was the building built?"

"Well, as it turns out, my dad said the building was built in the mid-1970s so that tracks, but between you and me, I can't shake the feeling that CCA is some kind of clue. I just don't know what, though."

"Why'd the EPA ban the chemical?"

"I guess it's a carcinogen but they didn't know that until later when people who were exposed to it started getting cancer."

Clint nodded. "A lot of building materials were later found to be dangerous around humans. Did you know the EPA has only banned nine chemicals in spite of the thousands on the American market?"

"That seems an underwhelming use of an agency created to protect people from chemical harm," Jordana said.

"Well, chemical makers aren't in a big rush to admit that their product could be dangerous. Proving that a chemical is harmful to humans is a long and lengthy process. Polychlorinated biphenyls, or PCBs as we call them, were banned in 1978 but you can still find some banned chemicals coming in from China where the regulations are different."

Jordana frowned. "How would you know if something was treated with an illegal chemical?"

"Aside from testing it, you have to rely on the honesty of the seller where you're getting your materials."

"Why would anyone buy tainted materials?"

"Money," he answered with a shrug. "Cheaper materials lower the bottom line. I remember Alex and I getting into a disagreement about some tech parts we were sourcing and he wanted to buy from a Chinese distributor, but even though they were cheaper materials, I didn't get a good vibe from the distributor as far as their chemical compound usage. Ultimately, we passed and went with a different distributor."

"You didn't trust Alex to make the right choice," she surmised.

"No, I guess I didn't. As it turned out, Alex had a bit of a moral and ethic ambiguity that didn't mesh with mine."

She reached out to squeeze his hand, assuring Clint, "He's going to get what's coming to him."

Clint nodded, appreciative of her gesture. "So that's the only lead so far?"

"Yeah, it's a little disheartening. My dad is up my tail-pipe, pressuring me to release the crime scene so he can demo the building, but I can't do that until I can solve those murders."

"Cold cases are notoriously hard to solve," he said. "I can understand your dad's frustration. As a business owner, I'd go nuts if I couldn't do my job because of someone else being in my way."

"And if that someone is his daughter, he feels it's perfectly acceptable to harass her at a family dinner," she said. "Totally ruining my mom's apple pie reveal."

"I'm sorry, babe."

"I feel bad for my mom. My dad is a tyrant some days. I don't know how she put up with him all these years. Oh, and my uncle Shep is moving into the carriage house, which has further put my mom on edge—not that she needed help in that department—and my dad seems oblivious to anything that doesn't directly affect him and Colton Construction."

"Does your dad care that none of his kids went into the family business?"

"Oh, yes. It's a point of contention but he mostly saves that beef for my brothers. Thankfully, they know how to let it roll off their backs."

"I can't see Ty being bothered by something like that." Clint chuckled.

"No, Ty is his own man. On one hand, I'd think my dad would be proud that his sons and daughters are so independent but he only wants us to be headstrong with other people, not him. With him, he wants us to jump when he snaps his fingers."

"As stressful as that all sounds, having your family around is a blessing. I wish I had siblings to argue with or a father to butt heads with over nothing. It's weird what you end up valuing. Alex was the closest I had to a brother. Now, he's gone, too."

"I'm so sorry, Clint," she murmured. "I wish things had turned out differently."

"Me, too. You know, I was half expecting the culprit to be a disgruntled employee or maybe even my assistant."

"Jeana? She's practically perfect," Jordana said, chuckling. "And she has a mad crush on you."

"You know… I think I figured that out, too. She's a good woman but, well, boundaries."

She blushed. "Is it terrible that I hate the idea of you dating anyone but me?"

"Yes," he said, shocking her. He grinned, showing that he was joking. "Hey, you're breaking my heart by leaving. The least you could do is suffer the heartburn of knowing that I might be out there dating."

"You're the worst," she chided around a laugh just as their food arrived. "You, sir, have been saved by the server."

He chuckled and watched with pleasure as she moaned after her first bite. Mission accomplished. At least he knew that the eggs Benedict hype was real. They made some small talk while they finished their breakfast and then, after paying the bill, they walked arm in arm out onto the sidewalk.

The weather was nearly perfect today. Birds skimmed across blue skies like skipping stones on water. The temperature was moderate, almost vacation weather. But on the day he was saying goodbye to the love of his life, it ought to be raining like the apocalypse was about to crash down around their ears. He glanced up at the sky with a subtle scowl but he couldn't blame Mother Nature for his bad luck.

Parking for this particular restaurant was always a

bear, but instead of using the car service, he wanted to drive Jordana himself. Something about the act of driving made him feel more in control of the situation, even though it was an illusion.

It didn't matter if he drove or the car service drove, Jordana was still going to head to the airport.

But as it turned out, the parking garage wasn't exactly the kind of place he would've chosen. Even to his own eyes, the place wasn't well-lit and there were too many dark areas for his comfort. Still, it was broad daylight— what could happen?

They were nearly to the car when, out of nowhere, someone wearing a ski mask popped from the shadows, the glint of a knife catching his eye before he went down to the ground with a hard thud. Jordana screamed and he realized his attacker had come prepared. Another man held Jordana while the man on him tried to gut him like a fish.

They scrabbled against the filthy cement. Clint struggled to keep the knife blade from his throat. Sweat broke out across his body as adrenaline powered the fight-or-flight defense mechanism. He could hear Jordana struggling with her attacker but he was too busy himself to help.

Please don't let me die like this.

"You know why I picked a knife?" the man said between grunts as Clint tried to overpower him. "Because it's more personal. You've been a real pain in my ass. I'm going to enjoy spilling your insides and then I'm going to have fun with your hot girlfriend as a bonus."

But just as the man went to shove the knife deep into Clint's chest, he went flying to land in a crumpled heap, knocked out cold.

Jordana stood, bruised and bloodied, looking like an avenging angel with a helluva roundhouse kick, the other assailant suffering the same fate as the first.

"Jesus, you're a badass," Clint breathed, wiping at his bloody nose, surveying the scene. "This must be the hit man or there's someone else out there who hates me enough to want me dead."

Jordana wiped the trickle of blood from her mouth with a wry smile and pulled her cell to call 911. While they waited for police to arrive, Jordana found some rope in Clint's car and quickly bound the men like trussed-up pigs ready for the fire.

Clint couldn't stop staring at Jordana.

"Are you okay?" Jordana asked, starting to check him for knife wounds, but he stopped her with a gingerly placed kiss around bruised lips.

"I will be," he answered. "Right now, I just want to kiss you until you tell me to stop. You saved my life. Again. If I wasn't so damn happy to be alive, I'd be embarrassed as hell that you had to save me instead of the other way around."

Jordana barked a short laugh as if he were ridiculous, saying, "Baby, kicking ass and saving lives is equal opportunity." She blotted at her bleeding lip with the edge of her shirt. "But I think I'm going to need stitches."

"Is it weird that I think that's the hottest thing I've ever heard you say?"

She laughed, howling as her lips protested. "Yes. Very."

He grinned, pulling her into his arms just as the cops screeched into view, lights and sirens blaring as if they were the ones saving the day.

They shared a wry look, both thinking the same thing, before pointing to the prone men tied and ready.

Chapter 30

Clint managed to convince Jordana to stay a few more days while her lip healed but soon enough she was mended and it was time to return to Braxville.

The last few days, aside from healing from a brawl, passed with little drama or stress. They ordered takeout, made love, laughed, watched movies, talked about the mysteries of the universe and forgot about the rest of the world outside of their four walls.

It was magical. But it was also unsustainable.

The outside world awaited even if they had no interest in participating. Jordana knew that Clint thought everything had changed but it hadn't.

Finally dressed after four days of minimal clothing, Jordana met Clint's gaze and prepared for the heartbreak of goodbye.

"What are you doing?" he asked, perplexed. "Do you want to go out to eat this time? I thought we could order Greek tonight."

"Clint, as much as I would love to stay in this apartment, in your bed, for a lifetime, eventually real life would intrude. We both have lives we have to get back to. Now that I know you're truly safe, I can leave with a clear conscience."

"Whoa, hold up, not so fast. Let's talk about this."

"No, nothing has changed. I have a job to return to, an investigation that I'm up to my eyeballs in with my family, and I can't just bail. They need me to figure out what happened."

"I thought, maybe, things were different now," he admitted. "Felt different."

She cupped his face, meeting his sad gaze with equal misery. "I love you, Clint. I always will. You are probably the love of my life and I have to let you go. Our lives are so different. Eventually, one of us would become resentful of the other, no matter what decision was made. If I stayed, or you came to me, it would end the same."

"You don't know that," he said, stubbornly refusing to listen. "You're making a judgment on the future, and as far as I know, neither of us has a crystal ball."

"No, but I have experience. I know who I am and I know I already ignored my misgivings to follow you here only to have it end in the same way."

"I was distracted and I didn't give you the attention you needed. I'll be better this time."

"Stop." She held a finger to his lips with a stern expression. "I'm not a fickle houseplant that needs constant tending or else I will wilt. But I'm also not the kind of person who can be idle. I need a purpose, a job, a reason to greet the dawn with enthusiasm. I can't get that here."

"You could get a job at the Chicago PD."

"I don't want a job with the Chicago PD. I have a great job in Braxville."

"It feels like you're running away."

"I'm not."

"Then what is this?"

"It's being responsible enough to ignore the pain in my heart and doing what's best for both of us."

"That's very saintly of you," he said with a harsh look that cut her to the core.

"Don't be ugly," she pleaded, hating that his pain was coming out with a harsh tongue. "Don't make this harder than it already is."

His expression lost some of its anger. "Baby, I don't know how to watch you leave. You're a part of me. You might as well lop off an arm or a leg. It'll feel about the same."

She reached for him, resting her forehead against his. "I know. I feel the same. We both know in our hearts this is the right decision. I don't want to ever see resentment in your eyes when you look at me, and I don't want to feel it when I look at you."

"So a preemptive strike is the best option?" he asked in disbelief. "Preparing to fail?"

"No, just honest about life and how it usually turns out when people ignore the reasons why they shouldn't uproot their lives for someone else."

Jordana stepped away, tears stinging her eyes. "Please don't make this harder than it already is."

"If you're asking me to make it easy to leave me, I won't."

"C'mon, Clint…this isn't fair."

"Damn straight it's not fair. Not fair to either of us. I'm asking you to give us a shot. You're saying what we have isn't worth it for you to take the risk."

"I'm not saying that," she disagreed on a cry. "How can you say that?"

"Because that's what I hear you saying. There are no guarantees for anyone. Sacrifices, compromises, they're all part of a functioning relationship. You gotta try, put in the work, do everything you can to meet your partner in the middle. That's how things work out in the end."

"Really? How would you know that, Clint? Your parents are dead. My parents are stuck in a dysfunctional marriage, eaten up by resentments, and only sheer stubbornness keeps them tied together, not love. I've known for a long time, and I swore I'd never have that kind of relationship."

"And we won't," he said, bewildered. "We love each other."

"You think my parents didn't start wildly in love? Oh, trust me, they were at one point. You don't have six kids without being into one another at some level. But it changed. Life changes people. Circumstances out of our control changes people. Why would I start a life with someone that I'm almost guaranteed to end up resenting at some point because one or both of us were required to give up something important to the other to make it work? I just won't do it. I can't."

"I won't resent you."

"I'm not willing to take that chance."

He groaned with frustration. "We're going in circles."

"Exactly." She bent to pick up her luggage. "I was hoping you'd drive me to the airport but maybe it's best that we just part ways here. I can call an Uber."

"That's cold," he chided. "Seriously, Jordana. Don't be ridiculous. Of course I'll drive you."

"Thank you," she said, wishing she didn't have a golf-ball-size lump in her throat. "I appreciate it."

Clint just shook his head, muttering, "Give me a few

minutes to get dressed," and then disappeared into the bedroom.

She supposed that was as good an ending as she could hope for.

Still hurt like a bitch.

True to his word, he saw Jordana off to the airport, but he didn't kiss her goodbye. He didn't think he could do that without embarrassing himself in front of strangers. He left her there with a curt goodbye, walking away before he could see the tears shining in her eyes. She was leaving as a preemptive strike against a possible future breakup. It was crazy and messed up but he couldn't change her mind.

He wasn't ready to admit that he'd lost her. Wasn't ready to lose.

Losing his memory had been an incredible experience. He'd been able to rediscover who he was and who he didn't want to be.

He wanted to be a better person. But he couldn't—and wouldn't—beg a woman to be with him if she was determined to leave. If Jordana couldn't see that he was the only man for her and vice versa, there was nothing he could do to change her mind.

For God's sake, he'd never had to think twice about finding a date for an event or an evening of no-strings-attached sex. But then Jordana came along and changed everything.

Damn her for cracking open his heart and showing him what love was really about. He'd never been in love with Iris. Breaking up with her had been a blessing to them both. To be fair, he didn't think Iris had loved him, either, but a love match in certain circles wasn't as important as connections, similar backgrounds and matching goals.

Why couldn't he have loved Iris? It would've made his life easier by half.

Of course, there was no way Iris would've been able to roundhouse kick his assailant into next week, either. They both would've died gruesome deaths if Iris had been the one walking beside him when they were attacked.

He shuddered.

So what happens now?

He goes on with his life as if he hadn't fallen in love with his soul mate?

Yeah, sure.

In the short term, he had a company to keep afloat in the aftermath of Alex's actions and investors to keep assured that it would continue to be business as usual at Broadlocke. He had lawyers to meet with, financials to break down and, at some point, to testify against his former best friend and business partner.

On the surface, it would seem falling in love with a woman from tiny town in Kansas would be bad timing. But wasn't that life in general? Was there ever a good time to fall in love? Love was complicated and messy. It burned with the same fire that lights your soul from within. By its very nature, it can't be tamed.

For all her bravery in the field, Jordana was afraid of getting her heart broken. It was better to be the one breaking hearts rather than the one getting broken.

He had no way of proving to her that he would've held her heart in the most gentle of hands. She would've needed to take that leap of faith. Faith was something Jordana didn't have—and he couldn't give it to her.

Hell, maybe she was right.

Even so, why did he feel the urge to buy a ticket and follow her stubborn ass right straight back to Braxville?

He'd put a ring on her finger, give her babies, build a farmhouse, whatever...if only she'd say yes.

In the end, he forced himself to keep walking. Just as Jordana had done.

It was truly over.

And he'd have to find a way to get over it.

Chapter 31

Back in Braxville, Jordana spent days trying to piece together her life without Clint in it. Her house was spotless. *Thanks, Mom, for passing on the neurosis.* However, no matter how hard she scrubbed, reorganized and decluttered, nothing seemed to brighten her day or let her forget that the ache in her heart wasn't going anywhere.

Bridgette showed up on her doorstep on her day off, dressed in sneakers and her hair pulled in a ponytail. "Get dressed. We're going for a hike," she announced with a cheery smile.

"A hike?" Jordana repeated, confused. "What do you mean?"

"Not a complicated statement. You need to get out of this house before you start tearing down walls and trying to rebuild something when you don't have the time for that kind of DIY project."

Bridgette had a point. Just this morning she'd been

eyeing her dated tile countertops, wondering how difficult it would be to demo and replace by herself.

A person could find how to do anything on YouTube, right?

"You know me too well," Jordana said with a sigh. It wasn't worth the effort to lie when Bridgette saw right through her. "Okay, give me a minute to get dressed."

"Excellent."

Jordana found her hiking shoes and exercise gear, dressed and climbed into Bridgette's rental car.

"I thought you were going to drive Dad's old truck while you were here?" Jordana commented, snapping her seat belt into place.

"And listen to Dad bitch about how I'm not driving properly in his beloved Ford? Hell, no. I'd rather pay half my salary in rental fees than listen to that noise. Besides, that Ford is a gas-guzzler. This baby will drive forever on a full tank of gas."

She chuckled as they hit the road, saying, "Fair point. Sometimes I think Dad only offers things that he can use as leverage later."

"That's our dad for you."

"Have you ever wondered if we're bound to have 'dad' issues when looking for partners? You know, they say that the most difficult parent is the one you'll end up marrying in the form of someone else. I'd stab myself in the eye if I married someone like Dad."

"Henry wasn't anything like Dad," Bridgette reminded her. "Henry was kind and gentle, compassionate and sweet. Can you honestly imagine someone using those words to describe Dad?"

"No. Not even in my wildest imagination."

"So, I don't know if that theory tracks for everyone."

"Or maybe you're just more well-adjusted than I am?"

Bridgette laughed. "Maybe. You are a hot mess."

"Hot mess? How so?"

"Look, don't get your feathers ruffled but I think what you're doing with Clint is stupid. You love him and he loves you but you broke it off because…you might resent each other later? Nobody knows what the future holds. You could be wrong and losing the love of your life on a possibility."

"I know it's hard for you to understand. You and Henry had a fairy-tale marriage until he died. You've seen our parents. I won't end up like that."

"Please don't compare anything to our parents' marriage. They've been unhappy for years but neither will do anything about it," Bridgette said. "And don't paint me and Henry as some paragon of married life. We had our moments just like anyone else."

"Yeah, but you were so in love."

"No more so than you and Clint," Bridgette pointed out. "I think you're cutting your nose off to spite your face."

"Trust me, I'm not. Clint isn't a househusband. He's used to commanding a big tech company worth millions. He's not going to be happy in the long run moving to a tiny town in Kansas without a true purpose."

"But you don't know that. You ran away before you even gave him a chance to figure things out on his own."

"Damn right I did. I don't have to be hit on the head to know that it will hurt. I wasn't going to stick around so I could get my heart broken when he finally came to his senses. No thank you."

"I never knew you to be such a pessimist," Bridgette said, shaking her head. "Where's your sense of optimism, that starry-eyed belief in the power of love?"

"Please, I'm not a teenager. I'm not looking for a

prince to sweep me off my feet." Although the times Clint had done exactly that had stolen her breath. He had a body that haunted her dreams. Shaking off the direction of her thoughts, she added, "Besides, with some distance and time to reflect, we'll both come to the same conclusion that not all love stories end with the white picket fence, two dogs and a few kids running around."

"Since when do you like dogs?" Bridgette quipped.

Jordana laughed. "You jerk, I like dogs. As long as they're not too yappy, too big, too small, needy or shed too much."

"Please stick to cats."

They pulled off the road and parked. This spot was a favorite among locals. The trail was easy enough and the view was glorious. Jordana took a big, cleansing breath of the fresh air and smiled. "This was a good idea," she admitted. "I needed a change of scenery."

"I know."

Jordana rolled her eyes. "I love how humble you are."

Bridgette grinned, gesturing with wide arms. "Why be humble when you've got all this?"

Jordana wasn't sure if Bridgette was talking about the vista or herself but she didn't have time to question because Bridgette had already set off at a brisk pace.

"Hold up, speed racer," she grumbled, jogging to catch up.

They walked in silence, enjoying the view, making small talk in between breathing heavy through the hilly terrain, and when they popped out at the top of the low-rise ridge, they had an excellent view of the grasslands below.

"Some people don't know the beauty of Kansas," Bridgette murmured, appreciating the landscape. "I miss this."

"Yeah? I thought maybe you might not enjoy coming home again."

"No, I've missed Braxville and you guys, but I don't miss enduring the constant tension between our parents. I swear they never get along. I wish they'd just divorce and get it over with."

"You know Mom will never divorce Dad. She's still stuck in a more traditional time where divorce was shameful."

"She needs to get over it. Dad is unbearable these days."

Guilt stabbed at Jordana. "It's because he's so stressed about the investigation. I think he's really in trouble."

"What kind of trouble?" Bridgette asked.

"Financial. I know he doesn't like to talk about those things with us but I think he's been struggling for years and this is the final blow. I think he blames me for how the investigation is going."

"It's not your fault."

"I know but I can't help but feel that I'm letting him down. I don't know what else to do."

Bridgette reached for her hand. "Something will pop up. You're a good detective. Trust your process."

Jordana wished she had Bridgette's confidence. She drew a deep breath, scanning the vista. The light breeze kissed her cheek. She closed her eyes, trying to soak in the calm, letting it permeate her soul to allow some semblance of peace, but Clint was always there in the background, reminding her of what she'd given up.

Tears sparked her eyes as she admitted to Bridgette, "I loved him. I mean, really loved him."

"I know you did," Bridgette said with true sorrow in her gaze. She went into her sister's arms for a tight hug. There weren't enough beautiful vistas in the world to make her forget that simple fact. She supposed she'd just have to let time do its thing.

And try not to break down and sob with each new day that he wasn't there with her.

Clint left his attorney's office numb to the emotions battering his soul. He had to stay focused. One foot in front of the other. Trudging forward like a solider on a mission.

Soldier.

Navy.

Arrgh. Why did everything he thought of lead him back to Jordana?

He entered the building and went straight to his office to find Jeana waiting for him with a full schedule on the books, which suited him just fine because it kept his mind occupied.

Jeana, business as usual, didn't pry about the details regarding Alex but Clint felt it was only fair to let her know all the gory details, even up to the attack in the parking garage.

"Oh, heavens," Jeana exclaimed, her hand flying to her throat in alarm. "Thank goodness Miss Colton was there to handle those miscreants."

He smiled. Jeana was born in the wrong decade, but he appreciated her soft-spoken efficiency and Victorian sensibilities. He found her comforting in a world that had been tipped upside down.

"Yes, very fortunate," he murmured in agreement. "The upside is that the man who attacked me, both in Braxville and here, is in custody and I don't have to keep looking over my shoulder anymore. Police have assured me he's not going to be released on bail so I feel good about moving forward with a clean slate."

"Excellent, sir." She paused before asking, "And will you be joining Miss Colton in Braxville?"

He looked up and held Jeana's gaze, realizing she was asking if she was going to have to start polishing her résumé.

"My business is here," he answered, hopefully putting to bed any fears she might have. "But I've come to realize that it's important to place value on the people around you. I've decided to give you a raise."

"A raise?" Jeana's eyes widened. "Oh, sir, that's not necessary. You're already quite generous."

"Not generous enough. For everything you've done, you deserve so much more."

She blushed. "I'm flattered. I enjoy working here at Broadlocke and with you."

"Good. I don't want to lose you to someone else waving more money at you."

"I would never—"

"Better safe than sorry," he cut in, refusing to take no for an answer. This was the right decision, especially when he found out that Jeana was living on such a modest salary considering her level of importance to his company. "I want to do this for you, Jeana. As a thank-you for being there for me."

She blushed a little harder but jerked a short nod. "My pleasure."

"I've already talked to payroll, so you should see your raise on your next check. I'm doubling your annual salary and then we'll work from there."

Jeana gasped, her knees wobbling a bit and causing her to reach out to steady herself. "Double?"

"Yes, and that might not be enough, either. The truth is, with Alex gone, I'm going to lean on you heavily in the coming months. It's going to be rough waters and I need you to help me keep the ship afloat. It's only fair to compensate you for your time."

"I don't know what to say."

"No need to say anything. It's what should've been done a long time ago. I'm sorry it took me so long to figure out who was worth keeping around."

Her eyes took on a shiny glaze but she held it together. Stiffening her back and squaring her shoulders, she said, "It's an honor to work with you, Mr. Broderick. You've always been fair and honest. In this day and age, those qualities are hard to find in someone of your stature."

He smiled, accepting the compliment. "Thank you, Jeana. Coming from you, it's high praise that I'll work to keep deserving."

Jeana, not one to gush or simper, settled back into work mode, saying, "You have a ten o'clock waiting. Shall I show them in?"

He nodded. "Conference room, please."

"Excellent." She turned on her heel and started to leave, only to pause to say, almost haltingly, "Even if you were to leave for Braxville, we could make it work. Broadlocke is a well-oiled machine. It will weather any adjustments."

And then, having said her piece, she went to collect his next appointment.

She was saying that if he wanted, he could make changes and it would still be all right. Was it true? What if he leaped to move to Braxville and Jordana still sent him packing? She'd already made it clear that she didn't want him uprooting his life for her. He understood her concerns. He didn't want to admit it but in the back of his mind he had the same worries.

He couldn't say without a shadow of a doubt that he wouldn't resent the move at some point.

Braxville was a huge difference from Chicago. He liked his conveniences.

But he loved Jordana.

He chewed on the dilemma for a moment longer before shelving it completely and heading to his meeting.

Chapter 32

"Jordana, just the person I wanted to see."

Jordana mentally cringed at the sound of her father's business partner, Dex. When they were growing up he was Uncle Dex because he was around so much, but now that they were adults, he was just Dex.

She'd hoped to talk with her mom about Uncle Shep but she was waylaid before she could slip out of reach.

"C'mere, girl," Dex said with a good-hearted chuckle as he wrapped her in a hug that she allowed but wished she could disappear. She knew why he wanted to talk to her and there was nothing she could say. "You're a sight for sore eyes. Why are you still single? You're much too pretty to be all alone."

Only Dex could make her cringe like this. She forced a smile, answering, "Just haven't found the right one, I guess."

"You gotta get out there, put on a pretty dress, a little

makeup. You'll catch a keeper eventually but you better hurry or else you'll end up on the shelf."

She couldn't resist. "That's sage advice—if it were the 1800s. Times have changed, Dex. Try to keep up."

Jordana caught her father's expression, and if she weren't mistaken, she saw a sliver of amusement shining in his eyes. Maybe he got tired of Dex, too.

Sobering, Dex said, "Actually, I was just talking to your dad and he said we're still holed up with the demo on the warehouse. What's going on? I don't understand what the holdup is?"

"It's an active investigation. We can't release the site until we're through with the investigation."

"Honey, these people have been dead for quite a long time from what I understand. They can't get any deader."

"It's not that—the site is an active crime scene. We still have forensics searching for anything that might be tested for DNA."

"DNA? Like what?" Dex screwed his expression into a perturbed frown. "Like eyelashes or something?"

"Something like that. We're still processing," she said, hoping Dex dropped it.

But her luck wasn't that good. "Now, now, honey, that's just not going to work. Surely your daddy has told you that we're losing business on this holdup? That's no lie. We're in some hot water and we gotta get moving or we're all going to lose our shirts. You don't want that, do you?"

She ground her teeth, hating that Dex was smothering her with guilt she didn't need. "Yes, my dad has told me that the investigation is hurting the bottom line. There's nothing I can do to speed things up unless you want to tell me who killed those people?"

"Well, honey, you know I don't have that kind of information." Dex huffed, adjusting his belt. "But surely I would tell you in a heartbeat if I thought it would move things along any faster."

She smiled. "I don't doubt it. But we're moving as fast as we can. Forensics isn't like they show on television. It's a slow process."

"Let's get real here. I could make a call to the mayor and see if there's anything he can do help but I was trying to give you the chance to do your thing. I just don't see how much longer we can wait around."

"She said she's doing all she can," Fitz interjected with a sharp rebuke. "Stop hounding the girl."

Jordana could forgive her dad calling her a girl because she was too shocked that he'd taken her side instead of Dex's on this issue. Particularly when he'd taken a chunk out of her ass just the other day about the same subject. She supposed her dad didn't care for someone else disparaging his daughter.

"It's time to put this to bed," Dex growled, undeterred. "We're getting a black eye all over town over this situation. You have no idea how I'm trying to keep our heads above water all the while little missy here is dumping buckets back in the pool."

"She's not doing that, she's doing her job." Fitz folded his hands across his chest. "We'll talk about this later."

The tension between the two men grew to an uncomfortable level until her mom breezed in with a bright smile, announcing she'd just made a fresh pot of coffee to have with her famous coffee cake. "Dex, I know you can't resist my coffee cake," she said, giving him a look that dared him to refuse.

But of course Dex caved with Lilly. She had this way about her that managed to disarm most difficult men. Maybe that was her secret or superpower.

"You know me too well," Dex admitted, breaking into a smile. "I'll have me a slice, darlin'."

"Fitz?"

Fitz grunted with a nod, dropping into his chair to wait for Lilly to serve them.

This was her chance to bail. She'd have to talk to her mom another time. Checking her watch, she made her excuses, kissed her mother's cheek and practically ran out of the house before Dex could start all over again.

Forensics would be finished soon, she told herself when the fear and guilt became too heavy to bear. She had to be patient. Rushing would help no one.

Especially not the two dead people who were still waiting for justice.

Clint wasn't sure what he hoped to gain by visiting Alex in jail while he awaited his arraignment but he supposed he needed some kind of closure.

Cook County Jail wasn't a place he'd thought to visit, and after being thoroughly searched for any contraband, he was certain he never wanted to return.

The razor-wire cyclone fence enclosing the drab facility was a reminder that no one was getting in or out without clearance. It was a far cry from what Alex was accustomed to. The reality that Alex was going away for a very long time hit him in the gut. He shouldn't but he felt bad for the guy.

Hell, it was hard to forget that he'd been his closest friend. As much as he wanted to, he couldn't.

Alex shuffled into the visitor booth. His ill-fitting khaki scrubs hung from his frame as if he'd lost twenty pounds in the weeks since he'd been arrested. Dark circles ringed his eyes and his head was shorn. Alex picked up the receiver and Clint did the same. The jail smelled of sweat, urine and sadness.

"You look like hell," Clint said, leading with the easiest observation. "What happened to your hair?"

Alex ran his hand over his nearly bald head. "Lice outbreak. It's easier to shave the inmates than treat the lice. One and done, problem solved." He paused a beat, then asked, "What are you doing here?"

"I don't know," Clint admitted, feeling like an idiot. "I just wanted some closure, I guess."

"I've already told you everything. My lawyer said I'm not supposed to say anything else."

"I'm not looking for a confession."

"Then what are you looking for?"

"I don't know," he answered. "Still trying to wrap my head around what happened. What you did."

"Yeah, welcome to my hell. If I had an answer for myself, I'd give it to you. I don't know. Addiction is a terrible thing. It takes your normal thought process and turns it upside down."

Clint nodded. It was an honest answer. "You okay in here?"

"Hey, it's my reality and I earned it. I'm not shying away from what I did. Whatever happens is my karma."

"Stop being so damn apologetic," Clint growled, knowing he sounded irrational. "It's hard to hate you when you're all pathetic behind this glass."

"I hate myself enough for the both of us. I got you covered, buddy."

In spite of everything, Clint chuckled. "Good." His smile faded. "Everything else okay?"

"I've been put in solitary for my safety. I'm considered a white-collar criminal, and since I paid someone to do my dirty work, I'm real low on the totem pole. My lawyer is working on getting me transferred to a different facility. One that's not quite so rough."

"I hope it works out for you," he said, meaning it. The threat was over. He couldn't hold on to the hatred eating him up inside. Alex messed up and he was paying for it. Even though Alex had done something terrible, Clint couldn't hate him.

"You okay?" Alex asked, surprising him. "Are you safe?"

"Do you mean is your hit man still out there gunning for my ass?"

"Not in so many words, but yeah."

"You can sleep easy. Your hit man tried to attack me in a parking garage with a buddy. Jordana took them both down. Chicago's finest came and arrested them."

Alex seemed relieved. "I'm sorry. I wish I could take it all back."

"You and me both. You still owe me for that stupid bet you lost. I'm never going to see that money now."

Alex chuckled. "I guess I'll just have to catch you in twenty years when they let me out."

"Do me a favor, keep it. I'm not sure I'll be inviting you over for dinner," Clint quipped with dark humor. When in doubt, make a joke to lessen the tension. Old habits died hard. "It's not the same without you. I landed the O'Hare account but I could tell I wasn't the show-man you were."

"You never gave yourself enough credit. You'll do fine without me."

Clint shrugged. "I guess I have to. Not a lot of choice in that decision."

"I'm sorry."

Clint waved away his apology. He had to keep his

composure even though his best friend had betrayed him and his girlfriend had left him to go back to Kansas.

As if honing in on Clint's private thoughts, Alex asked, "What's the situation with Jordana? Nothing hotter than a badass woman, right?"

He agreed but admitted, "She's gone, went back to Braxville."

"You doing the long-distance thing?"

"Nope." Was he discussing his love life with a prisoner behind safety glass? Man, his life had taken a weird turn. "She said she couldn't stay and I couldn't leave—one of us would end up resenting the other. She's probably right. Hell, I don't know anymore. Nothing makes a lot of sense in my life right now."

"What do you want?"

"I want her," Clint answered.

"So stop whining about it and go get your lady."

"My lady doesn't want to be gotten. I'm not going to chase after someone determined to push me away." He exhaled a long breath, adding, "And I'm not sure taking advice from you is the best thing. You never held on to a relationship longer than six months."

"Exactly. I know why I couldn't keep a girl and it has nothing to do with your issue."

"Which is what?"

"You're used to women throwing themselves at you. This one you have to work for and you're bailing. C'mon, man, I've seen you fight harder for a parking space than the fight you're putting up for the love of your life."

He had let her walk away. Even though everything in him shouted to follow and convince her that she was wrong.

"How am I supposed to be in two places at once? Braxville isn't a short commute to Chicago."

"A two-hour flight," Alex told him "You can make it work. Split your time between Braxville and Chicago. Let's face it, Broadlocke can be managed via telecommute if need be. All you need is a solid person at the Chicago office to manage the day-to-day and then you can conference call most of the client meetings."

Clint stared at Alex. How had this man just solved his problem? This is what Alex had always been good at: creative problem-solving. Tears welled in his eyes but he sniffed them back, pretending that he had something in his eye, but Alex seemed to understand.

"I'm sorry," Alex said quietly. "I can't say it enough. I wasn't thinking straight."

Clint nodded, needing to go. "Take care of yourself," he said, rising. "Do you need anything?"

"A file, some dynamite and a new identity if you've got 'em," Alex quipped, forcing a chuckle from Clint. *Same ol' Alex.* Smart-ass to the end. Alex offered up a brief, pained smile before adding, "Money on the books would be nice. I might be able to save my ass if I can trade something."

"Sure thing, buddy."

Replacing the receiver, he took one last look at his best friend before walking away.

No one told him closure would hurt like a bitch.

Chapter 33

Jordana walked into Bridgette's makeshift office to pick her up for lunch. It was nice having her sister home again. They used to be so close but then distance and busy lives had gotten in the way of their relationship.

Of her two sisters, she got along the best with Bridgette. Yvette, the baby, had a personality that tended to rub Jordana the wrong way at times, but Lilly always seemed to favor her, which also stuck a thorn in Jordana's side.

So even though Yvette lived in town, they rarely spent time together unless it was a family dinner at their parents' house.

Bridgette looked up and waved her over with a smile. "Sorry, I just have to finish up these notes before I lose my train of thought. My superior is asking for an update and I want to get everything down."

"Have you had any breakthroughs?" Jordana asked.

"Well, right now we're taking soil and water samples,

preliminary stuff. Then we'll start talking to neighbors who are situated near the clusters. We need to document how many people were potentially affected, which means a lot of interviews."

"Except with the people who have already died," Jordana said, frowning. "Have you ever heard of the chemical CCA?"

"Chromated copper arsenic? Of course, it's one of nine chemical compounds banned by the EPA for commercial use." She glanced up in question. "Why?"

Jordana vacillated between sharing privileged information or not with Bridgette. Given the fact that Bridgette was an investigator for the state, she relented. "Well, CCA was found on the bodies."

"Interesting. When was the building built?"

"In the mid-1970s so it was grandfathered in, I suppose."

"I wonder how many other buildings have CCA-treated building materials?" Bridgette mused, mostly to herself. "I think I'll look into that."

Alarm spiked Jordana's voice as she asked, "Why?"

"Well, we have a documented case of esophageal cancer that might be connected to exposure to CCA. I'll need to follow up."

Jordana voiced her secret fear. "What if Dad is somehow involved in all this?"

"How could he be?" Bridgette asked, confused. "Dad would never knowingly do anything that would hurt anyone."

"I know but something about this case gives me a bad feeling."

"You're just under a lot of pressure. It's twisting your perspective. Dad is probably fine. Now Dex, on the other hand—he's always seemed shady to me."

She wasn't going to argue that point because she wondered the same. "Dad would never let Dex do anything that would come back on his family," Jordana said, clinging to that hope. "But what if Dad is somehow affected by all this? Dad said he felt his own family was attacking him right now."

"Dad is being dramatic. It's all procedure. He got hot under the collar because I told him I needed to take samples near Ruby Row."

"Why?"

"I don't know. He doesn't trust all this "cockamamie science BS' as he calls it. He does things old-school and doesn't like being told how stuff needs to be done now. Honestly, I've said for years that Dad should retire. Maybe this will be the thing that forces his hand."

Jordana made a face. "Can you imagine Dad without a job to occupy him? He would be unbearable to be around."

"Speaking of, please tell me you know of a rental I can look into? I can't live with them much longer or I'll go Lizzie Borden on their asses."

Jordana laughed. "We don't want that to happen. I'll keep an eye out. Do you think our parents will divorce someday?"

"Not a chance. Mom would never leave Dad. No matter how grumpy he gets. You do realize, our dad is going to be that stereotypical grouchy old man who's always railing about 'those damn kids' as he waves his cane at them."

Jordana, affecting a crotchety old man voice, croaked, "Get off my lawn!" and they both laughed because they knew it was like looking into the foreseeable future. "Can you imagine Dad being young and happy? I mean, people don't spring up out of the dirt angry old men."

"Mom was beautiful in her day. He had to do something to charm her. I'm sure she had her pick of eligible bachelors back in the day."

"Oh, God, you just made me think of the reality that our parents used to have sex."

"Used to? You think they don't anymore?"

Jordana quipped, "Don't you think Dad would be less grumpy if they were?"

Bridgette gagged. "Please, you're ruining my appetite."

But Jordana was enjoying this and teased Bridgette, "Hey, you're living with them. Have you heard them going at it late at night?"

"Oh, my God, Jordana, I would pour hot oil into my ears if that ever happened. And thankfully, no, I haven't heard any late-night nookie." She shuddered. "That would be enough to put me off from ever having sex again."

Jordana laughed, enjoying messing with Bridgette, but she was starving and her lunch hour would be over if they didn't hurry up and get to the restaurant. "C'mon, you prude. Lock up and let's go. My stomach is starting to eat itself."

Bridgette made quick work of closing down her office and they popped into their favorite deli for a quick bite.

Afterward, Jordana dropped Bridgette off and headed back to the station. She worked hard to keep thoughts of Clint at the back of her mind but there were times when it seemed nearly impossible to stop the intrusion of memories.

Today reminded her of the day they went to Wichita and rock climbed. That'd been the best day. She and Clint had been compatible is so many ways, except the most important—where they called home.

Privately, in her weakest moments, usually late at night

when she couldn't sleep, she entertained the fantasy that everything had worked out between them and she got the privilege of falling asleep in his arms every night.

The fantasy gave her momentary pleasure until reality popped the bubble. She couldn't imagine Clint enjoying Braxville full-time. He hadn't minded visiting but to live here? He'd go insane.

That painful circle of reason was usually the point where she reminded herself that she'd made the right decision and tried to forget.

It never worked.

No matter how hard she tried, shaking free of Clint's ghost was damn near impossible.

She supposed this was her life now. Forever pining for the one who got away. The one she pushed away.

Yay, me.

Big decisions shouldn't be made on the fly, but after seeing Alex, Clint realized what he wanted to do. There was still the fear that Jordana would reject him, but he had to take the chance. Otherwise, he'd spend his life wondering what might've been if he'd just grabbed his balls and went for it.

Hell, when he and Alex started Broadlocke, they hadn't much between them aside from a determination to succeed shared by a common goal. If he could create a multimillion-dollar company, survive three different attempts on his life and put away his best friend, he could do anything.

His dark sense of humor was turning out to be a good coping mechanism for what he'd had to endure. But he couldn't deny—didn't want to deny—that he missed Jordana in a way that wasn't going to fade if he gave it more time. He knew the signs of real love even if he'd never experienced it before now.

They had a kind of love that burned down to the soul, leaving a mark for the rest of a person's days. If he didn't do his best to convince Jordana that they were meant to be together, he'd live in regret for what could've been. After everything he'd been through, he wasn't going to live half a life.

He'd convince Jordana's stubborn ass that she was meant to be with him and vice versa. The only trouble was he didn't know how he'd make that happen, only that it needed to. Creative problem-solving had been Alex's field of expertise.

Alex would say one problem at a time. He had to find someone he could leave in charge while he was in Braxville, someone he trusted. The obvious choice hadn't been so obvious, but once the lightbulb went off, it was nearly blinding. He just had to put his plan in motion and pray he wasn't doing it all for nothing.

Chapter 34

Another painfully tense family dinner. She needed to come up with a reasonable excuse to bow out the next time her mom sent an invitation. The only problem with bowing out was the guilt of leaving poor Bridgette to face their parents alone. For some reason the boys always got out of family dinners, but the girls were expected to show up.

Well, except Yvette. The baby always got special treatment. Mom never badgered Yvette for not showing up. It seemed that judgment was reserved mostly for Jordana these days.

The emotional toll of spending time with her parents when the investigation was all but stalled was excruciating. She never thought she'd long for the days when all she had to deal with was her parents' ordinary gripes about her never settling down—as if they were living in the Victorian era and she was in danger of becoming an old maid.

Jordana fell back onto the sofa with a groan, wanting to veg out on some mindless television before bed.

An idle thought crowded her mind as she flipped through channels.

What kind of impression would Clint have made on her parents? Her mom would've immediately been impressed by his wealth. Her father would've been his usual standoffish self, and if Dex were around, he'd probably sniff out any potential investing possibilities.

Dex was always hustling.

She supposed she shouldn't give Dex too hard of a time. If it weren't for Dex always looking for the next bid, Colton Construction would've gone under a long time ago.

"Uncle" Dex was an integral part of Colton Construction, no matter how he irritated her most days.

She grabbed her cell and began flipping through her photos, looking for the ones with Clint. Logically, she knew she should've deleted them. The best way to get over someone was to remove reminders.

She couldn't do it.

Her memories with Clint were the secret fuel in her engine. Only in the privacy of her thoughts could she openly admit how much she missed him. She couldn't count how many times she'd stared at her phone, so close to calling yet ultimately didn't because there was nothing more to say.

Hearing his voice would be a knife to her heart.

She missed his laugh; the low rumble deep in his chest when he chuckled was the sexiest sound she'd ever known. Not to mention how he made her bones melt when they were alone.

Jordana grabbed a throw pillow and hugged it to her chest. Had she made a mistake? Had she pushed away the one she would've happily grown old with? How was she to know that she hadn't taken a gamble on the wrong flip of the coin? The military taught her to never second-guess her instincts, but she wasn't so sure that she'd been listening to her instincts but rather fear.

Fear of ultimately losing a part of herself if and when Clint realized he couldn't make a life work as her partner. Fear of putting in the work to only discover they were truly incompatible. Fear of looking like a fool when she didn't fit in with his circle of wealthy friends.

Jordana exhaled on a groan, her mind spinning in circles. "No sense in looking backward when you know you're not going that way," she murmured to herself as she tossed the pillow, restless.

She glanced at her phone. It works both ways. She hadn't called him but he hadn't called her, either. Was he even missing her? Had he washed his hands of everything they'd been to each other? Yes, it was unfair for her to criticize his methods of closure, but she didn't care. If there was one lesson that'd been hammered home from the time she was young, it was that life wasn't fair.

Just once, she would've liked the pendulum to swing her way.

Enough with the pity party, she admonished, rising. Her gaze roamed her tiny house. There had to be something that needed cleaning or reorganizing. Maybe she would start that tile project, after all. She'd always wanted granite countertops.

No time like the present. Especially when her brain wouldn't let her rest, her heart ached like a bitch and guilt dogged her every step for not being able to close this case.

Adulting was hard.

Right now, she wanted to crawl under her blanket fort and block out everything and everyone.

Seeing as that wasn't an option...*tile project, it is!*

* * *

Clint walked with purpose into the office, his plan set in his mind, his feet ready to put the plan into action. He asked Jeana to join him in his office and to shut the door behind her.

Perplexed, Jeana followed his instruction, awaiting his disposition. "Have I done something wrong, sir?" she asked, concerned.

"I'd say so," he answered, steeling his fingers. "I did a little digging into your personnel file and discovered you have a degree in business management with a minor in robotic tech. Tell me…why are you my assistant and not on my development team?"

She blushed when she realized he was paying her a compliment. "I applied for a management position when I first came on board with Broadlocke but Mr. Locke thought I should spend some time as your assistant to learn how Broadlocke operates. I was lucky to land a position with Broadlocke and I was grateful for the opportunity to prove myself."

"That was five years ago. How long were you supposed to 'learn' the ropes?" Clint asked, confused. "Alex never mentioned your qualifications. If I'd known I would've rectified that oversight way before now."

"At first, I was a little disappointed that I wasn't headed straight into management as I'd hoped but there was some wisdom in Mr. Locke's direction. I did learn the ins and outs of Broadlocke in ways that gave me a particular insight."

Clint could see the value, but he didn't like that Alex had been a little sexist by throwing a highly capable female employee in the assistant role. Well, that was about to end. "Here's the thing, I can't do anything about the past but I'm looking toward the future and I need someone here who can help keep Broadlocke running smoothly when I'm not around. Someone I trust."

"Sir?" Jeana blinked, cocking her head to the side in question. "Are you hiring someone new? Should I contact the headhunting agency?"

"Nope. I did my headhunting, but as I turns out, I didn't have to hunt all that far."

"Oh. Okay?"

"You, Jeana, I want you to operate the Chicago office and not as my assistant."

Jeana's lip trembled as she swallowed. "Are you serious?"

"As a heart attack," he answered solemnly. "Look, you're already the engine that makes sure that this office is a tight ship but what I didn't realize was that you weren't being used to your best potential. If you're willing to take a lead role in the management side, it will come with a substantial raise, some perks, as you know, and a lot more work. Are you up for that?"

She didn't even hesitate. "Yes. Oh, yes!"

He nodded, pleased. "Good. Then you need to start headhunting for your replacement because you're going to need a 'you' by your side as you move into more responsibilities."

Jeana, beaming, took a moment to contain her happiness, then asked, "May I assume you will be opening a Braxville location?"

"You assume correct. A two-hour flight is nothing if I'm needed here. It's time I start creating a solution to my problem instead of just staring at it."

"Seems like a sensible course of action, sir."

"And another thing, no more 'sir,'" he admonished. "As soon as you sign your paperwork for HR, you're on my level. From now on, it's Clint. With Alex gone, I'll be needing a new partner. Understand?"

She smiled, nodding. "I do."

"Excellent. Glad that's settled. Now, if you wouldn't mind me asking you a tiny favor…could you book me a flight to Braxville on the next available plane? I've got a woman to woo and I've got my work cut out for me."

Jeana's smile grew. "I would be delighted to book you a flight. Consider it done."

Jeana spun on her heel and left his office with a little more spring in her step and it did Clint's heart good to make a positive difference in someone's life. Especially someone who deserved good things.

With the decision made, he no longer felt any reservations. He'd never give much thought to where he would raise a family if he were to have one, but he knew now that Chicago wasn't where he wanted his roots to grow. He wanted for his kids what Jordana had had growing up—stability and a firm understanding of where they came from.

He wanted to complain about small-town life, such as a neighbor with a noisy rooster, or a pig that'd escaped the farmer's pen to root around in his vegetable garden. Hell, he wanted to learn how to grow vegetables and plant fruit trees.

He wanted to attend Friday night football games for the local high school and get to know the townspeople on a real level. The kind of life that entails knowing people by name and being able to chat with them in the supermarket aisles. And he wanted it all with that stubborn, hot-as-hell detective who haunted his dreams and made him realize what he'd been missing all those years. He wanted the white picket fence, the DIY projects, the PTA meetings and corny office Christmas parties.

As long as Jordana was by his side, he'd do it all.

Now, time to problem-solve the biggest obstacle to that promised land: Jordana.

Well, he had a two-hour plane ride to figure something out. Good thing he'd always been light on his feet. And he didn't plan to leave Braxville until he'd convinced Jordana she was The One.

Even if it took a lifetime.

Chapter 35

"You look like someone just ran over your dog," Reese commented, prompting a sour look from Jordana. "Case in point. What's eating you, Gilbert Grape?"

She hadn't slept well. She might've dipped her toe into insanity last night, admitting, "I demoed my kitchen around ten o'clock last night."

"What?"

"And accidentally broke a water pipe," she answered, wincing at the nightmare her kitchen had become. "I managed to get the water main shut off but now I need a plumber to come and take a look to repair it."

"Your dad's in construction—can't he do it for you?"

"I don't dare ask my dad for anything right now," she said, shuddering at the thought. "I'd rather pay the money for someone else to take care of the problem."

"You don't think your dad would put aside petty grievances to help you out?"

"You haven't met my dad, have you? And no, I'm already on thin ice because of the investigation."

Reese seemed to understand. "You're doing everything you can. We're going to get a lead soon. Something will pop up. They always do."

"From your mouth to God's ear," she quipped, hoping it was true. She needed a win at some point or else her relationship with her dad might be forever ruined. Difficult personality aside, she still loved the man.

For her sake, Reese moved on. "Okay, my next question is fairly obvious…why in God's name are you starting a demo project in the middle of the week at ten at night? Are you doing crack? Cooking meth? Should I be worried? You know they drug test here."

"I'm not doing crack or meth, you idiot," Jordana said, rolling her eyes, but the motion gave her a headache. She rubbed at her temples. "I think drugs would be easier to explain. I kinda went a little nuts last night. I wasn't planning to start the demo for the countertops but I wasn't able to sleep, and one thing lead to another and before I knew it I was swinging a mallet like a crazy person."

"Which is how you burst a pipe," Reese guessed, to which she confirmed with a nod. "Okay, so maybe some therapy instead of wrecking your home before you know what you're doing?"

"Thanks for stating the obvious. I already told you that I kinda went crazy, but to be fair, I've been under a lot of pressure. Eventually, the top is going to pop."

"Most people do normal things to let off steam, like garden or watch true-crime documentaries on serial killers."

She leveled a sardonic look at Reese. "That's only you. Nobody else does that."

He countered, "I'm fairly certain they don't go full-on

wrecking crew late at night completely sober. At least tell me there was alcohol involved with your poor judgment."

She sighed. "Sober. Not even a glass of wine."

Reese chuckled, shaking his head. "Do you have a countertop replacement picked out?"

"Nope."

"Do you have a project budget?"

"Nope."

"So you basically got a wild hair up your butt and started swinging?"

"Yep."

He exhaled a long breath, pinching the bridge of his nose as he implored, "Jesus, Jordana. Just call the guy already."

Jordana stared, wishing she wasn't so transparent. Also wishing she hadn't lost her cool and raged at her poor kitchen without an actual plan as to how to finish the project. Now she had a nonfunctioning kitchen, water damage and no idea how she was going to put it all back together again. If that wasn't a metaphor for her life, she didn't know what was. She glanced away, finally saying, "I can't call him."

Reese sighed. "And why is that?"

"Because you don't get closure by repeatedly opening a wound. He needs time to heal, too. I wouldn't disrespect his privacy by badgering him for no discernible purpose."

"You make a lot of excuses for a woman who is normally pretty straightforward about things."

"I do not."

"You do. Look, I'm your partner. Trust is an essential component of our relationship. I wouldn't lie to you. So you can trust me when I say, you're better *with* him than without. And you're driving everyone crazy with your dour Eeyore routine. It's a bit of a drag."

Jordana glared Reese's way, not because he wasn't right but because she hated that she was *that* person. "Getting over Clint is turning out to be harder than I thought it would be," she admitted. "I just need more time."

"Maybe you can't get over him because you're not supposed to get over him. I don't think anyone would accuse me of being overly romantic but, you know, you and Clint seem pretty well-matched."

She snorted. "Not hardly."

"Forget all the surface stuff—I'm talking about the way you act with one another. He brings out the best in you, which is how it's supposed to work. At least, if rumors are to be believed, of course. Anyway, all I know is that you're making a big mistake by holding a line you drew in the sand over something colossally stupid."

"Did you just call me stupid?"

"Pretty much." Reese shrugged, giving zero "effs" as they would say. "I call it like I see it."

"You should mind your own business," Jordana told him.

"Sorry, can't. You're my partner so I'm forced to deal with you and whatever nonsense you manifest, both good and bad."

"Is there such a thing as good nonsense?" she asked, mildly amused.

"Sure, like your near-baffling belief that *The Wizard of Oz* is one of the best films ever made. That's bull that, although inherently wrong, is harmless, which is *good*. Get it?"

"Your logic is dizzying and you're wrong—*The Wizard of Oz* is a classic in film history. Anyone with a brain would agree."

"My point being, I'm willing to deal with all of it because I'm your partner and I'm tired of seeing you sad all the time. Even when you're pretending to be happy, I know you're not."

Jordana's eyes welled unexpectedly. *Don't do this here.* Her throat closed up and she couldn't manage a comeback. "I—"

"*The Wizard of Oz is* a classic," a voice with authority said behind her, choking her words in midsentence. She jumped from her chair to see Clint standing there, a half grin on his face, that adorable dimple popping out. "If we're throwing around facts, that is."

"What are you doing here?" she found her voice to rasp, but she was so happy to see him that all she could do was stare. "I mean… Chicago…why?"

He started to walk toward her, and her gaze never left his. The station seemed to disappear around them. Her soul stared with hunger at the man she wanted above all others. Reasons for why it wouldn't work, logical arguments against being together, all the things she had clung to in his absence, dissolved like mist in sunshine. He was here. Standing in front of her. Like the answer to an unspoken prayer.

And she couldn't say a thing.

Clint seemed to understand and reached for her hands to hold in his grasp, his stare never leaving hers. She was mesmerized by those eyes, drinking in his presence like a woman dying of thirst.

"Well, this is awkward," Reese broke in. "But I'm going to stay because I need to know how this turns out. Carry on."

That break was the catalyst to cause her to blink and come to her senses. After shooting Reese a look, she asked Clint again, "What are you doing here?"

"Coming to convince the love of my life to stop pushing me away so we can start our lives together."

Her heart stuttered. "What do you mean?"

"I mean, I'm looking to put down roots with you. Right here in Braxville."

"You can't do that," she protested, flushing with distress. "I told you that was a bad idea."

"Well, I gave it some thought and I realized you were partly right."

"She was?" Reese asked, surprised.

Jordana whirled on Reese. "I swear to God, if you don't shut up I'll shoot you."

Reese held up his hands in mock surrender. "Fine. So touchy."

Returning to Clint, she tried to understand what he was saying. Impatience colored her voice as she said, "Please clarify."

"You said if either of us moved permanently for the other, it would cause resentment. I couldn't deny that could be true. Then I realized I'm not giving up Chicago. I can live wherever I want and telecommute or hop a plane if need be, and be at the Chicago office in two hours. That's hardly giving up Chicago."

Jordana's heart sped up at the implication of his solution. Was it possible that she and Clint could make this work? She didn't want to get her hopes up but…the possibility filled her with elation. "But what about your Chicago office? Who will run it with Alex gone?"

"Turns out Jeana is the most qualified. I leave Chicago in highly capable hands. Probably even better than before. I'm excited to see what she can do. Powerful women are sexy as hell."

She trembled as the full import of what he was saying hit her. "So you're saying…"

He pulled her to him, and she immediately softened. When Clint wrapped his arms around her, she felt home. "What I'm saying, Miss Colton," Clint said in a low rumble, "is that I want to make a life with you here. In Braxville. What do you say to that?"

She felt the tension in the room as everyone seemed to wait for her answer. There wasn't time to be embarrassed at being the center of attention. Her future happiness depended on her answer.

To say yes would be to throw caution to the wind and embrace the now, regardless of the potential outcome.

To say no would be to condemn herself to knowing she'd pushed away the man of her dreams out of fear of the unknown.

She wasn't a coward. She needed to stop allowing fear to dictate her actions.

Jordana slowly looped her arms around Clint's neck, smiling as her heart fluttered with joy, saying, "I say... how good are you at kitchen demo?"

"I'm pretty good at writing a check," he answered with a grin. "But if it's something you want to do together... I'll figure it out."

That was exactly the right answer. As she lifted her mouth to his, the station erupted into applause. The loudest being Reese, the cheeky bastard. Partners were a pain in the ass but Reese was a good one.

"Take her home," Reese called out. "She needs a good...well, I think you can figure it out."

Clint hoisted her up on his hips and carried her out of the station amid the laughter as he called out over his shoulder, "I know exactly what she needs!"

And boy, did he.

Sigh.

* * * * *

Don't miss the next romance in
The Coltons of Kansas miniseries:

Colton's Secret History *by Jennifer Bokal*

Available from Harlequin Romantic Suspense!

Great. She'd get to endure another visit with the dubious
sheriff. Except now he'd be hard-pressed to doubt her
claims. Clearly she must have seen something to make
the hole digger feel he needed to close loose ends.

Julien ended the call. "While we wait for the sheriff,
why don't you go get dressed and pack some things? You
should stay with me until we find out who tried to kill
you."

He had a good point, but the notion of staying with
him gave her a burst of heat. Conscious of wearing only
a robe, she tightened the belt.

"I can stay with my parents," she said. "They can
make sure I'm safe." Her father would probably install a
robust security system complete with guards.

"You might put others in danger if you do that."

Her parents, Corbin and countless staff members might be in the line of fire if the gunman returned for another attempt.

"Then I'll beef up security here. I can't stay away from the ranch for long."

"All right, then let me help you."

"Okay." She could agree to that.

"Don't worry, I don't mix my work with pleasure," he said with a grin, giving her body a sweeping look.

"Good, then I don't have to worry about trading one danger for another." She smiled back and left him standing there, uncertainty flattening his mouth.

Don't miss
Her P.I. Protector by Jennifer Morey,
available September 2020 wherever
Harlequin Romantic Suspense
books and ebooks are sold.

Harlequin.com